READY-TO-TELL
TALES

J
398
.2
0973
Ready

Ready-to-tell tales : sure-fire stories from America's favorite storytellers / edited by David Holt & Bill Mooney. -- Little Rock : August House Publishers, 1994.
224 p. : ill.

07611048   LC:94027184   ISBN:0874833817 (pbk.)

1. Tales. I. Holt, David. II. Mooney, William.

2367   94DEC22   53/to   1-01038351

READY-TO-TELL
TALES

SURE-FIRE STORIES FROM AMERICA'S FAVORITE STORYTELLERS

EDITED BY
David Holt & Bill Mooney

August House Publishers, Inc.
LITTLE ROCK

Permissions are included in the
Acknowledgments following the text.

Printed in the United States of America

10 9 8 7 6 5 4 3 2 1 HC
10 9 8 7 6 5 4 3 2 1 PB

LIBRARY OF CONGRESS CATALOGING-IN-PUBLICATION DATA

Ready-to-tell tales : surefire stories from America's favorite storytellers /
collected and edited by David Holt and Bill Mooney — 1st ed.
p.   cm.
Summary: A multicultural collection of traditional tales contributed by more than
forty of America's most experienced storytellers, with tips for telling the stories.
ISBN 0-87483-380-9 : $24.95 — ISBN 0-87483-381-7 (pbk.) : $16.95
1. Tales. [1. Folklore. 2. Storytelling—Collections.]
I. Holt, David. II. Mooney, William.
PZ8.1.R233   1994
398.2'0973—dc20   94-27184

Executive editor: Liz Parkhurst
Assistant editors: Jan Diemer, Sue T. Williams
Design director: Ted Parkhurst
Cover design: Harvill Ross Studios Ltd.

The paper used in this publication meets the minimum requirements
of the American National Standards for Information Sciences—
permanence of Paper for Printed Library Materials, ANSI.48-1984

For all our children—
Zeb and the memory of Sara Jane,
Sean and Will and Beth Ann

Contents

Introduction

The question is often asked, "What makes a good storyteller?" The answer is ... good stories. All the technique in the world can't bring a bland tale to life, but a good story simply told will captivate any audience.

This is a collection of multicultural stories from some of the nation's best and most experienced professional storytellers. Every story presented here is *ready-to-tell*. It is tried and true. That is what makes our collection different from most others. Each one of these tales has been told and retold again and again to widely divergent audiences, and has proven its worth many times over. The tellers have told these stories often enough to figure out which parts "work" and which parts don't. They have pared away the extraneous parts, honed each section to a razor sharpness, retaining only the lean, streamlined version that you read here. These stories are meant to be told. When you read them aloud, you will notice they were written for the ear.

We also asked our contributing storytellers to include special tips on how you can enhance the telling of each story. In addition, they discuss what made them choose their particular story and where they found it. In many cases, if you decide to tell a story, you will be directed to the teller's primary sources. Each storyteller alters a story somewhat to fit his or her own personality and style. We anticipate that you will wish to do the same, so our contributors have contributed, wherever possible, information about their sources.

We live in a multicultural society. Stories tell of our similarities and differences, our strengths and weaknesses, our hopes and dreams. They have the power to teach us understanding and tolerance. This is a powerful tool. This collection brings together tales from diverse cultures around the world and presents them ready-made for oral retelling to modern audiences.

A teller always chooses a story because it means something to her or him. The story strikes some sort of responsive chord in the teller, perhaps because it is moving, or funny, or has a moral. The reasons for being drawn to a particular story are as varied as the storytellers themselves. (Actually, many tellers will say that a story chooses them, not the other way around.)

We have included stories for the beginning storyteller and and the seasoned professional. Most are easy to tell; some will be more of a challenge—but all will deliver enjoyment to the audience and the teller. We have selected tales that will appeal to a variety of age levels from children to adults, with an emphasis on stories that any age group will enjoy.

Moreover, we have selected stories that the authors are happy to see other tellers perform. The tales in this book are not the authors' "signature stories" and do not rely on force of personality or "tricks of the trade" for their effectiveness. These tales are truly ready for anyone to tell.

Hooking the Listener

Every storyteller represented in this collection understands the importance of having stories that grab the audience's attention early. Today's audiences will not sit politely if a story takes forever to unfold. Just like a fisherman with his rod and reel, the storyteller has to have an enticing lure. The story has to gain the audience's attention right away. Not only must it grab their attention, but it must hook them fast. We all know the moment when a story "kicks in." That is the moment when the audience bites. Then the teller sets the hook and begins the fun of reeling them in.

Each one of these stories "kicks in" fast. They hook the audience and keep them dancing on the line until the moment the story is over. They are stories that anyone can tell successfully.

Even if you are not a teller, but simply a reader, you will have a wonderful time browsing through these terrific tales. We know you will enjoy taking a swim through our book and letting each one of the wonderful stories hook you and leave you wriggling with delight.

When the storytelling revival started in the early 1970s, there was common agreement among the few of us that called ourselves professional storytellers that we would not "steal" each other's material—that is, use it without permission. The circle of tellers and audience members was too small. We also recognized that part of the job of a professional teller is to continually create or find new stories. This ethic still holds true today even though storytelling has grown into a nationwide movement.

We do not intend to address the intricacies of copyright law in this book. There are many, many instances in which one storyteller should seek permission from another before telling his or her story in performance.

The great advantage of this book is that the contributing storytellers offer these stories to the larger community. They want you to enjoy them, tell them, use your own words, make them your own. (Note that many tellers have included their original sources so that you can familiarize yourself with other versions of the stories in order to create your own.) All they ask is that you give them credit as your source when you tell the tale. Even though many of the stories are from folk tradition, they have been worked up and "arranged" for oral retelling by the authors. Tell them all you want, but if you want to record or publish any of these versions you will need to contact the author of the tale for permission.

Storytellers cannot rely on mass media to spread the word and the work. The movement has always depended on word of mouth. We make it a point to tell audiences about other storytellers and give them credit for their efforts. So, when you tell one of the tales from this book, tell a little about the teller you got it from as well. In this way we lift each other up, one story at a time.

I often pick up new sto-
ries from people I meet when I
am traveling. Mr. Dasgupta, a
musician from northern India,
told me an interesting tale
about a king and a riddle of
three dolls. I later developed the
following retelling from Mr.
Dasgupta's tale.

DAVID NOVAK has been telling stories professionally since 1978. He has twice been featured at the
National Storytelling Festival as well as many other festivals around the country. He makes hundreds of appearances throughout the year. He has produced programs
for The Lincoln Center Institute in New York and the
Los Angeles Music Center on Tour. He holds a BFA in
Theater Arts from Southern Methodist University and
an MFA from the University of California, San Diego.
David lives in Golden Hill, San Diego, with his wife,
Courtney, his son, Jack, one cat, one fish, and lots of stories.

The Three Dolls

David Novak

A STORY FROM INDIA

There was once a king who considered himself a great and clever king. He would proudly stroke his long beard and proclaim: "Ah! I am a clever king! To demonstrate my cleverness, I invite anyone to challenge me with a riddle or puzzle to solve."

One day, this king received a package containing three dolls, and a challenge which read: "Oh, King, if you are as great and clever as you maintain, please be so wise as to tell the difference between these three dolls."

The king announced: "Aha! I am a great king and a clever king, and I shall easily solve this little riddle."

So the king stroked upon his beard and hummed to himself as he studied the three dolls: "Hum-hum-hum, hum hum-hum, hum-hum-agh!" He pulled upon his beard in frustration, for he could see no difference between the dolls. The three dolls were exactly alike, in every form and feature, down to the minutest detail.

"Aha!" thought the king. "I am a great king and a clever king. And it is said that a great king will keep a wise man nearby to help him solve his problems. I have such a wise man." Then he called for the wise man.

The wizened old wise man hobbled into the court. Leaning upon his staff, he bowed before the king. "Majesty. In what wise matter may I be of service?"

"Wise Man," said the king, "I have before me three dolls, exactly alike. What is the difference between them?"

The wise man bent to examine the dolls. After a great deal of consideration, the wise man thought to tell the king this matter was not worth his time. He thought to tell the king many other things, too, but finally he wisely said nothing. For it is wise to keep your thoughts to yourself, especially in the presence of a powerful monarch. The king sent the wise man away.

"This wise man is of no use to me," thought the king. "He is too shrewd. But I am a great king and a clever king, and it is said that a great king will– sometimes listen to the council of a fool. For a fool will rush in where wise men fear to tread. I have such a fool." Then he called for the fool.

The fool indeed rushed in, slapped the king merrily upon the back and said, "Hi ya, King! How'ya doin'?"

"Fool," said the king, "I have three dolls exactly alike. What is the difference between them?"

The fool did not listen. He saw the three dolls and only thought to play with them. "Whee! Dollies! Let's play pretend! Let's pretend we're going on a picnic!"

But before the fool could have much fun, the king sent him away.

"This fool is of no use to me," thought the king, "for this fool is a fool! But, I am a great king and a clever king, and it is said that a great king will retain a storyteller. For the tellers of tales carry in their stories many words of wisdom." He called for the storyteller.

Into the court came the storyteller, bowing low with a great flourish. The storyteller began to speak at once. "Majesty, how may I serve you? A fable, perhaps? Or a recitation of the glorious deeds of your greatness in verse and song? Or perhaps—"

"Enough," commanded the king. "Storyteller, don't get started. Today I have a riddle—"

"Ah! Such as the riddle of the Sphinx?" the storyteller interjected. "Or the riddle of the little man who spun straw—"

"Precisely!" The king held up his hand to keep the storyteller from speaking further. "Now listen: I have three dolls exactly alike. You are a teller, can you *tell* the difference between them?"

The storyteller studied the three dolls briefly and exclaimed, "Majesty, you cannot see any difference between these dolls!"

"That much I myself have already determined," groaned the king.

"Majesty," said the storyteller, "if you cannot *see* a difference between these dolls, the answer must be much like the story of the three caskets: their outward show is greatly different from that which they contain. Likewise, the differences between these three dolls must be within."

"Ah, very good," said the king. "But how can you show these differences?"

"Majesty, there must be many ways to reach inside a person. However, the one way with which I am most acquainted is through the ears. If you will permit me." The storyteller reached up and plucked a hair from the king's beard.

"Ow!" exclaimed the king. "How dare you?"

"Forgive me," begged the storyteller. "But as you shall see, it was most necessary." He then lifted the first of the three dolls and began to thread the king's hair into the doll's ear. The hair went in and in and in the doll's ear until it was gone. "Majesty," said the storyteller, "this doll must be a wise man: what it hears, it keeps to itself!"

"Very good," said the king. "And what of these others?"

"If you will permit me," said the storyteller, and again he plucked a hair from the king's beard.

"Ow!" winced the king.

Now the storyteller lifted the second doll and began to thread the hair into its ear. The hair went in and in and in. But as he was threading the hair in one ear, it came out the other. "Majesty, this doll is obviously a fool: what goes in one ear comes out the other."

"Very good," said the king. "And this last one?"

"If you will permit me."

"Ow!"

Once more the storyteller plucked a hair. Lifting the third doll, he began to thread the hair into its ear. The hair went in and in and in. It did not come out the other side, but it did not stay altogether in, either. For as he was threading the hair into the doll's ear, it came slowly out the doll's mouth. "Majesty, this doll is a storyteller: what it hears, eventually it tells."

The king looked at the three dolls. "Storyteller, you have solved this riddle. But I see you have given me a new riddle to consider. For when you put the hair in the doll's ear, it is a straight hair. Yet, when the hair comes out the doll's mouth, it is all curled. Why?"

"Majesty," said the teller, "no storyteller worth his salt will ever tell a tale exactly as he heard it. We must always add a special curl of our own devising in the retelling of the tale!"

And so have I done in retelling this tale for you.

TELLING TIPS: Your voice makes many sounds. Use voice sounds for coloring. Use sound effects for animation. Turn the sound off for sudden surprise silences. Silence can grab the attention of a wiggly listener when noise fails. The silence says: *Who turned off this story? Where are we? What are we waiting for? What happens next?*

Vary the rate at which you tell. A sudden change of pace keeps the story interesting.

A young child can be easily intimidated by a big storyteller in a wild costume towering overhead. Work from the child's level. Start sitting down and being more or less eye-to-eye. Storytelling is an intimate art form. Even with a large crowd, if you sit for a moment, you can shrink the story to a more comfortable, intimate size, and this can be quite refreshing. As a general rule, the smaller the audience, the more you work from a seated position.

IRENE YOUNG

My introduction to
Judith Gorog's story is simply
to state conspiratorially: "You
know how stories usually
begin—'Once upon a time ...'
Well, this one doesn't! This one
begins ... "

Although **CAROL BIRCH** has appeared internationally in Singapore, Australia, and Europe, performances across America are the core of her life as a storyteller. In addition to her own recording, *Careful What*
You Wish For, she has just produced an ALA Notable
Recording, a package of stories told by nearly forty
storytellers at the 20th National Storytelling Festival.
Presently, she is co-editing a book on the aesthetics of
storytelling, in which several models for discussing the
art of storytelling are explored and developed.

Those Three Wishes

Carol Birch

AN ADAPTATION OF A STORY BY JUDITH GOROG

No one. No one ever called Melinda Alice nice. That wasn't the word they used. Melinda Alice was clever and witty. Melinda Alice was clever and cruel. Her mother had noticed how cruel she was, and frankly she hoped—she hoped she'd out grow it. Her dad didn't think anything was the matter. He liked it that his little girl was pretty. He liked it that she got good grades, and as far as he was concerned everything was just fine.

It was Melinda Alice back in the eighth grade who had labeled the shy myopic new girl "Contamination." And she was the first to pretend that anything or anyone touched by the new girl had to be cleaned, inoculated or avoided. High school had merely given Melinda Alice greater scope for her talent.

There was a surprising thing about Melinda Alice—her power. No one trusted her. But no one avoided her either. She was always included, always in the middle. But behind her back her friends didn't call her Melinda Alice, they called her Melinda Malice. If you had seen her, pretty and witty, in the center of a group of students walking past your house you'd've thought, "Wow, there goes a natural leader."

Now, Melinda Alice did get good grades. It was because she went to school early every day. She had a special place where she would go and study before the others arrived. And one day she was hurrying to school because she had heard that there was going to be a math test and she wasn't prepared. And as she was walking along she almost accidently stepped on a snail. And she thought, "Gross!" She didn't like to accidently kill things; purposefully killing things gave her pleasure. And so she stopped and she lifted her foot, she was about to squash the snail into nothing when the snail said in true story fashion, "Don't."

"What?"

"Don't," said the snail. "If you don't kill me I'll give you three wishes."

"Get real!" said Melinda Alice.

But the snail said, "Try it."

Well, he was offering three wishes. The first thing she wanted was more wishes. But she wanted to see if it was working. Her father wouldn't allow Melinda Alice to have pierced ears, and so her first wish was for small gold pierced earrings, and she had them in her ears just like that. No pain. Oh, she tossed her head with the light.

She thought about other things her dad wouldn't let her have. "My second wish is," she said, "I want a sleek red Ferrari that's all my own." And just like that, no pain, there was a beautiful sleek red Ferrari there at the curb. She grabbed the keys from inside that car. She checked, she checked to make sure there was an owner's card and an insurance card with her name on it. She was a very careful girl.

And then, oh then, she walked around her car admiring it. When she got back to the vanity plate, she saw that it didn't say "Melinda" and it didn't say "Alice"—it said MALICE. And she thought, *That stupid snail can't spell.* When she came around to the front, she got in the car … and you know a car like that has real kick and power, and she sat there revving the engine, and as she did she yelled back to the snail, "My third wish is I want my next ten thousand wishes to come true." And she took off.

She forgot about school; she forgot about the math test. She started driving up and down the streets, and for one minute she had a wave of altruistic feelings. For one minute she thought about all the good things she could do in the world with ten thousand wishes. She could wish for peace, that no one would be homeless, that no one would be hungry. She could wish for a cure for cancer. She thought, *I could take people who are old and ugly and sick, and with ten thousand wishes I could make them young and healthy and beautiful.*

And then she thought … *Nah, people who are young and healthy and beautiful, who I don't like, I could wish they were old or ugly or sick,* and it was ugly thoughts that held her till she suddenly remembered school. She pulled into the parking lot, she slid into her seat just as the bell was ringing. And the guy beside her leaned over and said, "Hey, did you study for that math test? 'Cause I heard we're having one first period."

"Oh," she said, "that stupid snail made me forget all about that math test. I am never going to pass that test. Oh, I wish I were … dead."

And that is the story of *those three wishes.*

18

TELLING TIPS: Though the wishing is startlingly modern, this is an old-fashioned "jump" story. It works well as the first story of a program because of its surprising twist. The more wry the delivery, at the beginning especially, the more effectively it piques the attention of middle- and upper-school students. It is most important that your audience have a clear idea of exactly who Melinda Alice is *and* how dastardly you think she is.

ABOUT THE STORY: Judith Gorog wrote the original story "Those Three Wishes" in the book *A Taste for Quiet: Ten Disquieting Tales* (Philomel, 1982). If you compare this version with hers, you'll notice the wishes, and therefore many words, have changed. These changes evolved over the years as audiences offered their wishes to the tale. In spite of the changes in the path through the story, both Ms. Gorog and I feel the *story* hasn't changed. It remains her distinctive tale in tone, intent, plot, setting, character, point of view, and fundamental style. In moving from print to performance, the words may have changed but not the story. Judith Gorog also *tells* the story differently from the exact way she *wrote* it. She joins me in the wish: *May the next one tell it better!*

SUSAN WILSON

I was looking through dozens of folktale books, looking for a story that grabbed me, one that had repetition and vivid language, and the word "Squintum" jumped out at me. When I tell this story, I give it no introduction. I simply start singing the song. That serves to gather the audience's attention. I agree with what Gamble Rogers said: "If the words speak for themselves, don't interrupt."

BILL HARLEY is a singer, songwriter, and story-teller who works primarily with family audiences. He has won awards for his many recordings and is a regular contributing commentator to National Public Radio's "All Things Considered."

Fox's Sack

Bill Harley

A STORY FROM ENGLAND

Once upon a time there was a fox that was very hungry. He hadn't eaten for a long time. He had a sack, but there was nothing in it. "Oh," he said, "if only I had something in this sack. Something to eat."

And just then a bee buzzed by. *"Bzzzzzz."* He grabbed the bee, and put it in the sack. He said, "This is not enough to eat, but soon what's in my sack will make a very nice snack."

He put the sack over his shoulder and walked down the road. As he walked down the road he made up this little song.*

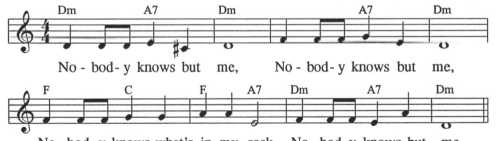

No-bod-y knows but me, No-bod-y knows but me,
No-bod-y knows what's in my sack, No-bod-y knows but me.

Fox walked down the road until he came to a house. He walked up to the front door, knocked on the door *[knocking sound]*. The door opened and there was a very small woman. She said, *"Aaaah!* Hello, Fox." She was afraid of Fox.

He said, "Hello. I'm going to the house of my friend, Squintum. I'd like you to keep this sack until I come back."

She said, "Rrrrright."

He said, "Very well, but whatever you do don't look in the sack."

She said, "Whawhawhat's in it?"

He said, "Don't look in it!"

She said, "All right, all right." She said she wouldn't. She took the sack, she put it down by the door. Fox turned around and walked off, and as he walked off he sang, just loud enough for that woman to hear,

> Nobody knows but me,
> Nobody knows but me,
> Nobody knows what's in my sack,
> Nobody knows but me.

And that very small woman heard that song. She looked at Fox walking off down the road, getting farther and farther away, and she looked down at the sack by the door. She looked at the Fox again. She looked at the sack and then she said,

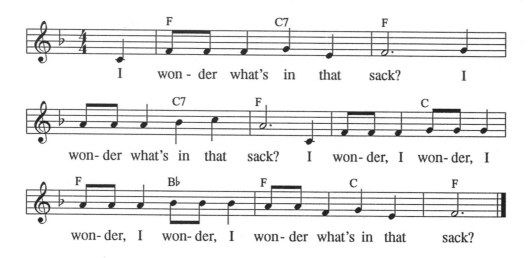

She saw Fox a long way off. She said to herself, "He'll never know. He's so far away." She tiptoed over to the sack and she opened it up. *"Bzzzzzz."* Out flew the bee. She said, "Oh, my goodness." She tried to get it, but it went out the window. She ran into the yard with the sack, but her hen was in the yard, saw that bee—*"gulp, burp"*—and swallowed the bee. "Oh, no!" she said. She went and put the sack back and went about her business. And in a little while, *Fox came back [knocking sound].*

"Oh, no," she said, "it's Fox." She opened the door. She said, "Hhhhiii fox, ththere's your sack."

Fox went over and picked up the sack. But then, he did what she hoped he wouldn't do—he looked in it. He said, "I had a bee in here and it's gone. Did you look in this sack?"

She said, "Well, y-y-yes, I did."

"I told you not to!"

She said, "I-I-I-I-I know, but I heard you sing that song and I got kind of curious, and I looked down, and when I looked in the sack the bee flew out and I tried to get it back, but my hen was in the yard and-and-and it swallowed it."

"Oh," said Fox, "so your hen swallowed my bee. Then I'll just take your hen." He grabbed the hen—"*brawk!*"—and put it in the sack.

That little woman said, "But that's not fair."

And Fox said, "What's fair is fair. What's not is not. What's in my sack goes in my pot."

And he walked out the door, down the road, until he came to the second house on the street. He walked up to the door *[knocking sound]*. The door opened and there was a big tall woman, "Wwwwwhhhaaa! Hi, Fox." She was afraid of Fox too.

He said, "Hello. I'm going to the house of my friend Squintum. I'd like you to keep this sack until I come back."

She said, "Sh-sh-sh-sure, whatever you say."

"Very well," he said, "but whatever you do, don't look in the sack!"

She said, "What's in it?"

He said, "Don't look in it."

She said, "All right, all right. Don't be so touchy."

She took the sack, she put it down by the door and Fox turned around and walked off. As he walked off he sang just loud enough for that tall woman to hear,

> Nobody knows but me,
> Nobody knows but me,
> Nobody knows what's in my sack,
> Nobody knows but me.

And that tall woman heard that song. She saw Fox walking off, farther and farther away. She looked down at the sack, she looked back up at the fox, she looked at the sack again, and she said,

> I wonder what's in that sack?
> I wonder what's in that sack?
> I wonder, I wonder, I wonder, I wonder,
> I wonder what's in that sack?

"He'll never know. He's so far away."

She tiptoed over to the sack, she opened it up. *"Brawk!"* Out jumped the hen. "Oh, my gosh!" she said.

It went right through her legs. She ran out in the yard to get it, but her pig—*"snort, snort"*—was in the yard—*"snort, snort"*—and that pig—*"snort,*

snort"—chased that chicken—*"brawk!"*—right down the road, away. She said, "Oh, my goodness." She put the sack by the door, and in a little while, *Fox came back [knocking sound].*

"Noooo, nooo," she went and opened up the door. She said, "Hi, Fox. Here's your sack."

Fox walked over, picked up the sack, looked inside and said, "Oh, my goodness, I had a hen in here and it's gone. What happened to it? Did you look in this sack?"

She said, "I did."

"I told you not to."

She said, "I know, but I heard you sing that song and I got a little curious and I wanted to take a little peak inside and I looked in … and well, the hen jumped out and I tried to get it back, but my pig was in the yard, and my pig does not like hens and it chased it away."

"Oh," said Fox, "so your pig chased my hen away. Then I'll just take your pig." He grabbed the pig by the hind legs—*"wheeee"*—put it in the sack.

The woman said, "That's not fair!"

And Fox said, "What's fair is fair, what's not is not. What's in my sack goes in my pot."

He put the sack over his shoulder, walked out the door, down the road, until he came to the third house on the street *[knocking sound]*.

A very skinny woman opened the door, she said, "Aaaah!"

He said, "Hello. I'm going to the house of my friend, Squintum. I'd like you to keep this sack until I come back."

And the skinny woman said, "All right."

He said, "Very well, but whatever you do, don't look in the sack."

She said, "What's in it?"

"Don't look in it."

"All right, I won't."

She took the sack. She put it down by the fireplace. Fox turned around, walked off down the road and you know what he sang. He sang,

> Nobody knows but me,
> Nobody knows but me,
> Nobody knows what's in my sack,
> Nobody knows but me.

And that very skinny woman heard that song and she looked down at the sack, and she saw Fox walking off down the road. She said, "I'm not going to look in there. I don't know what's there, but I'm not going to look." And she went back in the kitchen. She didn't look. No, she didn't.

But in a little while, her little boy came back inside. He'd been playing outside. He walked into the living room and there by the fireplace he saw a large sack. He said, "Hmmmm … Hey, Mom, what's in this sack?"

From the kitchen she called back, "Don't look in it."

He said, "Who is it for?"

She said, "Just don't look."

He said, "Oooooh! Maybe it's for me." He looked at the sack. His mother was in the kitchen, he said,

> I wonder what's in that sack?
> I wonder what's in that sack?
> I wonder, I wonder, I wonder, I wonder,
> I wonder what's in that sack?

"She'll never know," he said, "she's so slow." And that boy tiptoed over to the sack. He opened it up. *"Wheeee, wheee!"* Out jumped the pig. He said, "Oh, a pig!" He grabbed a stick, he chased it out of the door, down the road, and in a little while, *Fox came back [knocking sound].*

That skinny woman said, "Ooohhh, it's that fox. I don't like him." She went over, she opened up the door, she said, "There's your sack."

He walked over to pick it up, but it was empty. He said, "Look, this sack is empty. There was a pig in here. Did you look in this sack?"

She said, "No, I didn't."

"I told you not to and someone did. Who did?"

"Well, it wasn't me. And I …" She turned and looked. She saw her boy standing there by the door, she said, "Did you look in the sack?"

He said, "Yes."

"I told you not to."

He said, "I know, I thought maybe it was for me. There was a pig in it. And I know you don't want a pig in the house, so I chased it out the door and down the road."

And Fox said, "Oh, so your boy chased my pig away, then I'll just take your boy."

The woman said, "That's not fair."

He said, "What's fair is fair, what's not is not. What's in my sack, goes in my pot." He grabbed the boy *[scream]*, put him in the sack, walked out the door, down the road, until he came to the last house on the street. Fox walked up to the door *[knocking sound].*

A big, stout woman opened up the door. She looked down at Fox. She said, "Fox, what are you doing in my neighborhood?"

Fox said, "Hello. I'm going to the house of my friend, Squintum. I'd like you to keep this sack until I come back."

She looked at Fox, she said, "I'll keep it, but I won't keep it for long."

He said, "Very well, but whatever you do, don't look in the sack."

She said, "It's not my sack, it's not my business."

She took the sack, she put it down by the fireplace, she started to walk back into the kitchen and as she walked by the door she heard Fox sing as he walked off,

> Nobody knows but me,
> Nobody knows but me,
> Nobody knows what's in my sack,
> Nobody knows but me.

That big stout woman shook her head and went back into the kitchen where she was making cookies with her two daughters. They were making gingerbread cookies and had the batter in a big yellow bowl. They rolled the batter into little sticky balls. They put them on a cookie tray which they had oiled, they turned the oven on, they opened up the oven door, they put the tray of cookies in the oven and they closed the oven door and they sat down at the kitchen table to wait for the cookies, because it doesn't take long for cookies to bake. In a little while the smell of the gingerbread filled up the kitchen, filled up the living room, filled up the whole house.

One of her daughters couldn't wait any longer. She said, "Mom, I want a cookie."

And the second daughter said, "Me too."

And from out in the living room all three of them heard someone say, "Me too!" [muffled]

The big stout woman said, "Who said that?"

The first girl said, "I did."

The second girl said, "I did."

And the living room said, "I did!" [muffled]

That stout woman said, "What's going on here?"

She walked into the living room by the fireplace. She saw that sack, she said, "What's in Fox's sack?" She walked over, she opened up the sack and there was the little boy. "Hi!" he said.

She said, "What are you doing here?"

He said, "I don't know. Fox put me in here."

She said, "Fox is up to no good and we're going to play a trick on him." She looked at the little boy. She said, "You run into my bedroom over there and you hide under the bed."

"Great!" said the little boy who loved to hide under the bed.

Then that stout woman walked over to the door. She opened up the door and she whistled. "Buster," she called, "hey, Buster, come here." Buster was her watchdog. Buster came in the door *[sniffing, grunting sounds]*. She said, "Hi Buster, come here. I have a little job for you." She led Buster over to the sack. She said, "Buster, could you climb in the sack for just a minute?"

Buster said, *"Rowf!"*

She put Buster in the sack. Buster was just about the size of a small boy, if you know what I mean. Buster climbed in the sack, the woman tied it up, and she left it by the fireplace. It looked just like a small boy in a sack, but it wasn't. And in a little while, *Fox came back [knocking sound]*.

The big stout woman said, "The door's open, come on in." Fox opened up the door. He saw the sack, saw that it was still full, went and picked it up, heard something say, *"Ggrrrr ...!"* but he didn't think anything about it. He thanked that stout woman and walked out the door down the road singing to himself,

> Nobody knows but me,
> Nobody knows but me,
> Nobody knows what's in my sack,
> Nobody knows but me.

He walked down the road, thinking about what he was going to have to eat when he got home. He got hungrier and hungrier until he didn't think he could wait any longer. He said, "I'm going to eat him right now."

He put the sack down, opened it up, and stuck his paw in, "Ouch, oh that nasty little boy bit me."

He looked in the sack and there was not a little boy at all. There was a big watchdog! *"Growl!"* The fox said, "What are you doing in my sack?"

But Buster didn't answer. He just jumped out at Fox. Fox turned around on his tail and headed off into the woods with the dog right behind him. *"Rowf!"* Deeper and deeper into the woods they went until the fox got to his den. He jumped in the den, and just as he did Buster reached out and *"Ruff!"* bit him right on the rear end.

The fox was in his den, safe. Buster knew he was not going to get the fox, so he turned around and he ran all the way back home. He came in the back door, right into the kitchen, and there in the kitchen the cookies were sitting and cooling, ready to eat.

The stout woman saw Buster come in. She said, "It's time to eat!"

She gave one cookie to one of her daughters, one to another. She called the boy out from underneath the bed and gave one to him. She had one herself, and she gave two to Buster the watchdog.

Of course, there was none at all for Fox, who sat at home with a sore tail, singing to himself,

> Everybody knew but me,
> Everybody knew but me,
> Everybody knew what was in my sack,
> Everybody knew but me.

TELLING TIPS: I tell this story to primary grades. It works well because of the repetition involved, and the mix of people and animal characters. It's important that each woman develops her own personality in the few short lines that she has, and that Fox does his work at a leisurely pace. He's very confident. As with all stories, it's also important to take your time. Fight the inclination to rush through each incident after the stage has been set. There is a tendency among beginning storytellers to gloss over lines or incidents that happen time and time again. In a story like this, it's crucial to *emphasize* those lines and incidents. The children delight in the repetition, especially when the lines are repeated in each character's own particular way.

ABOUT THE STORY: I have put this story together from several different versions, most notably Joseph Jacobs' *English Folk and Fairy Tales* (G.P. Putnam's Sons, 1898) and another version by author/illustrator Paul Galdone. I've written the little songs and much of the rhymed repetition. It's the tellers' job to add their own changes, and give credit where it's due.

CAP FRANK

This story intrigues me because it is a story that deliberately challenges the stereotypes about stepmothers when many traditional tales (at least at first glance) reinforce those stereotypes. It is a healing story, a story about bridging troubled waters. I find it works with audiences of all sizes.

LEN CABRAL lives in Cranston, Rhode Island, with his wife and two daughters. He is the great-grandson of a Cape Verdean whaler who immigrated to America in the early 1900s. He grew up listening to Creole being spoken (through the stories of the Cape Verde Islands) and Creole music being played. He began his storytelling while working in a day-care center in Providence back in 1972. Being in charge of fifteen five-year olds, it was a means of survival. Twenty years later, it's still a means of survival, but also a way of life. In addition to telling stories around the country at festivals, museums, schools, theaters, and libraries, Len has co-founded the Sidewalk Storytellers, a childrens' theater company, and Spellbinders, the Rhode Island story-telling collective. He has served on the board of the Rhode Island Council of the Arts and as regional advisor to the board of the National Storytelling Association.

The Lion's Whisker

Len Cabral

A STORY FROM EAST AFRICA

Once there was a boy who was about ten years old, and his mother died. He was very sad that his mother died. He was angry that she died and he was confused about her death. And after about a year's time, his father remarried.

He married a woman who came from the highlands. Her name was Sonya and she loved the boy very much.

But the boy … he was so sad that his mother died, he was angry that she died, and he was confused about her death … and now he felt threatened by Sonya's presence. He felt his father would not love him as much because of Sonya's presence, though Sonya loved the boy very much.

She'd make beautiful clothing for the boy, but the boy would wear the clothing and run through the briars and rip them.

She'd make wonderful meals for the boy, but the boy wouldn't touch the food.

Try as she would, she could not win this boy's love.

One morning the father got up and went hunting. Sonya said, "Today I'm going to talk to my stepson about our feelings toward one another. For I love him dearly and I need for him to return that love to me."

And Sonya went into the boy's room. Now that boy, he was sitting on his cot and he had a feeling that Sonya was going to come in and talk to him about his feelings. He didn't want to talk about his feelings. He was sad, he was angry, he was confused. He felt threatened. He didn't want to talk about his feelings.

Sonya came into the room and said, "Son, I want to talk about our feelings toward one another."

He didn't even let her finish. He jumped off that cot and said, "I hate you. You're not my real mother. I'll never love you. I'm running away."

And he ran away.

This crushed Sonya. Sonya sat down and she cried and she cried.

Finally her husband came home, and she said, "Our son, he ran away."

Well, the father went down to the riverbank, where many boys and girls would go and spend time, and sure enough the boy was there throwing rocks into the water. He wasn't trying to make them skip or anything. He wasn't even throwing flat rocks. He was throwing round rocks.

The father walked over to the boy and placed his arm on his shoulder, and they sat down on a log and they talked for a long, long time. And then they walked home arm in arm.

When they returned home, Sonya had prepared a wonderful meal for them. They sat down and they ate of that meal. And after that meal they all went to their rooms, all except Sonya.

Sonya left that house. She walked out of the village, down a dirt road into the bush. Sonya went to the home of the witch doctor.

Now a witch doctor is a man of the village and knows the ways of the mind as well as the ways of the heart.

Sonya said, "Witch Doctor, you must give me a love potion, so that I may give it to my stepson so he will learn to love me, for I love him dearly and I need for him to return that love to me."

The witch doctor looked at Sonya and said, "First you must bring me a whisker from a furious mountain lion."

"Come again?"

"I said you must bring me a whisker from a furious mountain lion."

"But how can I do that?"

"Use your wits."

Well, Sonya returned home and she thought about that all night long.

Very early the next morning she left that house, and the only thing she took with her was a sack with four pieces of meat in that sack.

And Sonya, she walked away from the lowlands to the highlands, to the mountains and then the cliffs, and Sonya saw a cave. And she said surely there must be a furious mountain lion living in that cave.

Sonya reached into the sack and took out that first piece of meat. She walked up to the cave and placed that meat in front of the cave, and then she went back a hundred yards and hid in the bushes. And sure enough, a furious mountain lion came out of that cave, smelled the meat, ate the meat, and went back into the cave.

Sonya reached into that sack and took out that second piece of meat. She placed it in front of the cave and went back fifty yards. This time she did not hide in the bushes, she stood in the open. The mountain lion came out of the cave, looked right at Sonya, smelled the meat, ate the meat, and went back into the cave.

Sonya reached into that sack and took out the third piece of meat. She placed it in front of the cave and went back twenty yards. The mountain lion came out of the cave and looked right at Sonya. Sonya was frightened. She was shaking like a leaf, but she was a brave woman. The mountain lion smelled the meat, ate the meat, and went back into the cave.

Sonya reached into that sack and took out that last piece of meat. She placed it in front of the cave and took three short steps back. The mountain lion came out of the cave, looked right at Sonya, smelled the meat, and started to eat the meat. Sonya inched forward. She leaned over, she reached out, grabbed ahold of one of the whiskers and pulled. The mountain lion was still eating the meat. Sonya inched away until she got around a clump of bushes and then she ran.

She ran all the way back to the witch doctor's house, knocked on the door, and said, "Witch Doctor, here, here is a whisker from a furious mountain lion. Now give me my love potion so that I may give it to my stepson, so he will learn to love me, for I love him dearly and I need for him to return that love to me."

The witch doctor reached over and he took that whisker and he said, "Indeed, this is a whisker from a furious mountain lion."

"Yes, it is. Now give me my love potion."

"I'll not give you a love potion."

"But you said, you said—"

And he silenced her and said, "You must approach your stepson the same way you approached the lion."

Sonya thought about that and she said, "You mean, slowly and patiently?"

And the witch doctor nodded.

Well, Sonya returned home and she did approach her stepson slowly and patiently. And in a matter of three weeks the boy started to smile at her. In five weeks' time he helped her out around the house. In seven weeks' time they started going for long walks. That boy showed her how to skip rocks across the water, the nice flat rocks. In ten weeks' time they became best of friends.

That boy never forgot his real mother, but now he found room in his heart to love his stepmother also.

And that's the story of The Lion's Whisker.

TELLING TIPS: This story works well with audiences from sixth grade up. Because it is a story about breaking down prejudice and stereotypes, it can be used as an effective teaching tool. If you tell it in a classroom or with a small group, you can follow up with a discussion on prejudice. But if you tell it with a large audience, the story is strong enough to make its point with no discussion at all.

Resist the temptation to make this story too rambunctious. This story is most effective when told quietly and straightforwardly.

ABOUT THE STORY: My telling is based on *The Lion's Whiskers: Tales of East Africa* compiled by Russell Davis and Brent Ashabranner (Little, Brown, 1959).

JUDITH BLACK has twice been featured at the National Storytelling Festival and appears often at many other festivals throughout the country. This past year she taught and told stories in Colorado, Nebraska, Tennessee, and Minnesota, and developed the narrative line for the premier of The New American Music Ensemble. She has created original stories to both accent and accompany classical works, and has been a featured solo artist with the North Shore Philharmonic Orchestra, at Boston Conservatory, and as part of numerous regional concerts. She is a founder and board member of The Three Apples Storytelling Festival, New England's oldest and largest storytelling festival.

Lynn, Massachusetts, which saw its heyday well over half a century ago, is thought by many to be a dying city inhabited primarily by new immigrants and aging Americans. An economics bust is a storyteller's boom. After I shared tales at an old Lynn synagogue, a man who fit comfortably into this world made his way over to me. "Would you like to hear a story my father told me?" The following tale is one passed from his father to him, and from Meyer to me, and from me to you. Please do keep the chain evolving.

The King's Child

Judith Black

A JEWISH STORY

There was once a king whose sorrow was unending. Even though he was loved by his queen, worshiped by his subjects, and feared by his enemies, he still had no child. "Who will carry on my work, my power, my memory? I must have an heir!"

A reward was offered to anyone who could help the royal couple fulfill their dream. Many tried, many died, and the king and queen remained bitter and childless.

It was one cold day an old woman came to the king and queen. Shown into the throne room, she proclaimed that a child could be theirs if the king did just one thing.

"And what is that?" The king became anxious, and filled with hope. The tzaddikah* spoke.

"Your Majesty, because there is no system for washing out the human waste, there is much sickness in the land. All waters are the same. Use your army and dig canals through the cities and villages so that the waste may go to one place while the water for drinking and cooking is taken from another source."

The king was perturbed. "And this will bring me a child?"

The old woman smiled. "It is assured, Your Majesty."

It was done. The pestilence that had attacked them for generations was gone, but after many months there still was not a sign of quickening. The old tzaddikah was called back before the throne.

---

* Tzaddiki/Tzaddikah: a man or woman, in the Jewish tradition, of great virtue and righteousness.

35

"You have lied to me. I did as you said and yet no child is ours. Prepare to die."

But the old woman spoke quickly.

"My good king, you have only fulfilled part of the requirement. You must now parcel out the land to the serfs and peasants, allowing each a lot large enough for both sustenance and sale."

"Why should I give what is mine?" the king roared.

"So that you might have one with your name to follow," she said softly. The image of that "one" spoke so deeply to the king, he did as the old woman instructed. Every able-bodied peasant and serf was given his own lot. They could, for the first time in memory, feed their families and guests with ease. Then, the king and queen waited. But, no child grew between them. The king's blood boiled beneath his skin as he demanded to have the old woman brought before him, and he condemned her to death.

"Your Majesty, you may kill me, but then you will never know if the last requirement will bring fruit."

"The last?" Suspicion rolled with hope.

"Yes, Your Majesty, one last thing will ensure you an heir. Of this I am sure."

"If it does not," he spoke with a shaking voice, "your heirs will be denied their mother."

"Have no fear. The last thing you must do is to dismantle your army. For the last two decades our kingdom has fought war after war. Make lasting treaties with your neighbors and dissolve that force that once protected your aggression."

"But my army!"

"I give you no choice, Majesty."

And so it was done. For the first time in the memory of many, young men remained home behind plow and anvil, and children danced safely by the borders. The king, having sacrificed so much, was sure that now he would receive his heart's desire; but days turned to months, and months turned to a year, when the king had a scaffold erected in the throne room and the old woman was sent for.

"Now, you will die. Do you have anything to say?"

Her eyes looked towards a window and she spoke quietly. "Your Majesty, your wife was barren, as was the land. Your people died of sickness, starvation, and war. Look now at your land. You have given your people health, wealth, and the security of peace. You have given them a better life and your name is spoken with reverence. It is bestowed upon the children of your subjects and will be passed down to their children and their children's children. And it will be always a name spoken with honor. You, through acts of loving kindness, will be the father of and remembered by all the children of this land."

The king, whose eyes had followed the old woman's, gazed at the new landscape he had created. Taking her hand, he knew she was right. His children now would number with the stars and he would be remembered forever.

TELLING TIPS: Instead of pretending to be these characters and finding yourself using inflated, unreal voices, search for their real feelings within you. When the king is desperate to not leave this earth without a sign that he has been here, what is he feeling? How can you feel this same yearning along with the king and bring that feeling to his vocal quality and words? When the tzaddikah makes a promise to the king, is she trying to trick him—or empower him? How does this affect what she says and how she says it? Allow yourself to enter the characters' world and situation before finding what they say and how they say it.

This is one of the easiest to remember-and-tell stories that I know. I grew up with this version in County Down in the north of Ireland, but there are other versions in Ireland, England, France, and Germany. A few years ago I even heard an Italian one. But the Irish, as I'm sure many of you already know, are grand folks for telling the rest of the world how to act.

MAGGI KERR PEIRCE was born in Belfast, Northern Ireland, but has lived in the United States since 1964. She has taught many classes on the art of story-telling and was Artist-in-Residence in Bonner County, Northern Ireland, in 1986. Since 1980 she has been a familiar performer at the National Storytelling Festival in Jonesborough, Tennessee. She is the author of *Keep the Kettle Boiling, Storyteller's Guide,* and *Christmas Mince,* and is presently writing a novel for young girls. She has five cassettes of storytelling on the market. In 1988 she received a finalist award from the Massachusetts Arts and Humanities Artists Foundation for excellence in her field of storytelling.

The Story of the Half Blanket

Maggi Kerr Peirce

A STORY FROM NORTHERN IRELAND

There was this farmer and his son owned a tidy wee farm in the valley of Slievenaman (sleeve-nah-*mahn*). They had sheep on the high hills, a cow in the byre and a wheen of chickens in the yard. The mother had died many years before, but the household of two males kept things going very well and there was never a hard word between them.

The father would keep the house and yard tidy and in order, and the young man would roam the mountaintops after the black-faced sheep, as happy as the day was long. And although the house could have been a bit tidier, the oul' man could bake the grand soda bread on the griddle and there was always fresh buttermilk from the churn and the lovely brown eggs on a Sunday morning.

The father and son were content—until that is, the young man set his eye on a sonsy fine girl in the next parish. Before you could say "Jack Robinson" she was brought back to the valley as his blooming bride— and just in case some of you may think that this lassie is going to be making trouble between her menfolk, you have another think comin' to you! For D'il the bit of it.* Instead she made their lives all the better. Currant cake on a Sunday, lamb stew on a Thursday, I'm tellin' you they made a happy household, and then to make their joy complete—nine and a half months to the day—wasn't a baby born in their midst.

But what was the horror of it, for you won't believe what I'm tellin' you, the child made a terrible difference. The young man suddenly felt the heavy responsibility of fatherhood on his shoulders and he turned from being a happy-go-lucky chap to a complainin', disagreeable man.

---

* "D'il" is a shortened term for *devil* in Ireland.

And it was not on the wife or the wean he turned. No, it was on his poor oul' dad.

"Will you stop snuffling when yer atin' at table, do you think yer at a trough?" "Stop spitting in the fire, you'll teach the child bad manners." "Yer getting' too old for the yard work, you move like a snail." And on and on he would go, chandering and whinin' until he would have given you a pain to listen to him. And through it all, the poor oul' father said nothing, trying to keep out of his son's way, doing his best, trying to eat less, trying to disappear in the evening, no matter how cold it was, so that he wouldn't take up any room by the peat fire.

Finally, one night the son ups and says, "Father, there's nothin' else for you, the house is getting too small for us all, there's food only for us. It's to the poorhouse ye'll go tomorrow." And his wife tried to speak to him, but he thundered, "That's final!"

So the next morning he says to Mary, for that was the wife's name, "Get down that blanket that you brought with you for your dowry and we'll give it to Da to take with him." And with many a sad glance in the old man's direction, Mary tearfully brought down the lovely woolen blanket that she'd woven with her own hands.

Now in those far off days blankets were woven so long that they would be double on the bed when laid flat, and when himself saw the glory of the blanket and the fine length of it, he changed his mind. "Augh, that's too good a blanket to take with him to the poorhouse. Cut it in half," he ordered.

This time Mary was ready for him. "I will do no such thing," says she. "I brought this blanket into the marriage and your old man has been kindness itself to me all the days I've been here. Ye'll give him the whole blanket, and that's final," and the young man, hearing the note of authority in her voice, went to nod his head in agreement, when suddenly, from the cot on the hearthstone, there arose a small, piping voice.

"Daddy," the newborn baby said, "do no such thing. The half blanket will be fine and enough, but Mammy, be sure you put away the other half in a safe place, so that when I'm sending my Daddy to the poor-house, I'll know where it is."

Do you know, you would have thought that a ton o'bricks had hit that young man. "Sit by the fire, Father, make yourself comfy. Mary, put the whole blanket in the top cupboard and make a cup o'tea for us all." And from that day to this, the old man and the wee family lived together in peace and contentment, and the word "poorhouse" was never uttered again in the Valley of Slievenaman.

TELLING TIPS: Have fun in the telling. Only the child needs to have a wee squeaky voice; otherwise no change in tone is required. If any of the words are too strange to you as teller, use your words that you're comfortable with. Please give my name for this particular story but emphasize that it is known throughout the British Isles and Europe, as that always adds to the knowledge of the audience.

ABOUT THE STORY: In the many versions of this story I have encountered, the object is not always a blanket. In the Italian version, it was a dragon who remembered the old man being tipped into a garbage dump instead of a poorhouse. But the idea is always the same, and the young man always learns his lesson. In the French version, the "baddie" is the young wife, but I'm glad that in Ireland it isn't the woman—even though they *always* say, "It's true that the women are worse than the men!"

IRENE YOUNG

GAY DUCEY is a freelance storyteller who performs throughout the United States and teaches storytelling at the University of California, Berkeley, and at Santa Rosa Junior College. She is also a children's librarian at the Oakland Public Library. Ms. Ducey is the former chairperson of the National Storytelling Association, and is also the founder and director of the Bay Area Storytelling Festival. She was a commissioned artist in 1992 at the Smithsonian Institution's National Museum of American History, where she researched, developed, and performed an original piece. She was recently named an "Outstanding Woman of Berkeley" by the Berkeley, California Women's Commission.

"Lazy Jack" seems to work with almost all children between kindergarten and the third grade; it strikes the universal funnybone. When I first encountered it, though, I was concerned by Jack's portrayal as stupid in many versions.

Perhaps I was uneasier than most. Jack's attempts at following directions with those comically disastrous results had a familiar ring. Our son has Attention Deficit Disorder (ADD), a neurological disability. He was plagued by the misunderstandings and lapses typical of the disorder, especially during early childhood.

As my telling evolved, the mother's cry of "stupid" or "slow" became "Jack, I know you can learn."

This story is widely told, and for good reason; it is hilarious to young listeners.

Lazy Jack

Gay Ducey

A STORY FROM ENGLAND

Once there was a boy that everybody called Lazy Jack. And there's a reason they called him Lazy Jack. Because he was *laaaazy*. Jack spent each summer lying out in the meadow, smelling the sweet grasses, and watching the sun cross the sky. Sometimes he would bestir himself when he saw his mother. "Mother? How about some milk and bread? Apples?" And often his mother would oblige him.

Things changed for Jack when the weather got colder. He came inside and tucked up in front of the fire, warming his backside, and waiting for his mother to fetch him some fine meat. And often his mother would oblige him. But not always. For she loved her son, and wished him to grow strong and independent. And neither of them was getting any younger. So one day she said to him:

"Jack … I want you to get a job."

"A what?"

"A job, Jack."

"What's that, Mother?"

"Well, you go somewhere, work all day long, and at the end of the day, you're given something for your work."

"Oh no! I think not, Mother, I am ever so content as I am."

"Jack, I *know* you can learn, and it's time you worked for a living. So out you go, and tomorrow."

As Jack loved his mother as much as she was devoted to him, he did seek work the next day, and found it at a farm. All day long Jack dug and planted. Jack had never worked before, and he thought it the greatest fun. At day's end the farmer said, "Jack, you're a good lad, and here's your pay." And into Jack's hand he put a few shiny coins. But Jack had never had need of money, and knew nothing about it. Off he went,

43

saying, "My mother *will* be pleased!" But as he crossed a brook, he fancied to skip one of those coins and it was gone. The second he threw as high as he could, and so had only one left. "I shall save this for my mother." He held on as tightly as he could, but his hands began to sweat and the coin slipped from his grasp.

When he arrived home he had nothing but the story to tell his mother. She said, "Never you mind, Jack, I *know* you can learn. Now listen: that's not what you should have done with what you got. You should have put it in your pocket."

"Really! Is that what those are for? Never you worry, Mother, I'll remember, that I will."

And the next day Jack went to work again. But this day he hired on to a dairy farm. Jack led the cows to pasture, brought them back, milked them, and at the end of the day the dairy farmer gave Jack a tall jar of fresh, sweet milk. Now Jack liked milk as well as the next boy, but he remembered just what his mother had said. So he poured that milk down into his pocket and started the walk home. Soon the milk began to ooze down Jack's pants leg, and then to slide into his shoes, to sop up his socks, and slip between his toes.

When Jack's mother saw him she smelled him too! "Jack! I *know* you can learn! That's not what you should have done with what you got. You should have put that jar on your head and held it there till you got home."

"Really? What a good idea! I'll remember it, Mother, that I will!"

And the next day Jack went to work again. This time he worked for a cheesemaker. Jack spent the day salting the cheeses and turning them round. He was pleased when the cheesemaker placed a fresh round cream cheese in his hands as payment. But Jack remembered just what his mother had said. So he placed that soft cheese on his head and started the long, hot walk home. At first the cheese simply sat, and shaded Jack's face. But soon it began to melt and drip down Jack's face, and squish into his ears, and stick in his hair.

When his mother saw him she knew just what had happened. "Jack! I *know* you can learn. That's not what you should have done with what you got. You should have wrapped it in wet leaves and held it out in front of you, and not put it down."

"Really! What a good idea, Mother. I'll remember it, Mother, that I will."

On Thursday Jack worked at a bakery. For hours Jack smelled the pies, cakes, cookies, bread, muffins, and scones. He just knew something special was coming. And so it was, for into Jack's hands the baker put a nice, round, warm, fat … black … tomcat!

Now Jack remembered exactly what his mother had said. It took Jack quite a while to wrap the poor cat in those wet leaves; then Jack took the cat's ears in one hand, and its tail in the other and started on the path to home. At first the cat simply lay there in shock, but then it got mad, and started to yowl and jump. After a bit of a tussle Jack continued home, bitten and scratched.

When he arrived home, his mother said, "Jack, I *know* you can learn! That's not what you should have done with what you got. You should have tied a string around its neck, and pulled it along behind you."

"Really! What a good idea. I'll remember it, Mother, that I will."

On Friday Jack worked at a butcher shop. He was sure he would bring home some bit of meat, and he knew his mother would be pleased. Jack worked as hard as ever that day, hoisting sides of beef, legs of lamb. Tired at the day's end, Jack waited for his pay. The butcher brought out a fine ham. Jack was pleased … until he remembered just what his mother had said. So he tied some twine around the ham, laid it in the dirt, and started home. At first the ham skipped and tumbled beside him. But then it hit a mud puddle. Horrible! And a pile of leaves! Worse!

By the time Jack got home that meat wasn't fit to eat. Jack's mother was so upset she began to cry just a bit. "Oh, Mother, don't cry. I *know* I can learn."

"I know too, son. Here's what you should have done with what you got. You should have put it on your shoulder and not put it down at all."

"What a good idea, Mother. I'll remember it, that I will."

On Saturday Jack went to work for the driver of a donkey train, which carried people's bundles from one village to another. The day was busy, the road long, and when evening came they were far away from home. The donkey driver felt badly. "Jack, I meant for us to get back. You'll have to spend the night here and then return tomorrow." Jack did that very thing.

Before Jack left the next day, the driver said, "I will give you more than wages for staying overnight. I'll give you one of my finest donkeys."

But Jack remembered just what his mother had said. "No, no, that's all right, I'll just take my pay." But the driver insisted. And so Jack had a donkey. It took all Jack's strength to hoist that donkey up on his shoulders. First the front end, then the hind end. Jack was bent double from the weight, and the donkey's ears waved in his eyes, and the donkey's tail switched his ears, and that donkey smelled *baaad*.

Off Jack went very slowly, from one village to the next, making his way home. Now unbeknownst to Jack, along the way there lived a very rich man, whose only child, a daughter, had never laughed in all her life. Her father had consulted many doctors and wise people, but no one was able to make her laugh. She was spending that day as she spent all the others, gazing out of the window, sighing, moping.

But as she looked out she saw an astonishing sight. At first she thought it was a tiny old man, struggling under a tremendous weight. But as it came closer she saw it was a young man ... and that it was not a man riding a donkey but a donkey riding a man! And a tiny sound escaped her, something very close to a giggle, followed by another, and another, and then a real laugh. People came running to see what had caused her, at last, to laugh. She could not tell them, she could only point and scream.

"Bring that young man to me," said her father. "For I promised a fortune to anyone who could make my daughter laugh." And when Jack came in, the father handed him two great bags of gold. Jack remembered just what his mother had said. And he did not put that gold down until he brought it home to her. When his mother saw him she shouted, "Jack, I *knew* you could learn!" And she was right.

Jack built his mother a fine house and paid for it with that gold, and there was plenty left over. Jack hasn't changed much since then ... He still spends the summers out in the meadow, and in the winter you'll still find Jack lying in front of the fire. But, you know, it's a funny thing. Ever since Jack got all that gold, no one calls him Lazy Jack anymore. No. Now they call him *Mister* Jack. And that's what happens on the journey from being poor to being rich.

TELLING TIPS: This story lends itself to an active telling. I often mime Jack's plight, whether it is dripping cheese or holding the donkey aloft. I also extend the "a" in Laaazy Jack as long as bearable, and children often join me. Although the mother says much the same thing throughout the tale, emotionally I progress from mild annoyance to comic grief upon the arrival of the spoiled ham. When the girl begins to laugh, I find it much more effective to laugh myself than to describe it. I begin with a small giggle which escalates into a belly laugh, and I place my glance over the heads of the listeners and on Jack in the middle distance.

ABOUT THE STORY: I have changed the ending of this story, something I very seldom do. But I do not think the tale is diluted if Jack gets the gold, and not the girl. There are many other variants in these printed sources: *Obedient Jack: An Old Tale* by Paul Galdone (Franklin Watts, 1972); *Chimney Corner Stories: Tales for Little Children* by Veronica Hutchinson (Minton, Balch & Co., 1925); *English Folk and Fairy Tales* by Joseph Jacobs (G.P. Putnam's Sons, 1898); *Idle Jack* by Anthony Maitland (Farrar, Straus & Giroux, 1977); and *The Three Bears & 15 Other Stories* by Anne Rockwell (Crowell, 1975).

GREG NYSTROM

PLEASANT DeSPAIN, "Seattle's Resident Storyteller," is a former literature instructor at the University of Massachusetts and the University of Washington. He has hosted his own television show featuring storytelling, called "Pleasant Journeys," and written a syndicated newspaper column by the same name. He is the author of four books published by August House, *Twenty-Two Splendid Tales to Tell, Volumes One and Two; Thirty-Three Multicultural Tales to Tell;* and *Eleven Turtle Tales: Adventure Tales from Around the World.*

Folktales are told in the common language of world literature and usually express the common dreams, hopes, and aspirations of humankind. The husband and wife in this story are simple and hardworking folk—until the pot, which duplicates whatever is placed within, enters their lives. The quality of greed takes over, changing their lives dramatically.

After this tale I often hear, "Wow! I want one of those pots!" Materialism must be a timeless and multicultural trait!

The Magic Pot

Pleasant DeSpain

A STORY FROM CHINA

Once a poor but hardworking woodcutter was walking home from the forest, with an ax strapped to his back. Suddenly he came upon a large old pot made of brass. It was the biggest pot he had ever seen.

"What a fine pot!" he exclaimed. "But how will I get it home? It's too heavy to carry … Wait, I know …" He untied his shoulder strap and dropped the heavy ax into the pot. He proceeded to tie one end of the strap through one of the pot's handles and the other end around his waist. Then he began the hard work of dragging the clumsy pot down the path to his small house.

The woodcutter's wife was most pleased to see the pot and said, "What a fortunate day, Husband. You found a wonderful old pot and another ax."

"No, Wife, I just found the pot. I had the ax before."

"But there are two axes in the pot," she said.

The woodcutter looked inside and was speechless. Two identical axes sat side by side. As he leaned down to pull them out, his straw hat fell from his head and into the pot. Now two hats rested near the axes.

"Wife! The pot is haunted!"

"Or it's magical!" she said happily. "Let's put tonight's dinner inside and see what happens."

One dinner became two.

"Quickly," said the wife. "Get our savings from the jar on the shelf!"

The handful of coins doubled.

"It is magical!" cried the woodcutter. "What shall we put in next?"

"The money, of course," said his practical wife. "Let's get rich while we can."

They placed the coins inside repeatedly, and the amount doubled each time. An hour later every jar, pan, basket, pocket, chest, shelf, and shoe they owned was filled with money. They were, indeed, rich!

"Dear Wife," said the woodcutter, "we can build a fine house and have a big vegetable garden, and I won't have to work so hard from now on. I'm so happy that I could dance!"

Then he grabbed her around the waist and began to dance around and around the small room. Suddenly he slipped on some loose coins and accidentally dropped his wife into the pot! He tried to pull her back out—but it was too late. He now had *two* wives. They stepped out of the pot and looked closely at each other. It was impossible to tell them apart.

"What have I done?" cried the woodcutter. "Can a man live with two wives at the same time?"

"Not in my house," said the first wife.

"Not in my house," said the second wife.

Both women smiled and grabbed the woodcutter and made him get into the pot. Two woodcutters climbed back out.

"Can two families live in the same house?" asked both of the men.

"No," said the first wife.

"No," echoed the second wife.

Half the money was given to the second couple and they built an elegant house. It was right next to the first couple's fine, new house. Ever since that time, the people of the village have remarked on the strong resemblance of the woodcutter and his wife's new relatives, the ones who must have brought them all that money!

TELLING TIPS: I've told this tale for fifteen years and found that it works well with all ages, including adult audiences. When introducing it, I ask my listeners a few questions: "What would you do if you found a purse and discovered that it had the power to double any amount of money that you placed inside, as often as you wanted? Would you try to find the rightful owner? Would you keep it for yourself? Would you toss it away?"

Then I throw them a curve: "Don't answer until you have heard my story." The resulting discussions are always lively, enlightening, and entertaining.

Allow the gentle humor resulting from the story's end to settle upon your listeners with a modicum of grace. Pause after the final sentence and watch the smiles spread as your listeners put the resulting scene and logical solution together in their minds.

ABOUT THE STORY: This telling is my adaptation of a variant found in *The Arbuthnot Anthology of Children's Literature* by May Hill Arbuthnot (Scott, Foresman & Co., 1961).

RUTH STALMAKER

DAVID HOLT is an award-winning musician and storyteller. He is best known for his appearances on The Nashville Network and as host of the PBS series "Folkways" and American Public Radio's "Riverwalk." In 1984, Holt was named in *Esquire* magazine's Register of Men and Women Who Are Changing America. He has four award-winning storytelling recordings and four music recordings, including Grammy nominee *Grandfather's Greatest Hits.* A native of Garland, Texas, Holt has lived in the western North Carolina mountains for two decades.

BILL MOONEY starred for many years as Paul Martin in the ABC daytime serial "All My Children" and is a two-time Emmy nominee for that role. His one-man show of humorous frontier stories, *Half Horse, Half Alligator,* was recorded by RCA Victor and toured America and Europe for two decades. Mooney currently lives in East Brunswick, New Jersey.

We get together a couple of times a year to write original stories or work up traditional tales for telling. When we began working on our recording of animal stories, Why the Dog Chases the Cat, *we searched out every animal folktale we could find. We realized "Trouble" could have some wonderful characters and musical sound effects. We wrote the songs to spice it up and added slide guitar to give it a blues feel. It adds up to a fun story that warns the listener never to go looking for "trouble."*

Trouble!
(or, How the Alligator Got Its Crackling Hide)

David Holt and Bill Mooney

AN AFRICAN-AMERICAN STORY

Once, a long time ago, the alligators had beautiful smooth golden skin. They had the easiest life of all the creatures. During the day they swam around the swamp, fishing and eating. When they got tired of that, they would sun themselves on the banks, or chase rabbits for a snack. If it got too hot and tiring for them, the alligators would slide down into the water and cool off.

One hot summer day when all the alligators were lazing in the water, Rabbit came hopping along the bank. When he saw those alligators, he jumped back. You see, not long before, he'd had his tail bitten off by these same alligators. And he was coming to pay them back. So he started singing like he didn't have a care in the world:

Trou-ble, oh trou - ble, trou-ble's in the air,

Trou-ble, oh trou - ble, trou-ble's ev-'ry-where.—

Now, trou-ble is a teach-er, it's just— like a friend, It

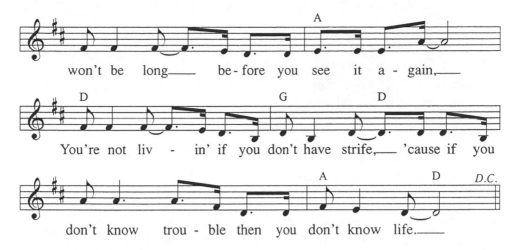

won't be long___ be-fore you see it a-gain,___

You're not liv - in' if you don't have strife,___ 'cause if you

don't know trou - ble then you don't know life.___

When the King of the Alligators heard that happy little tune he called out, "Hey, Rabbit, what's this 'trouble' thing you're singing about?"

Rabbit stopped in his tracks. "Trouble? You mean to tell me you never heard of Trouble?"

"Naw, never heard of it. We don't get outta the swamp much. We all just fish and eat and laze around in the sun all day. But we sure do like to hear about new things—things like this here Trouble."

"Oh, I can tell you about Trouble. I've seen it lots of times," said Rabbit.

> "I've seen trouble as wide as a river
> Or narrow as a sliver.
> Big as a sky
> Or small as a fly.

Once you see Trouble you'll never be the same."

"That sounds exciting," said the king. "Sounds like something I'd like to see."

"You want to *see* Trouble?"

"Yeah," said the alligator, "could you show me some?"

"Yes, I can show you *big* Trouble," said Rabbit.

> "Trouble so big, you'll dance a jig.
> Trouble so wide, you'll be goggle-eyed."

"Where can I see it?"

"Well, lemme think … You and all your family meet me in the center of the hayfield in the morning."

"Yes, sir," said the King of the Alligators. "We'll all be there, looking for Trouble."

[laugh] "See you then!

Trouble, oh Trouble,
Trouble's in the air,
Trouble, oh Trouble,
Trouble's everywhere."

The next morning, not long before the sun touched the top of the gum tree, the King of the Alligators got up on a big cypress stump.

He sang out in his big bass voice,

And the mama and papa alligators echoed:

"Alligators, gather 'round,
We're gonna see Trouble,
Won't you come on down."

And all the baby alligators answered:

"Alligators, gather 'round,
We're gonna see Trouble,
Won't you come on down."

So all the alligators gathered on the banks and started off. They were laughing and singing, running and playing. It was the finest jamboree of alligators that the creatures in the swamp had ever seen. Big ones, little ones, long ones, short ones all parading to the hayfield, their golden skin shining in the sunlight.

Rabbit was there waiting to meet them.

"Rabbit, have you got Trouble with you?"

"Yessiree bobtail," said Rabbit, "I brought you big Trouble! Just like I said I would. Gather all the 'gators in the center of the field and I'll send Trouble out to meet you."

So the alligators all bunched together in the center of the field where the grass was high and the grass was dry.

In the meantime, Rabbit hopped off to a far corner of the field. He pulled out a kitchen match and started a fire in the grass. Then he hopped off to another corner of the field and lit another fire. In no time, he had fires burning all around the edge of the dry hayfield.

One of the big alligators hollered out, "What's that pretty red stuff comin' this way?"

"That must be the Trouble that Rabbit is bringing to us."

The fire moved closer, and the fire got hotter.

> "My, my, my, it's warm and rosy.
> Trouble makes you feel all nice and cozy."

And the fire got closer, and the fire got hotter.

> "My, my, my, isn't Trouble hot.
> Feels like the sun on a big hot rock."

And the fire got closer still, and the fire got hotter still.

> "My, my, my, it's biting me.
> Trouble feels like a swarm of bees."

The King of the Alligators said, "I've enjoyed about as much of this Trouble as I can stand. LET'S GET OUTTA HERE!"

The alligators jigged to the left and to the right. They jigged forwards and backwards, but there was fire all around.

Then the King of the Alligators hollered, "Foller me." He lowered his head and plowed through the burning grass. All the other alligators followed along behind him.

Each alligator scrambled through the burning grass till at last they reached the banks of the river. One by one they slithered off the bank and flopped into the water, sizzling and crackling as they hit.

Aaah! That water was co-o-o-o-ol and ca-a-a-alm and comforting. Yessssir. They were *home.*

As they lay in the water feeling good, the alligators looked around at each other. Their smooth golden skin had turned dark grey-green, all covered with cracks and ridges and still smoking. The King of the Alligators started to sing in a slow bluesy voice:

> "Trouble, oh Trouble,
> Trouble's in the air,
> Trouble, oh Trouble,
> Trouble's everywhere."

As he was singing the blues, along hopped Rabbit.

"So how'd you folks like Trouble? I told you it was a good teacher."

"I don't want to learn anymore about Trouble, Rabbit!"

But Rabbit said, "Oh, it's too late for that now. The first rule of Trouble is: *'Never trouble Trouble, till Trouble troubles you!'"*

And to this day, the alligator stays near the water, so he can cool his rough cracked skin

> and
> stay away
> from
> TROUBLE!

TELLING TIPS: Even though the story was written to use David's musical talent, you can tell the story without a guitar or banjo. When Bill tells it, he sings the song *a capella* and makes the sound effects with his voice. It helps the telling if you characterize Rabbit as being sassy and smart-alecky, and the King of the Alligators as being bellicose and self-important. The mama, papa, and baby alligators are usually depicted by high and low voices.

ABOUT THE STORY: This story comes from the African-American tradition. There are many different versions of it dating back to its origin in Africa. David has heard several variations in North Carolina, and Bill learned a similar one when he was growing up in Arkansas.

When I read this story in Ruth Finnegan's Limba Stories and Storytelling, *I thought, "This is a story my audiences need to hear." When I saw yellow ribbons tied to every door in my community announcing support for the Gulf War, I thought, "I must begin telling stories for peace." It is a little thing. But it is something we storytellers can do.*

MARGARET READ MacDONALD was born and raised in southern Indiana and received her Ph.D. in Folklore from Indiana University. She has been a children's librarian and storyteller since 1965 and draws on that experience for her many folktale/storytelling publications. Her *Storyteller's Start-up Book* and *Twenty Tellable Tales* are popular with beginning storytellers; *Look Back and See: Twenty Lively Tales for Gentle Tellers* and *Peace Tales: World Folktales to Talk About* provide tellable tales for many tellers' repertoires; and *The Storyteller's Sourcebook: A Subject, Title and Motif-Index to Folklore Collections for Children* has become a standard reference for all storytellers. Dr. MacDonald has offered her "Playing with Story" workshops throughout the United States and in Europe, New Zealand, and Canada.

Strength

Margaret Read MacDonald

A STORY FROM THE LIMBA PEOPLE OF WEST AFRICA

The animals decided to have a contest
to see who was the strongest.
   This contest was Elephant's idea.
   "Everybody meet on Wednesday.
   We'll see who has STRENGTH."

First to arrive was Chimpanzee.
Chimpanzee came in jumping around.
   "Strength!
   I've got strength
   See these ARMS!
   Just wait till they see my strength!"
Chimpanzee sat down.

Deer arrived.
   "Strength!
   Look at these LEGS!
   I have SUCH strength."
Deer sat down.

Next came Leopard.
Leopard was showing his claws and growling.
   "Strength!
   Look at these CLAWS!
   I ... have STRENGTH!"
Leopard sat down.

In came Bushbuck.
Bushbuck lowered his strong horns.

"Strength!
See these horns!
THIS is strength."
Bushbuck sat down.

Elephant came in.
Elephant moved so slowly.
"El … e … phant …
MEANS
Strength."
Elephant sat down.

They waited.
They waited.
One more animal to come.
They waited.
At last Man came running in.
"STRENGTH! STRENGTH!"
Man was showing off his muscles.
"Here I am
We can START now!"

Man had brought his gun to the forest.
Man had been hiding his gun in the bush.
That is why he was late.
Elephant took charge.
"Now that *Man* is finally here, we can begin.
Chimpanzee.
Show us strength."

Chimpanzee jumped up.
He ran to a small tree and climbed it.
He bent it over and tied it in a knot.
He climbed back down.
"Strength! Was that strength?!!
What strength!"

The animals cheered.
"Strength! Strength! Strength! Strength!
THAT's strength!"
The animals calmed down.
"Well …

Chimpanzee
SIT DOWN.
Who is next?"

Deer leaped up.
Deer ran three miles into the forest.
Deer ran three miles back.
Deer wasn't even out of breath.
    "There.
    Wasn't that strength!"

The animals agreed.
    "Strength! Strength! Strength! Strength!
    That was STRENGTH!"

    "Well …
    Deer
    SIT DOWN.
    Who's next?"

Leopard leaped up.
Leopard drew out his long claws.
He began to scrape at the earth.
    Scrung … scrung … scrung … scrung …
That dirt just flew!
The animals jumped back.
They were frightened.
    "Aaah!
    Wasn't that strength?"

    "Strength! Strength! Strength! Strength!
    That was STRENGTH!"

    "Well …
    Leopard
    SIT DOWN.
    Who's next?"

Bushbuck was next.
Bushbuck lowered his huge horns.
A cane field was there.
Bushbuck began to plow through that cane field.
    Shuuu … shuuu … shuuu … shuuu …

60

His horns just made a ROAD right through that field.
Bushbuck turned around.
 Shuuu ... shuuu ... shuuu ... shuuu ...
He plowed a road right back.
 "Wasn't THAT strength?"

The animals were impressed.
 "Strength! Strength! Strength! Strength!
That was STRENGTH!"

 "Well ...
Bushbuck
SIT DOWN
Who's next?"

Now came Elephant.
Many trees were there.
They were growing close together.
Elephant leaned his huge shoulder against those trees.
 Eeennhh ... eeennhh ... eeennhh ... kangplong!
Those trees fell right over.
 "STRENGTH! Was THAT strength?!"

 "Strength! Strength! Strength! Strength!
THAT was STRENGTH!"

 "Well ...
Elephant
SIT DOWN.
Who's next?"

Man's turn.
Man ran to the middle of their circle.
Man started whirling around.
He turned somersaults.
He turned cartwheels.
He did handsprings.
That man was twirling all over the place.
Man stopped.
 "Strength! Strength! Wasn't that STRENGTH?!"

The animals looked at one another.
 "Well ... that was exciting."

"But … was it strength?"
"Not really …"
"Is that all you can do?"

Man was insulted.
"Well then, watch THIS?"
Man climbed to the top of a palm tree
So fast! So fast!
He threw down palm nuts.
He climbed back down again.
"Strength! Strength! Was that strength?!"

The animals looked at him.
"Would you call that strength?"
"He just climbed a tree."
"That's not really strength."
"Is there anything else …?"

Man was ANGRY.
"Strength? I'll show you STRENGTH!"
Man ran into the bush.
He grabbed his gun.
He ran back again.
Man pointed his gun at Elephant.
Ting …
He pulled the trigger.
Kangalang!
Elephant fell over.
Dead.
Dead.

Man was jumping and bragging.
"Strength! Strength!
Wasn't THAT strength?!"

"Strength …"

Man looked around.
The animals were gone.
They had fled into the forest.
"Strength! …"
There was no one left to hear him brag.

Man was alone.

In the forest the animals huddled together and talked.
  "Did you see that?"
  "Was that strength?"
  "Would you call that strength?"
  "No. That was DEATH."
  "That was DEATH."

Since that day the animals will not walk with Man.
When Man enters the forest he has to walk by himself.

The animals still talk of Man ...
That creature *Man* ...
He is the one who cannot tell the difference
  between strength
  and death.

TELLING TIPS: This retelling is easy to learn and powerful when told. Here are a few hints for the telling. The audience may enjoy joining in on the animals' chorus— "Strength! Strength! Strength! Strength!"—and the story can be developed as a lively participation event. However, though this story is energetic and humorous in its telling, the ending must be delivered in a serious manner, cutting directly across the audience's excited mood and expectations. Practice the ending carefully before attempting it, so that you are certain you can carry the audience through the tale's abrupt mood change at its end. Children often buy into Man's "triumph" at the tale's end and are brought up short when they realize that his actions were perhaps not triumphant after all. This powerful story is one that children need to hear.

ABOUT THE STORY: A fine variant of this tale appears in *Limba Stories and Storytelling* by Ruth Finnegan (Clarendon, 1967).

RAFE MARTIN is an award-winning author and storyteller. He has performed, spoken, and taught throughout the United States and as far away as Japan, appearing at such prestigious institutions and events as the American Museum of Natural History, the Vassar College Institute on Children's Literature, the Chautauqua Institute, the National Storytelling Festival, the American Library Association National Convention, the International Reading Association's International Convention, the American Booksellers' National Convention—to name just a few. His work has been featured in *TIME, Newsweek, U.S. News & World Report,* and the *New York Times Book Review.* His books, which include *Will's Mammoth* and *The Rough-Face Girl,* and his tapes, which include *Animal Dreaming* and *Ghostly Tales of Japan,* have received such recognition as the ALA Notable Book of Distinction, the Parents' Choice Gold Award, and the Anne Izard Storyteller's Choice Award.

This version of "Urashima Taro," the most well-known folktale in Japan, was recreated especially for this book and emphasizes directness of style and ease of telling. It's based on my own original telling (as recorded on my audiocassette, Ghostly Tales of Japan*). That telling is, in turn, based on the version first made available in English by Lafcadio Hearn at the turn of the century. Hearn's versions are still the classics. A more complex and literary retelling of "Urashima Taro" will appear in my new book,* The Snow Woman and Other Mysterious Tales of Japan, *available in 1996 from G.P. Putnam's Sons.*

Urashima Taro

Rafe Martin

A STORY FROM JAPAN

Once there was a poor but kind-hearted fisherman, named Urashima Taro. One day as he was walking along the beach towards his boat, his nets rolled up on his shoulders, he passed some boys throwing sticks and stones at something that was crawling in the sand. What could it be?

He went over and saw that they were throwing those sticks and stones at a gigantic sea-turtle that had crawled up out of the sea and was now trying to make its way back to the waves.

"Stop, boys!" he called. "Why harm this innocent creature? Indeed, the turtle is the messenger of the Dragon King who lives under the sea and is said to live ten thousand years. If you kill it, the loss of all those years will pile up on your own heads. It could be dangerous. Here, boys," he said, digging into a little pouch that hung by his side, "take these coins and let the turtle go."

Willingly the boys took the coins and let the turtle go. Just before diving down under the green sea, the turtle turned back and looked at Urashima Taro as if fixing his image in its mind. Then it dove down under the green sea.

Urashima Taro came to his boat. He put his nets into the boat and pushed the boat out, splashing through the waves. Then he jumped in, took up his oars, and began to row. He rowed and he rowed and he rowed.

And as he rowed the islands of Japan sank down into the seas.

Out on the sea the little boat rocked back and forth on the waves. And as Urashima Taro sat there in his little boat rocking gently on the sea he began to feel sleepy. And before he knew what he was doing he had put his head down on the side of that little boat and he fell asleep.

He had a dream. In this dream it seemed that a beautiful woman rose up out of the sea and began walking along the tops of the waves without sinking in at all. Her long black hair hung down behind her. Her robe was crimson and blue. And she was beautiful.

On she came across the water, closer and closer. She stepped into his boat, reached down and touched him on the shoulder and …

Urashima Taro awoke. And there she was, just the way he had seen her in his dream!

"Who are you?" he stammered. "What do you want?"

"Urashima Taro, Urashima Taro," she said, "I am the daughter of the Dragon King from under the sea. Because of your kind deed to my father's messenger, the turtle, he has sent me to you to be your bride. And we shall live together on the Island Where Summer Never Dies, if you wish."

He did wish. So she sat down beside him and she took up one oar and he took the other. And they began to row together. They rowed and they rowed and they rowed. And as they rowed, like a dream up before them rose the Island Where Summer Never Dies. They rowed through the surf. Urashima Taro jumped out, pulled the boat up onto the sand, and helped the princess step out upon the shore where strange creatures from under the sea awaited them saying, "Welcome, welcome, kind Urashima Taro." And Urashima Taro married the princess from under the sea and for three years he was happy.

Then, one day, in the third year it was as if he suddenly awoke from a dream. "My mother," he said, "my father, my family and friends. They must think I'm dead. I went out into the sea three years ago and never returned. How could I have done such a thing? And I miss them. I must return home and let them know that I am all right."

And he went to his wife. "My mother," he said, "my father, my family and friends. I left three years ago and never returned. They must think I'm dead. And I miss them. I must return to them for a short while. I must go home."

But she said, "Urashima Taro, Urashima Taro. Don't go. If you go you shall never return."

"Of course I will return," he insisted. "I would never leave you. I must just go back to my home for a short while and let my family and friends know that I am alive. I miss them and must see them and at least make a proper farewell."

But once again she said, "Urashima Taro, Urashima Taro, don't go! If you go I shall never see you again."

But, "Do not fear," was all he said. "I will be back soon."

When she saw that he was going to go whether she wanted him to go or not she turned, reached back, and gave him *this*.

It was a little black-lacquered wooden box tied with a silken cord.

"Take this box and keep it with you always," she said. "It will help you come back to me. *But you must never open the box!* Do you understand?"

"I, I do," he answered. "I will keep it with me always and I will never open the box."

Then, carrying the box, he ran down to the beach, put the box in the boat, pushed the boat out splashing in the sea, jumped in, took up his oars, and began to row. And he rowed and he rowed and he rowed. And as he rowed, the Island Where Summer Never Dies sank down into the sea and up before him once again, like a dream, rose the islands of his home, of Japan.

He rowed right through the surf, jumped out splashing in the water, pulled the boat up on the sands so it wouldn't drift away, lifted out the box and, what was this?

Something was strange. When he had left, only three years ago, the mountainside behind the village had been covered with trees. And now it was just bare stone. When he had left, only three years ago, the trees of the grove had been tall and straight, yet now they were all twisted and bent. The houses were strange. He had never seen houses quite like that before. The people's clothing was strange, like none he had ever seen. Holding that box, he walked up into the village. But the people's faces were strange to him too. This was his own home, his own village. Yet he didn't recognize a single soul.

"What's going on?" wondered Urashima Taro. "Why does everything seem so different? I'm going to go home." And he ran to where his house should have been. But when he got to where his house should have been no house stood there at all.

"What's going on?" repeated Urashima Taro, confused. "What kind of strange illusion is this?"

Just then an old man came hobbling down the lane leaning on a stick. "Old man," called out Urashima Taro, "old man, please help me."

"Eh?" said the old man. "What do you want?"

"Help me, please," said Urashima Taro, "to find the house of one named Urashima Taro. He grew up here. He lived here. His mother and father live here still."

"Urashima Taro?" said the old man. "Urashima Taro? Never heard of him." And he started off.

"Old man, wait, wait!" cried Urashima Taro. "I know he lives here. Please old one, think hard. Urashima Taro. Urashima Taro ..."

"Urashima Taro?" repeated the old man. "Urashima Taro! Why my father's father told him the story of Urashima Taro, the young fisherman who went out into the sea three hundred years ago and never returned. Urashima Taro! You want his home? It's the graveyard. You'll find his whole family there." And the old man hurried off.

"What kind of nightmare is this?" said Urashima Taro, but holding the box he hurried to the graveyard and there, in the oldest portion of the graveyard he found three large grave stones. They had been there for a long time for they were weathered, cracked and split. And they were covered with moss.

Urashima Taro went up to the first stone and rubbed the moss off. And there, beneath the moss, carved in the stone, he read his mother's name! He went to the second stone, rubbed the moss off the second stone and read—his father's name! He went to the third stone, rubbed off the moss—and there was his own name!

Overwhelmed, but still holding the box, he turned and wandered in a daze back down to the sea. And when he got there he said, "The secret of this nightmare lies in this box. I will open the box and find out what's going on. And I'll do it now!"

He untied the silken cord and put one hand on the top of the box. He took a deep breath, lifted up the lid, and *Whoooosssshhhh!* A thin white mist rose up out of the box and blew away across the ocean towards the Island Where Summer Never Dies.

All at once Urashima Taro felt very old, very tired and weak. His hands shook—and shriveled up before his eyes. His teeth loosened and fell out. His hair turned white. Then Urashima Taro, three hundred years old, collapsed onto the sands, turned to dust, and blew away across the ocean towards the Island Where Summer Never Dies.

TELLING TIPS: The key to success with a story like Urashima Taro is sensitivity to the tale's underlying rhythm—and to its elegant, eerie, and ultimately poignant atmosphere. When the princess speaks, her voice murmurs quietly, perhaps, like the sea. But when she hands him the box and says "But never open it!" that "BUT" is, at least in my way of telling the story, intense, loud, even startling. It can frighten. The contrast catches us by surprise. It is a change of rhythm. The rest of the story now takes place on a heightened level of interaction with the listeners, whose pulses may race and whose eyes may widen. The story also draws upon the awareness of aging we all carry deep within us and the recognition that there is really no going back home—for any of us. This is not just a story. One is saying by the act of telling, "This is true. Time changes all." So the ending, while strong, even visually horrifying, is also tender, quiet, and sad. It's a complex mood, but voice, pacing, and body language can carry it well.

J.J. RENEAUX, a musician and storyteller, grew up surrounded by the Cajun folklore and superstitions of southeast Texas and Louisiana. She has performed at festivals and universities around the world, including the National Storytelling Festival. She is the author of *Cajun Folktales* (recipient of the Anne Izard Storyteller's Choice Award) and *Haunted Bayou and Other Cajun Ghost Stories,* both published by August House. Her audiocassette, *Cajun Ghost Stories* won the Parents' Choice Award in 1992.

Mr. Laurence Mollere loved to tell this story about the "dancin' fiddle, the magic hat, and the shoot-'em-up gun." He especially liked the part where the boy gets the sheriff, the judge, and the rich man all dancing up a storm. The story would alway spark some boyhood memory, and one story faded surely into another, so that I hardly knew when one tale ended and another began. In later years I found other versions of the tale, but I have always like Mr. Mollere's story best.

The Magic Gifts

J.J. Reneaux

A CAJUN STORY

Leo was a poor boy who lived with his papa in a little run-down shotgun shack. His papa tried hard to make a living, but after many years he was getting too old and tired to keep on working so hard. Leo saw his papa was just about worn out with work and worry, so one day the boy went to him and says, "I'm almost a man now. It's time for me to find work and help earn a livin'. If you can hold on a while longer, I'll go and see what I can make of myself. If my fortune is good, I'll be able to take care of you, Papa. You can spend your days fishin' or sittin' in the warm sun out on the *galerie*. You've taken care of me, now I want to do for you." Papa gave his blessing and wished his son *bonne chance.*

Leo started out and traveled all over the countryside looking for work. Times were hard and nobody wanted to hire a boy to do a man's work. One day Leo was tired and discouraged. He was just about to give up when he remembered his ol' papa's face. *When Papa was tired, he didn't give up,* the boy thinks to himself, *and here I am actin' like a whupped pup. If I'm gonna be a man, I guess I better pick myself up and start actin' like one!* Leo started walking again. This time he wouldn't take no for an answer.

The boy came to a farm and asked the farmer if he needed a hand. Ol' farmer scratches his head and looks the boy up and down. Before he could say no, Leo claps his hands together and says, "Tell ya what I'm gonna do. Me, I'm gonna work for you for a whole year. If you don't like my work, you don't have to pay me. But if you think I've earned my pay, you can pay me then. What've ya got to lose?"

The farmer had to admit it was a good deal. The man and the boy shook hands and Leo went to work.

70

He proved to be the best hand the farmer ever hired. When a year had passed, Leo came to collect his wages. "If you're satisfied with my work," he said, "then I guess it's time for you to pay me and I'll be on my way."

The farmer was more than satisfied. In fact, he didn't want the boy to go. He told Leo that if he'd stay and work another year, then he'd pay the boy for two years of work when the time was up. Leo figured it was a good deal. He had no better offer and he got along just fine with the farmer.

As time went by, Leo became an even better worker, for he was growing taller and stronger and learning all the ropes. When the year was out, the boy went to collect his pay, but since the farmer still needed a hand, he asked the boy to stay on yet another year. He promised to pay him for three years when his time was up. Leo still figured it was a good deal. He trusted the old farmer, and besides, he didn't have any other offers. Times were lean and hard.

The boy worked another year. He grew even taller and stronger, and the old farmer taught him well how to bargain and trade. The year passed and he came to collect his pay. Farmer says, "You've been a good worker. I never thought a boy could do the job of a man, but I sure am glad you talked me into hirin' you. Now it's time for me to pay you and let you go on your way."

But the farmer didn't pay Leo in ordinary money. Instead, he gave him gifts that a clever boy could use to make a fortune. The first present was a special gun. No matter how it was aimed, this gun never missed its mark. The second gift was a fiddle. It played music so sweet that anybody who heard it was bound to dance until the song stopped. The last gift was a hat. Leo put it on and found that it made him invisible!

The boy told the farmer goodbye, took his gifts, and started down the road. He walked a long way, but the gifts didn't bring him any luck at all. *Well,* he thinks, *if Lady Luck won't come to me, I'll just have to go and find her!*

Leo put the hat on and made himself invisible. Coming around the bend in the road, he saw a rich-looking man firing a gun at a strange red bird flapping across the sky. Each shot was wide of the mark. Leo walked unseen right up to the man and heard him talking to himself. "Aw! Missed again! I've got to have that bird. It's worth a fortune! I'd pay a lot of money to get that bird down."

When Leo heard that, he knew he had caught up with Lady Luck. He took his magic hat off, and there he was standing by the rich man. He says, "I can get that bird down for you, but it'll cost you a thousand dollars." The rich man nearly jumped out of his shoes to see the boy suddenly appear at his elbow. "All right then," he agrees, "you get that bird down, and I'll pay what you ask."

Leo took aim, fired the gun, and the bird fell into a thicket of blackberry bushes. "There it is," says Leo. "Now pay me."

The rich man was greedy. He decided he would get the bird and not pay the boy a red cent. "It was a lucky shot. I coulda got it myself. You don't deserve a thousand dollars for a lucky shot!"

"All right then," says Leo, "go get the bird yourself." The man picked his way through the thorns and found the bird. But before he could get out of the thicket again, Leo started playing his magic fiddle. The song was so sweet and lively that the rich man couldn't keep his toes from tapping. Next thing he knows, his feet are dancing with a life of their own and the thorns are stickin', stickin', stickin' him! Rich man is cryin' and hollerin', "Stop, stop! I'll pay!"

Leo quit playing and the rich man stopped dancing. He paid the boy the thousand dollars, but he was mad as a wet cat. He went straight to the sheriff and had Leo arrested as a thief and a rascal. They took the boy to the judge to have a trial.

"You good-for-nothin' crook," the judge growls. "Thought you could cheat an honest man out of a thousand dollars, eh? Well, I order you to return that thousand and pay a fine of a thousand dollars more for cheatin', lyin', and bein' too smart for your britches. If you haven't got any money, then we'll throw you in the jail—or we'll take that shoot-'em-up gun, that tricky fiddle, and that magic hat for payment!"

But before they could lay hands on him or his gifts, Leo started playing the fiddle. In a second they were dancing all over the courtroom, hollering, "Stop! Stop that music!"

"I won't stop 'til ya'll pay me. A thousand for the bird, a thousand for false arrest, and a thousand for tryin' to ruin my good name."

The three men held out as long as they could until their feet were blistered and sore. "All right, we'll pay!"

Leo was too smart to let them go before they paid. He made them sign an IOU before he'd let them stop dancing. "Now, I'll expect this money to be waitin' on me when I get home. If it's not, I'm gonna put on my hat and sneak up on you, and I'll play my fiddle so fast, you'll dance 'til you melt into butter!" Then Leo packed away his fiddle and put on his hat. Quick as a wink he disappeared.

When Leo got home, his papa was overjoyed to see him. Three thousand dollars was waiting on him. He showed his papa the magic gifts. "You'll never have to work again, Papa," he says. "I've made my fortune. Your boy is gonna take care of you!"

"Ah, my son," the ol' man says, "these are fine gifts and your fortune is a blessing. But there is another gift you've earned that's more valuable than all this. You left here green and untried, but you took on the work of a man. You met all your troubles head-on and earned respect. My son, you left here as a boy, but today you come back as a man!"

Leo worked hard and had a good life. He never had to use the magic gifts again. He kept them locked away in a trunk for many years until, in time, his own son earned the gun, the fiddle, and the hat through hard work and courage.

TELLING TIPS: For me, storytelling is not what I *do,* it is *who I am as a person.* That is why I feel that it is important for storytellers to research the cultural roots of stories. I strongly encourage storytellers to do their work; take the time to learn more about Cajun language, history, and culture. Then, I urge them to find the point where their own life intersects the story. In discovering this point of universality, the teller may well discover a new personal story that can be a companion tale to "The Magic Gifts." Audiences respect a storyteller who is authentic in his or her knowledge and truthful in his or her personal connection to any story.

DOUG LIPMAN is a storyteller, teacher, scholar, and award-winning recording artist. He integrates music and participation into stories aimed at touching people deeply. Recognized both as a storyteller and a teacher, Doug specializes in coaching storytellers and others who use oral communication.

In Mexico, there is a whole day for the dead: the Feast Day of the Dead. You see, in Mexico, death is not a stranger but an everyday companion. Death is thought of as a merciful friend, for often the poor have no other. I usually introduce this story by talking about the Day of the Dead as a Mexican holiday, when families picnic in the graveyards and leave bread by the side of the road for Death, so that Death will not travel that road hungry. I sometimes talk about the different ideas of death: the celebration and welcoming of death as something that can end suffering when there is no other way.

La Muerta: Godmother Death

Doug Lipman

A STORY FROM MEXICO

Well, there was a poor peasant in Mexico named Antonio. He was so weak and so impoverished that if you wanted to hire him, you'd have to feed him for a week before he'd have strength enough to do a day's work. But this year, on the Day of the Dead, something happened in Antonio's life: to Antonio and his wife was born a new child. They had already eight, although four were in the Campo Santo and no longer needed to be fed. But to have a child born on the Day of the Dead—that was a good sign!

Antonio said, "This child will change things for us. I will go off and find a godmother, a *madrina*. I will make sure this one has the qualities we want. I will make sure she can offer him all the important things: justice and mercy and, especially, power."

So Antonio left his family and went off alone into the world to find a *madrina*. As he walked along he sang,

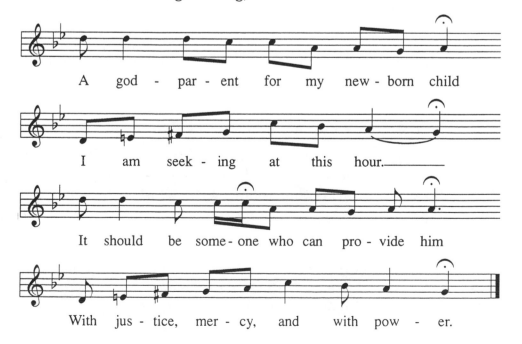

A god - par - ent for my new - born child
I am seek - ing at this hour.
It should be some - one who can pro - vide him
With jus - tice, mer - cy, and with pow - er.

Antonio saw a rich carriage pulled by splendid horses. It was the señora who owned the *hacienda*. The window of the coach opened.

"Antonio, why do you walk alone? Why are you not with your family on this day?"

"I have a new child, born today."

"Ah! Are you looking for a *madrina* for such a special child born on the Day of the Dead?

> I would make a fine godparent,
> My family's rich and old.
> We could surely give him riches and power,
> His toys would be made of gold."

For any other child, Antonio would have been honored to have this wealthy woman as *madrina*. But for this child he said, "You are rich and powerful, that is true. But you are not just and you are not merciful. Your children play with golden toys while mine, so close by, starve. No, this child deserves more than you can provide."

Antonio walked ahead into the day.

Off in the fields he saw a woman dressed in rags, but with a youthful shine to her face. Someone whom even the flowers and grasses noticed as she went by. Antonio recognized her as a holy woman.

"Antonio, why are you out today, alone?"

"I have a new child."

> "I would like to be *madrina*
> For your newborn child.
> You can be sure I would provide him
> With justice and mercy mild."

Antonio was honored.

"Yes, you could provide justice and mercy like no one else, but you are poor. And in this world, there is no power in poverty. No, this child must have something that even you cannot give him."

So Antonio continued on his way until there, in a barren piece of dusty land, he saw a woman he did not know by sight. She was tall and thin and so wrapped in cloth that even her mouth was hidden. She moved with the easy grace of someone who was used to going wherever she would. She looked at Antonio and said, "I know you have a new child.

> I would like to be *madrina*
> Such as you're seeking at this hour.
> You know I surely could provide him
> With justice, mercy, and with power."

"Who are you?"

"Antonio, do you not know me? Four times I have visited your home. I am *La Muerta.* I am Death."

"*La Muerta?* Yes! You are merciful. When wretchedness has no other outlet, you are there to put an end to it. You are just. You take from the rich and the poor alike. And there is no power on this earth that can stand to yours. Yes, you will be godmother."

And so Antonio turned home—if not happy, then satisfied.

His child, Julio, grew well and strong and quickly. When Julio was the age to be a man, his *madrina, La Muerta,* came to do her offices. She took him into the *campos,* and there in the woods she showed him the use of every healing herb—many of them unknown to us—so that soon Julio knew more of healing and the powers of herbs than any doctor in the land.

When his education was complete in this way, she said, "Julio, I have one more gift for you. I will show you this flower."

She showed him a pale yellow flower—a flower often overlooked when seen, yet seldom found when sought.

"This is *La Yerba de la Vida.* If you make a medicine from this and give it to the dying, they will come back to life. But two things, Julio: you must withhold it for charity when life would be more painful. And your eyes—your bright eyes—and the failing eyes of the dying one will see me at the foot of the bed. If I am there, you may give the dying one *La Yerba de la Vida.* But if you see me at the head of the bed, you must not give it, for I have come to claim my own."

Well, Julio took his knowledge and went out in the world. He went to the palaces of the rich and the hovels of the poor. Everywhere he became known as *Julio de los Remedios.* Many he cured and others he said, "It is more kind not to cure."

Still to others, he said, "No. Death has come for this one and there is no helping."

One day, word came that the king of that land was ill. Anyone who could cure him would get half the kingdom. Julio was finally sent for when all the other doctors failed. They sent for *Julio de los Remedios.* Julio thought, *This is why I was sent into my family. None of us—and none of our descendants—will ever again know the sharp pain of poverty.*

He went with confidence to the bed of the king carrying *La Yerba de la Vida.* But when he looked, he did not see Death at the foot of the bed. There by the king's head stood the tall, stern figure of *La Muerta.*

Julio thought, *If only I could cheat her this one time, I would own half the kingdom.* Then he shouted, "Air! Air! The king needs air! Quickly turn his bed so that his head is near the window."

Death was now at the foot of the bed. Julio gave the king *La Yerba de la Vida,* and the king stood up. All eyes were on the king, except Julio's. He looked into the stern face of his *madrina, La Muerta.* She extended her long arm toward him and said, "If you do that again, I will come for you."

Julio, who had been *Julio de los Remedios* in the hovels of the poor, was now Julio of the Court. He spent his days with kings and queens and princesses. One princess, the daughter of the king, won his heart.

They agreed they would be married. But one week before their wedding day, the princess fell ill. Julio felt that his world had shattered. Then he remembered that he was still *Julio de los Remedios.* He took *La Yerba de la Vida*—it had never failed before, it would not fail now—and he held it to the lips of his beloved. But when he followed her glance, it was not toward the foot of the bed, but to *La Muerta* there at the head.

Julio thought, *My godmother will not carry out her threat to me. And if she tries—this is my partner in life. This one time I will disobey her.*

He turned the bed around. Death was now at the foot. Julio gave *La Yerba de la Vida* to the princess. He waited for the hand of Death, but it did not touch him. *La Muerta* was gone.

A week later, Julio and the princess were married. They spent their wedding night in each other's arms. After Julio had drifted to sleep, there came a knocking at the chamber door. When he opened it, there was the tall figure of *La Muerta.*

She motioned to him, and he followed. He followed her along roads and streams he had never seen. At last they came to a large cavern. He followed her under the ground. They walked for what seemed like miles down through the twisting cavern, past rocks that shone of their own light, until at last they came to a large space. In it were lights, thousands of candles. One would flicker out here, another would burst into flame there. It seemed as if the flames danced from one place to another. Julio said, "What is this?"

"These are the lights of people's lives."

Julio looked down. There in front of him was a small candle that was nearly burned out. The wick had fallen over in the liquid wax and the flame sputtered, about to go out.

"Whose is that?"

"Julio, that is yours."

"Oh, please, *madrina* of mine, show me mercy!"

"Julio, I have shown you mercy."

"What mercy have you shown me?"

La Muerta pointed a finger at a large candle, solid and strong and round, the wick not yet charred, the flame just flickering into life.

"Whose is this?"

"Julio, that is the candle of your child."

"Please, save my life. I am to be a father!"

"Julio, I have shown you mercy. I have given you power. Now I must show you justice."

La Muerta's tall figure bent over and blew out the candle of *Julio de los Remedios*.

> "Farewell to those I love so well,
> Do not go searching for me.
> Farewell, my family and companions,
> I'm on my final journey."

TELLING TIPS: I think of *La Muerta* as an ideal story for fifth-graders. And of course, it's enjoyed by anyone older than that.

The tone of the story is almost understated. It forces the listener to come to the teller. Even though it deals with the scary figure of Death, it is not a story that you can profitably dramatize. It's not the kind of story where you want your listeners to be on the edges of their seats. Don't try to reach out and grab them. Lean back a little bit when you tell it. Simply imagine that a celebration has been taking place in the cottage this night. The fiddlers have had their time. The children are all asleep. And in the quiet, the old person by the side of the fire begins to speak. That's the mood. It's almost a confidential story.

ABOUT THE STORY: My attention was first drawn to this story when I read a version of it in Diane Wolkstein's *The Magic Orange Tree and Other Haitian Folktales* (Knopf, 1978). Later, I was asked to participate in a Halloween show, and someone suggested that I do that little five-minute story from Diane's book. But I like to research the stories I tell, and by the time I had finished, my version was considerably longer than five minutes. The story is an example of what Aarne and Thompson call Type 332 *Godfather Death*. I read through twenty or thirty different sources and chose the details I liked best. The single most important version for me was in a book called *Tongues of the Monte* (Little, Brown, 1947) by J. Frank Dobie. All the lovely Mexican cultural markers come from this version. Also helpful was Riley Aiken's *Mexican Tales from the Borderland* (Southern Methodist University Press, 1980). I borrowed the detail of Death herself blowing out the light from Marie Campbell's *Tales from Cloudwalking Country* (Greenwood Press, 1976).

I also incorporated into the story a combination of a *rogativa,* a prayer-song for the dead that is often sung for souls in purgatory, and a *despedimento,* which is a prayer-song usually couched in the form of a first-person address by the deceased to his parents, relatives, friends, and others. I found these in John Donald Robb's *Hispanic Folk Music of New Mexico and the Southwest* (University of Oklahoma Press, 1980).

Like Jack, **ELIZABETH ELLIS** grew up in the Appalachian Mountains of Tennessee and Kentucky. And like Jack, she went out in the world to seek her fortune. In 1969, she went to work for the Dallas Public Library, where she was a children's librarian for ten years before becoming a professional storyteller. She still tells stories from the Appalachian Mountains, as well as personal experience and family stories and tales of heroic American women.

My grandfather was a circuit-riding preacher in the Appalachian Mountains during the first fifty years of this century. He heard lots of stories, and many of them were about Jack. When I was younger, he told those stories to me. Like many great storytellers, he always took the starring role for himself. So, when he told Jack tales, they were always about himself and his two brothers, Steven and Taylor. When I was little, I thought all the things that happened to Jack in the stories I heard actually happened to my grandfather.

Jack and the Haunted House

Elizabeth Ellis

A STORY FROM THE APPALACHIAN MOUNTAINS

One time things got real bad at Jack's house. They got so bad that Jack and his mama thought they might starve to death. Finally, it was decided that Jack should go out in the world to seek his fortune. His mama cried to think about him leaving home when he was still so young, but she thought it was the best thing for him to do. She figured if he got work somewhere, at least he'd be able to eat regularly.

She had a little food left; there wasn't much of it. But, she divided it into two equal parts. She put her part back in the cupboard. She put Jack's part in a sack. He threw that sack across his back and headed down the big road.

The first day or two, that wasn't too bad. The sun was shining bright and pretty. When Jack would get tired, he'd lay down underneath a tree and take a nap. When he'd get hungry, he'd reach into the bottom of the sack and get something to eat. But, on the third day of his trip the sack was empty. So on the fourth day of his trip, so was Jack!

Then the wind began to blow. The clouds came in and covered up the sun. It began to rain a real cold rain that was running down the back of Jack's neck and making a puddle in his underwear. He felt like he might freeze to death.

He came into a little village. In the middle of the village was an inn. Jack said, "That's the kind of place I could get something good to eat. I could get a nice warm bed to sleep in … if I had any money." Jack didn't have any money at all.

He said, "I'll try my luck anyhow!" He went over and knocked on the door. When the innkeeper answered, Jack said, "Do you have any work you need done here? I'm good to work. Why, I could chop wood, build fires, feed your animals … any kind of thing that you need done. I sure wish you'd give me something to eat, and I don't know if you've noticed how wet it is out here."

The innkeeper said, "I don't remember seeing you around here before."

Jack said, "That's because I don't live around here. If I lived around here, I'd be smart enough to go home and get out of all this rain!"

The innkeeper asked, "Why did you leave home?"

Jack said, "I had to come out in the world to seek my fortune."

"Well," said the man, "if it's fortune you want, you don't want to stay here with me."

"I don't?" asked Jack.

"No. Look up on the hill. Do you see that great big empty-looking house?"

Jack said, "I'm hungry. I'm not blind!"

The innkeeper said, "The king says that anybody who goes in that house and spends the night can have the house and all the land that it sits on for his own."

"You mean I could have the whole thing," exclaimed Jack.

The man nodded.

"That's great!" said Jack. "But … what's the catch?"

"Well," said the man, "if you asked the people who live around here, they'd tell you the house is haunted."

"Huh!" said Jack. "I've never seen anything that could scare me."

"Good!" said the man. "I hope you say that again … in the morning!"

He thought he ought to give Jack something to eat, but this wasn't the kind of man that would give away anything that cost any money. He had some beans cooking on the stove. That was all, just beans. He took a cup, scooped some out into a little bucket of a thing … didn't even have a lid for it. He handed it out the door to Jack. Then I guess he got ashamed of himself for giving Jack so little to eat, because he got a big hunk of cornbread, too. He spread a lot of butter on it and handed it out the door to Jack.

Jack was so hungry, he was really glad to see those beans. He took the beans in one hand and the cornbread in the other. He started up the hill toward that big, dark, empty house. Since it had been raining, the hill was muddy. That made it slippery and slick. Jack was picking his way along real carefully because he didn't want to trip and spill his beans. He knew if he did he wouldn't get anything more to eat that night.

He made it all the way to the top of the hill … hadn't spilled a single drop. He was really proud of himself about it, too. He walked up on the porch of that house and knocked on the door. Suddenly he stopped.

"What am I doing?" he said to himself. "If nobody lives here, who's gonna come and let me in?"

He put his hand to the doorknob but jerked it back because the doorknob was so cold!

82

"That's because it's a metal doorknob," he said to himself.

He touched the wooden door and found it was just as cold as the doorknob had been. But he said, "I won't let that bother me."

He turned the doorknob and pushed the door. It c-r-e-a-k-e-d open. Jack went on inside. All he could see, everywhere he looked, were cobwebs, shadows, and lots of dust. He started groping along in the dark. Before long he found a fireplace and beside it, a big stack of dry wood. He figured that was his lucky day. That quick, he built a fire in that fireplace!

He put the little bucket of beans down by the fire to get warm. He put the cornbread down there. Jack figured when the butter melted in that cornbread, that was going to taste pretty good. He was just standing there in front of the fire, thawing out his fingers. He was thinking about how he was the onliest person to be in this big, dark, empty house in so many years ... when he thought he heard a voice.

It sounded like it was coming from up inside the chimney. It sounded like it was saying, "I'm gonna f-a-l-l! I'm gonna f-a-l-l! I'm gonna f-a-l-l!"

"FALL! And get it over with!" said Jack.

From out of the chimney there fell a pair of human legs. They walked out of the fire, shook the ashes off themselves. They walked across the room and sat down in a rocking chair that was there. The chair began to rock back and forth, back and forth.

"You better be careful," said Jack. "You nearly spilled my beans."

About that time, up inside the chimney, Jack heard that voice again. It said, "I'm gonna f-a-l-l! I'm gonna f-a-l-l!"

"COME ON if you're coming!" said Jack.

From out of the chimney there rolled a human body. It rolled out of the fire, shook the ashes off itself, rolled over to the chair, and fastened itself on those legs. Jack looked over at that thing. He said, "You better be careful. As hungry as I am, you don't want to spill those beans."

But, just then, up inside the chimney, he heard that voice again. It said, "I'm gonna f-a-l-l! I'm gonna f-a-l-l!"

"CAN'T you say anything else?" said Jack.

Plop! Plop! On either side of the chimney there landed a human arm. They fastened themselves together at the fingers. Just like a pair of legs, they walked out of the fire. They shook the ashes off themselves. They walked over to the rocking chair and fastened themselves onto that body.

Jack was beginning to get a little nervous by this time! He said, "Two of you was too much! That time you nearly did spill those beans."

Just then, the body jumped up so fast it turned the chair right over backward. It started running all over the room. It was pulling open cupboards, cabinets, and drawers. It was throwing things around in every direction.

"What are you hunting for?" asked Jack.

"My head."

"Well, where was it the last time you saw it?" asked Jack.

"Down in the cellar."

"If you will sit down, stop all that running around, I'll go down there and get it for you," said Jack. "Running around the room like that, you're gonna spill those beans for sure." With that, Jack marched across the floor and jerked open the cellar door.

Boy, it was dark down there!

Jack said, "I'll get it for you first thing tomorrow morning."

But the body pulled off its little finger and stuck it in the fire. Lit the end of it, just like it was a candle. Handed it up to Jack. Jack gulped and said, "Thanks."

He started down those steps. It was cold down in the cellar … damp … and musty smelling. On the floor of the cellar, Jack could see a head laying there. He scooped it up under his arm and started up the steps. At the top of the steps he could see the body was waiting for him. Very slowly, he held the head out to the body. Very slowly, the body took the head and set it right square on its shoulders. Those big eyes began to blink as it looked around the room.

The body said, "Jack, I've been haunting in this house for seven years. With all the people who have come here, trying to get my house and my land, you are the first one who ever tried to help me! When I was alive, I lived in this house. I buried all my gold down at the foot of the cellar steps … right where you found my head. You go down there and dig. You'll find enough money to make you rich for the rest of your days."

With that, the body was gone!

"Thank you," said Jack. "I'll go down there and get that money … first thing tomorrow morning!" Jack sat down in front of the fireplace. He didn't stop until he'd eaten every bean in that bucket … and every crumb of that cornbread.

The next morning, when it was bright and pretty outside, Jack went down in the cellar. He began to dig. Before long, in an old wooden box, he found gold. More gold than he could spend in his whole life. First thing he did with it was go home and get his mama. He brought her there to live in the house with him. Last time I heard anything about them, except for Jack's mama's arthritis, they were getting along pretty good.

TELLING TIPS: This story fills the bill when you want something scary to tell but you'd like it to be funny as well. It is a jump tale. In fact, there are three jumps in it, as each of the body parts falls down the chimney. To create the best jump, lower your voice slightly as you go into the set-up for the jump. Speak more slowly, too. Be subtle. You don't want your listeners to be conscious of what you are doing.

Use a loud, forceful voice on the words that are meant to startle people. It helps if you move toward them physically at the same time. If you are using a microphone, you will want to test all this by doing a sound check before your listeners arrive. Nothing spoils the mood of a good ghost story as much as electronic feedback.

ABOUT THE STORY: Most of the people who settled in the Appalachian Mountains came originally from western Europe or Great Britain. Of course, they brought their stories with them. Some of the stories from England and Ireland centered around a boy named Jack. After a few generations, the tales began to merge and become more Americanized. Many tellers used Jack as the hero even if he hadn't been in it before the tale came "across the ocean water."

This tale is one of those. It is an Appalachian version of "The Story of the Youth Who Went Forth to Learn What Fear Was" as collected by the Brothers Grimm. It has lots of other titles and lots of other variants in different cultures. The popular children's book, *Esteban and the Ghost* by Sibyl Hancock (Dial, 1983) is one set in the Hispanic tradition. M.A. Jagendorf includes a similar Appalachian version in *Folk Stories of the American South* (Vanguard, 1972).

We were all storytellers in our home. My brother Steamer could tell tall tales with the best of them, often holding forth at John Mauk's store. This story was one of his favorites, and it was my pleasure to hear him tell it at the National Storytelling Festival before he died in the 1970s. Now I tell it, and my daughter Hannah tells it too.

DOC McCONNELL was born near Tucker's Knob, a small farm community near Rogersville, Tennessee. He grew up telling stories on the front porch of his Hawkins County home and around a potbellied stove at John Mauk's store. He is the barker of his own Doc McConnell's Old-Time Medicine Show—a re-created show that he has performed throughout the United States. Doc has appeared many times at the National Storytelling Festival and helped found the National Storytelling Association. He tells stories and conducts workshops at festivals, conferences, conventions, schools, and libraries throughout the United States. He has appeared on "The Today Show," "CBS Morning News," "A Prairie Home Companion," and many other programs. Doc still lives in Rogersville.

The Storekeeper

Doc McConnell

A STORY FROM THE AMERICAN SOUTH

There was once a country storekeeper who had a reputation of making a profit any way he could. Some said that he would put his thumb on the counter scales when he was weighing out sugar, beans, or salt in his store. He would shortweigh the customer if he got a chance. Others said that he would shortchange you if you didn't watch out. He would tell a lie or two if he could make a profit. Folks knew his ways and traded with him with caution.

In spite of his reputation, folks still used his store because it was the only store within ten miles. Even when he overpriced his goods in the store, folks would call it to his attention and he would claim he had just made a little mistake in the paperwork. Folks wished that they could trust the old merchant and they would not have to watch him so close.

Some of his customers got together one day and decided that if the old storekeeper could get saved and start going to church, he would change his ways. They started working on the evil storekeeper. They urged him to get his life straightened out and to get saved. They had their best chance to get the storekeeper to get honest and go straight when the revival meeting came to the community. The Baptists had a protracted revival, and it drew large crowds and great response.

The revival had been running for about three weeks and was coming to a close. The last night was scheduled on Sunday night. The crooked merchant had not attended a single meeting of the revival nor did it look like anyone was going to convince him that he needed to attend and get saved and get his life straight. After much badgering and convincing and a final visit to his house on Sunday afternoon, the group persuaded the old merchant to go to church on the final night of the revival. At meeting time he sat on the front row just to please those who were so determined to get him to church and get him saved.

Needless to say, the church service was a lively one and the group so interested in the old storekeeper, they badgered and witnessed and dragged him to the altar. To please them, the old merchant claimed to have received the Ghost, got saved, and redeemed. The old merchant went home more stooped-shouldered than ever from the back-pounding for conviction and congratulations. He hoped that they would all be satisfied now and would quit bothering him about getting saved and changing his life.

The next day most of the usual crowd was at the store to watch the redeemed and saved storekeeper. They wanted to watch him be honest in his dealings, not cheat the customers, and deal on the square. They waited and watched. The old storekeeper went about the store trying to convince the group that indeed he was saved and had changed his ways, living for the Lord, praying for good, and taking up residence at the foot of the cross. He went about singing hymns, quoting scriptures, looking pious and putting on a good front. Most were not convinced because they knew a leopard cannot change its spots. A wolf in sheep's clothing is still a wolf, and actions speak louder than words.

It was about this time that a little boy came into the store. The storekeeper was never kind to children nor did he like them. When the little boy came in the door of the store the old merchant met him with a smile and asked, "What can I do for you, young man?" The boy wanted a nickel's worth of candy. The old storekeeper walked behind the counter and came out with a paper bag of candy well worth twenty-five cents. We watched to see what the old merchant was up to. He patted the boy on the head, gave the boy a friendly greeting and walked over to the cash box, looked up toward heaven, dropped the nickel into the box, placed the palms of his hands together, closed his eyes and said, "Suffer the little children to come unto me."

The onlookers were not impressed. The merchant went about quoting scriptures and singing church songs. About that time Mrs. Myers came into the store. Her ninety-year-old father was having a birthday and she had come in to buy him a gift. The storekeeper went behind the counter and got a bandana handkerchief, a barlow knife and a pair of sock supporters, and put them in a bag for Mrs. Myers. The gifts were well worth two dollars but he only charged her fifty cents. She thanked him and left. The storekeeper went over to the cash box singing "Just As I Am," dropped the coin in the box, and again closed his eyes and looked toward heaven and said, "Honor thy father and thy mother."

About ten minutes passed, and there was some loud noise outside the store. It was a big pick-up truck pulling a long horse trailer. A big heavy cowpoke came swaggering in with a ten-gallon hat on his head, high heel boots and a big belt buckle. The old merchant leaned over the counter and asked, "Kin I hep ye?"

The man responded, "I want a horse blanket." The old merchant saw an opportunity here to get rid of one of his old moth-eaten dirty blankets in the feed room. The store had not sold a horse blanket in ten years and it didn't look like another one would ever be sold.

The merchant went to the feed room and brought forth a brown dirty horse blanket worth about two dollars. He pitched it on the counter and said, "I'll give you a good buy on that blanket, Mister, I'll let you have that fine blanket for only nine dollars and ninety-eight cents." The customer claimed that he had a fifty-thousand dollar Tennessee Walking Horse in the trailer and that he wasn't about to put a nine-dollar blanket on it. He demanded a better blanket. The storekeeper didn't have a better blanket but he didn't tell the customer so. Instead he marched to the feed room in the back and brought out a green blanket of the same quality and said that this better blanket would cost only forty-nine dollars and ninety-eight cents.

The blanket customer demanded an even more expensive blanket for his valuable horse. The slick merchant saw an opportunity to make some big money, so he went again to the feed room in the back and found at the bottom of the stack of old cheap blankets a bright red one. He shook the dust and insects from the blanket and folded the faded side in with the bright side showing and brought it to the store counter where the anxious customer waited.

The storekeeper, with great skill, placed the blanket in front of the customer, gently stroked its surface, and said, "Now how is this for a fine blanket for such a fine horse as you have out there in that trailer?" The customer was pleased even more when the price of ninety-nine dollars and ninety-eight cents was quoted as the cost. The horse owner quickly paid with a hundred-dollar bill and said, "Keep the change," and left.

All of the observers in the store watched closely. They had watched the shrewd merchant try to impress with the candy for the little boy and the generous gift for Mrs. Myers, but they wondered how the old storekeeper was going to justify selling that old moth-eaten, dirty blanket, worth two dollars, to an unsuspecting customer for almost a hundred dollars. They waited and watched.

The slick storekeeper held the hundred dollar bill with the tips of his fingers in front of his face. He looked at the money and then began singing, "Just As I Am." He walked over to the cash box, looked up into the heavens, turned to the onlookers, closed his eyes, and said, "He was a stranger and I took him in."

TELLING TIPS: When telling a tall tale, the element of surprise is important. The teller needs to make the story sound realistic for as long as possible so that the exaggeration sort of creeps up on the listener. To make this story as authentic as possible, the teller needs to experience it rather than memorize it and retell it. Picture the store, and picture yourself in it. Envision the faces of the onlookers. Hear the voices of the storekeeper and the customer. Most importantly, picture yourself as being part of this story.

NICOLE KROEGER

GAYLE ROSS is a direct descendant of Chief John Ross, Principal Chief of the Cherokee Nation during the infamous Trail of Tears. Since 1979, she has traveled the country telling native American stories at schools, libraries, colleges, and festivals. She has recorded two audiotapes of Cherokee stories, and her stories have appeared on two educational videotapes. Her collection of Cherokee rabbit stories, *How Rabbit Tricked Otter,* is published by HarperCollins, Inc. Gayle lives with her husband, Reed Holt, and her two children, Alan and Sarah, in the Texas Hill Country town of Fredericksburg.

Of all the stories of the Ani Yun Wiya, the Cherokee, none are more important than the tales of Rabbit, the trickster. Rabbit embodies the many contradictory characteristics of human beings, by turns lazy and greedy, kind and caring, malicious and mischievous, cunning and curious. He tricks and is tricked; he wins and he loses. But he is always there. And though his sense of self-importance may make him a figure of fun, one must always remember that you only have to look at the changes he made in this world to realize that his power is indeed rare. Remember to honor Rabbit when you tell his stories.

Rabbit and Possum Hunt for a Wife

Gayle Ross

A CHEROKEE STORY

There came a time when Rabbit and Possum each wanted very badly to get married, but no one would marry either one of them. Possum, with his long, skinny, hairless tail, was considered to be a very ugly fellow, and everybody knew Rabbit's ways. Finally, Rabbit said to Possum, "Maybe if we look for wives together, our luck will change."

After they had talked about it for a while, Rabbit came up with a plan. He told Possum, "Let's travel to a different settlement. Everyone knows that I am the messenger for the council. I will announce that the council orders everyone to get married at once, and we will get wives." Possum thought this was a fine idea, and so they set out together.

Rabbit can travel much faster than Possum, however, and soon he was far ahead. He came to a town and told everyone to gather in the council house. When everyone had assembled to hear the messenger, Rabbit spoke. "The council orders everyone to get married at once!" he announced. Quickly, the animals began selecting mates, and Rabbit got himself a fine wife. When Possum finally arrived there were no more women who were not married and he was left without a wife.

Rabbit thought this was a pretty funny joke, but he pretended to feel sorry for Possum and told him that he would carry the message to the next settlement. "This time," said Rabbit, "you will surely find a wife." Rabbit hurried on to the next town, gave the message, and got himself a wife. Again, Possum traveled so slowly that he was left without a wife when he finally arrived.

By now, Possum was beginning to get angry, and this made Rabbit nervous about traveling with him. "Let me carry the message to another town," said Rabbit. "This time, I will make sure they know you are coming so there will be a wife waiting for you!" Rabbit sounded so sincere that Possum truly believed he wanted to help. So Possum told Rabbit to go on to the next town to give the message, and Possum would travel after him as swiftly as he could.

But when Rabbit gathered the people in the next settlement, he gave a very different message! First he talked at length of how long there had been peace in the land. "The council is very worried that everyone is getting lazy," said Rabbit, "so it has been decided that there must be war at once. A stranger to your village is coming right now. The council orders you to make war on him!"

Just then, Possum entered the council house and everyone jumped on him all together. Possum had given no thought to bringing weapons on a wedding trip, so he had no way to defend himself at all. He was beaten nearly senseless before he thought to fall over and pretend to be dead. At last, he saw his chance, and he jumped up and made his escape. So Possum didn't get a wife on that trip, and he and Rabbit never traveled together again. But, to this day, Possum will fall over and pretend to be dead whenever he is in a tight spot. This is what people call "playing possum."

TELLING TIPS: It is important to remember that we see the animals as people every bit as much as the human beings are. They are our relatives. Therefore, while the character of the animal participants may be developed through voice, body language, and facial expression, it is extremely important that they not be reduced by "cartoonish" caricatures in their portrayal. Even when they are exhibiting foolish characteristics (such as we humans often display) they must still be accorded the respect they deserve as people.

If you decide to make changes in the story, please make sure that you do not change the story in such a way as to make it inconsistent with Cherokee culture. If you do not know enough about Cherokee culture to recognize these inconsistencies, you probably shouldn't be making any changes!

Remember not to rush the story, and do not use a screaming voice. The spirit of Rabbit will come to hear his story told; he listens slowly, and you wouldn't want to hurt his ears!

ABOUT THE STORY: This is a Cherokee Indian story published by the ethnologist James Mooney in his *Myths of the Cherokee,* which appeared in the nineteenth annual report of the American Bureau of Ethnology, 1897.

BOB MARSHAK

LAURA SIMMS has been telling stories since 1968. She served for seven years as a member of the Board of Directors of the National Storytelling Association, and was the Artistic Director for the National Storytelling Festival. She founded the Storytelling Center of Oneonta at Oneonta, New York, in 1977, and in 1985, she co-founded the New York City Storytelling Center. She has produced a number of albums and audio- and videocassettes. She lives in New York City where she continues to perform, write, and teach.

This ancient tale is never outdated and perhaps at present more relevant than ever. I tell it to older students, fourth grade and upward into college. It stirs the heart and opens the listener deeply. We all know the heartfelt sorrow of unrequited love, and the desperate desire to be someone or something that we are not. It is at first glance a sad tale, but it serves to remind us in the most direct way that beauty arises from our authentic self, no matter how we outwardly appear, and not from a conventional or fantasy ideal. The sorrow that is generated in this tale brings the listeners together in a human way.

The Black Prince

Laura Simms

A STORY FROM EGYPT

One September, I was hired to tell stories in Bryant Park at 42nd Street behind the New York Public Library. I expected a stage, microphones, and chairs. I arrived in a backless flowered dress. There was no stage, no microphone, nor any chairs—only empty beer cans and this sordid, sordid group of people. Suddenly, a tall man with an oxford shirt, sleeves rolled, red tie, greeted me cheerfully. I asked, "Where do I perform?" He pointed, still smiling, towards Sixth Avenue, seemingly oblivious to the noise, the smell, the danger. He sat on the rim of the fountain.

I thought, I need the money. I'll tell a quick, funny story and go home. *A man sat down next to him, bare-chested, torn slacks, eating from a two quart container of fluorescent-colored ice cream. Our eyes met. I thought,* This man really needs a story. *A story that I rarely tell came to mind. A little nervously I said, "Ladies and gentlemen, I've been hired by the Parks Department to tell you stories today."*

Two strange characters, a female and a male, sauntered over, sat down on the well, and said, "Hey, you know there were two juggling clowns here yesterday reciting poetry."

I began. My eyes never left the eyes of the ice cream-eating man.

In ancient Egypt, there was a boy who was ugly, stupid, and lazy. The only thing he cared about was a wooden flute that he had carved. He would wander, play the flute, fall asleep. Even his mother said, "My son will come to nothing." She often said, "I expect that one day he'll fall asleep at the edge of the river and drown."

One day, while the boy was walking through the city, he came upon a white stone wall that he had never seen before. Beautiful green trees grew up behind the wall and, curious, he climbed to look into the garden. It was an extraordinary garden. But what truly caught his eye was a young woman, serene, beside a pool of water. The boy felt such longing that he wanted to play the flute. But the wind seemed to blow in the opposite direction.

He put the flute to his lips and he began to play softly everything he felt. When she didn't turn around, he was certain that she couldn't hear and he began to play everything he felt. He played all afternoon. And before the sun went down, she stood up and walked away, vanishing among the trees.

That night, he couldn't sleep. He couldn't stop thinking about the girl in the garden. And the next day he returned to the wall and waited. In the afternoon she returned. And once again, he played everything he felt. He returned to the garden every day.

He was falling in love. You know how it is the first time you fall in love. And each day he played the flute, played everything he felt. He fantasized that one day he would leap down into the garden, play music for her alone, and she would love him the way he loved her. He would ask her to marry him and she would go with him out of the garden to his mother's hut beside the river.

One evening, when he was returning home, he sat down by the well in the middle of the village to listen to the old women gossip. They were talking about a garden and he realized they were describing the very garden that he looked at every day. And the more he listened, the more he realized that the girl that he loved was none other than the pharaoh's daughter, the princess Thudmos.

He knew that a princess could not love a boy who was poor and ugly and lazy and stupid. He wandered through the city streets all night, broken-hearted. He couldn't go home.

Before dawn, he left the city gates, went out through the market, and there was a caravan of merchants. And the men bade him sit down with them and have some tea, and he did. And they told the kinds of stories that merchants tell, about magic. And he listened, all ears, as they described a magician named Habee: "He can do anything." And finally, the boy asked, "Can he change man's soul?"

"Oh, God willing, if he's alive, he can change a man's soul. He performs miracles!"

"Where would I find him?"

And they pointed to the desert and told him to walk three days and three nights without stopping.

With nothing but the clothes on his back and his flute, the boy walked through the sand. He walked for three days and three nights without stopping. And he came to an oasis. There was a tree with a donkey tied to it and an old hut. The door opened, and an old man came out—bald, eyes wide, toothless.

"Are you Habee, the magician?"

"And that is my name."

"I have heard that—"

"Boy, everybody hears about me. Everyone has a story. Rest. Refresh yourself. And then tell me your tale and what you would like."

The boy washed; he couldn't rest. And after drinking tea he waited until the magician sat down beside him. He explained who he was and how he had fallen in love with the pharaoh's daughter, and how she could never love him. And then he said to Habee, "Can you make me strong, powerful, charismatic, unrelenting, cruel—a soldier, a prince, a warrior?"

"Ha, ha, that I can do. But once I change a man's soul, I can never change it back again."

"All right," said the boy.

"What are you going to pay me?"

He had nothing but the flute. So the boy gave Habee the flute that he had carved.

Days passed in the city and in the village. The boy's mother searched for him and when she didn't find him, she said, "Alas, he must have fallen asleep at the edge of the river and drowned." They had a funeral and she mourned. "So be it," she said.

Three years passed. During that time, enemies attacked Egypt. The pharaoh lost almost all of his land and half of his wealth. His army was camped in the middle of the desert, about to surrender, when a young man was seen walking alone, across the sand, completely dressed in black. He asked to see the pharaoh.

His presence was startling. He was so handsome and so charismatic that the soldiers brought him instantly before the pharaoh. The Lord of Egypt was impressed himself. And the young man said that his name was the Black Prince. If the pharaoh would let him lead his army, he would win back all of Egypt and land beyond.

The pharaoh agreed. Within weeks, the Black Prince's strategy won back all of Egypt, lands beyond. He took over 10,000 soldiers prisoner. He had half of the soldiers' hands cut off at the wrist so they would never pick up weapons against the pharaoh again.

The pharoah thanked the Black Prince and told him that if he would come to his palace one month from that day, he would reward him. He could ask for power or wealth. He could lead the armies. He could share the throne with the pharaoh. The Black Prince bowed and said he would arrive at the palace one month from the day, and walked alone again on foot into the desert.

Word spread about the Black Prince. Women in the kingdom swept clean the streets, scattered white flowers in the pathways. And on the day of his arrival, the women stood behind trellised windows, watching. Men stood on rooftops. And when the Black Prince walked through the streets, every heart stopped beating. He entered the palace and the court of the pharaoh. He saw the ruler sitting on a gold throne and beside him, on another throne, was his daughter, the Princess Thudmos.

The pharaoh welcomed the Black Prince. He made his offer of power and wealth, of rulership. Without taking his eyes off the princess, the Black Prince said, "I want neither power nor wealth. I ask only for the hand in marriage of the Princess Thudmos." The princess stood up.

"Father," she said, "if it is your command, I will marry him, but please listen to my story. You see, I was so alone. Every day I sat in my garden. I had no one with whom to talk and share my feelings. Then one day, a boy appeared on the white wall. He didn't notice me. His face was so handsome, like the changing seasons. And he played the flute. Why, he played for the sky and the water, for the beautiful flowers, but everything he played were my feelings. I used to imagine that he would jump down into the garden and that he would love me as much as I loved him. We would spend our days together. And then I would ask him to marry me and he would come and live here in the palace. Then one day, he didn't return. I sent my servants and handmaidens out into the city and into the village. Everyone had heard the boy who played the flute. And then I heard that he had drowned. Father, I know that I can never love as deeply again, and I have sworn that I could marry no one but him."

The Black Prince listened and he looked long at the Princess Thudmos, and then he said, "I once had a love as deep as yours. I would never make you marry me."

And he turned and left the palace. And they say that the Black Prince walked back across the desert on foot and was never seen or heard of again.

The story ended. My eyes were still on the eyes of the ice cream-eating man. People had sauntered over and left. Some had made comments and tried to disturb us, but we were protected.

A few seconds after the story ended, the ice cream-eating man, spoon in midair, put his spoon back into the container and started walking toward me. Then I remembered that I was standing there in Bryant Park in my backless flowered dress. I panicked. He came right up to me, having no boundaries at all.

He said, "Lady, are you coming back here tomorrow?"

"They only hired me for today."

"Why'd he do it? Like, why did the boy do it?"

"Well, don't you remember what the magician said? That once you change your soul you can never change it back again."

He said, "Man, lady, that's real life. I better walk you out of the park."

TELLING TIPS: To create your own version, you might tell the story from each character's point of view so that you get under the skin of the story. It is a profound and emotional tale. The storyteller needs to take a somewhat impartial place in it and allow the whole array of each character's emotions to come out, so that you embody the depth of almost adolescent feeling that's inside the story.

The frame story is true. It happened to me in 1984. Thus, if you tell that story, the best way to tell it is in third-person, or use my name—"this happened to Laura Simms"—because it did not happen to you. A story about being authentic should be treated with honesty. The storyteller is not an actor, but an individual relating what has happened, what has been heard or read to someone else. Thus, you the teller gain the trust of your listener and the integrity of a honest performance. The potency of this tale arises from you when you visualize it, speak it from the heart.

VICTOR HALL

When I first read this story it made me think of my father, who told stories similar to this. I knew he would like it because it used lots of humor to address the conflict between two friends. It says a lot about the need to beware of good intentions. I shared this story with my father, and I knew from his appreciation of it that my instincts were right.

When she was growing up, **DIANE FERLATTE** heard wonderful stories on her grandparents' porch in New Orleans. But she didn't become interested in telling them herself until she adopted her son, Joey. She not only tells Southern and African-American stories, but those from many other cultures, sometimes utilizing her skill in American sign language. Her audiotapes have won awards from Parents' Choice and the American Library Association. One of these tapes, *Sapelo: Time Is Winding Up*, is a recording of her one-woman show based on her trip to the Georgia Sea Islands. Diane has been featured at the National Storytelling Festival and has toured in Austria, New Zealand, Australia, and Bermuda. She performed at Washington's Kennedy Center as part of President Clinton's inauguration.

The Horned Animals' Party

Diane Ferlatte

A STORY FROM ANTIGUA (BRITISH WEST INDIES)

You know, there's nothing like a good party. Everyone likes a good party. Well, it happened that one time all the horned animals decided they were going to have a party, but only the animals who had horns could come. Well, pretty soon the word started spreading around about that party.

[sing]

> Party*, party*,
> Did you hear about the party*, party*,
> Party over here, party over there,
> Party over here, party over there.
> Party*, party*,
> Party*, party*.

Pretty soon everybody heard about that party, even Bro'-dog and Bro'-cat. And they wanted to go. But how could they go? They didn't have any horns. Well, Bro'-dog, he thought high and he thought low.

[sing]

> He thought high
> and he thought low.
> He thought high
> and he thought low.

Finally he thought of a way they could go. What they did, they slipped on over to the graveyard and they dug up a goat's horn, and ol Bro'-dog, he said,

---

* Audience claps twice

101

"Woof, I'll wear the horns one half of the night, you wear the horns the other half of the night, that way we'll both get to go to the party!"

Bro'-cat said, "Sounds pretty good to me."

Well, the next night they slipped on over to where the party was going to be and hid themselves in the bushes and laid low. Bro'-dog, he slipped the horns on first and said, "I'll go in for a few minutes, then come out, and let you go in."

"That's fine with me."

Old Bro'-dog, he headed on up to the door and knocked *[knocking sound]*, and they let him in. Ooohhh, it was horns for days, and plenty of food, plenty to drink, and the best musicians and the best drummer. Bro'-dog couldn't believe it. He headed right over to the food. He started eating and eating, and had him something to drink. Pretty soon he started dancing and singing. Ooohhh, he was having a good time.

> Aboon da, aboon da
> Aboon da, tara boon da
> Woof, aboon da, aboon da
> Aboon da, tara boon da
> Woof, aboon da, aboon da

Ah, he was having a good time. And you know how it is when you're at a good party, you don't think about leaving, do you? Bro'-dog didn't give Bro'-cat a second thought. He just kept on dancing and singing.

[dance and sing]

> Aboon da, aboon da
> Aboon da, tara boon da
> Aboon da, aboon da
> Aboon da, tara boon da

Well, there was Bro'-cat outside saying to himself, "I wonder where Bro'-dog is. He should have been here a long time ago. Well, I guess he'll be here in a minute."

Do you think Bro'-dog was giving him a second thought. *Ha!*

[dance and sing]

> Aboon da, aboon da
> Aboon da, tara boon da
> Woof, aboon da, aboon da
> Aboon da, tara boon da

Bro'-cat, he got tired of waiting. So he tipped on over to the door, then went around the side of the house to the window. He could see Bro'-dog. He said, *[whisper]* "Bro'-dog, Bro'-dog, Bro'-dog, Bro'-dog."

Do you think Bro'-dog heard him?
[dance and sing]

> Aboon da, aboon da
> Aboon da, tara boon da
> Aboon da, aboon da

Oh-oh, but somebody *did* hear him. It was Mr. Bull, the boss of the party, and you know how bulls are. When they get mad, they start shuffling on the ground and their nose starts flarin' up. Oh, he was mad. He went to the front door and opened it and he said, "Mmmmm, get on away from here! There ain't no dog in here." And he slammed the door. He was mad.

Well, Bro'-cat was a little mad too. Oh, he was so mad he went up to the door and said, "Bro'-dog, *Bro'-dog,* BRO'-DOG!" This time Bro'-dog heard him. He started easing towards the door.

[dance and sing]

> Aboon da, aboon da
> Aboon da, tara boon da
> Aboon da, aboon da

He opened the door and he said, "Shhh, Bro'-cat, be cool. I'll be out in a minute. Shhh." Oops! Bro'-dog saw Bro'-bull looking at him and he said, "There ain't no dog in here," and he slammed the door.

Well, Bro'-cat, he had had it! He went back up to that door and he said, "Bro'-dog, *Bro'-dog,* owwww BRO'-DOG, *come on out of there.*" And when Bro'-bull heard that noise he got to thinking, "Maybe there is a dog in here. Maybe we should look."

And old Bro'-dog, he said, "Yeah, I'll help you look." And old Bro'-dog started easing himself toward the door.

[dance and sing]

> Aboon da, aboon da
> Aboon da, tara boon da
> Aboon da, aboon da
> Aboon da, tara boon da

He wasn't watching where he was going, and he hit the wall. His horns fell off. When Bro'-bull saw it was Bro'-dog, he turned to the other horned animals and he said, "Get him!" And all the horned animals started running toward Bro'-dog. And Bro'-dog, he took off out the front door.

Boogadie, boogadie, boogadie, boogadie, boogadie, boogadie, boogadie, boogadie, boogadie, *ooohhh,* but who did he run into but Bro'-cat—*ooohhh*—and the argument they had! They started biting and scratching and with hair flying every which away. Back and forth, back and forth, and there was old

Bro'-cat on his back on the ground. He was getting the worse end of this fight, when all of the sudden Bro'-cat just kind of reached out and scratched Bro'-dog right there in the corner of his mouth.

Have you ever seen a dog's mouth, how in the corner it always looks kinda raw and pink-like? Well, that's how come. And that's how come today Bro'-dog and Bro'-cat are not friends. Bro'-cat ain't never forgot about that.

[sing]

> Party*, party*,
> Did you hear about the party*, party*,
> Party over here, party over there.
> Party over here, party over there.
> Party*, party*,
> Party*, party*.

TELLING TIPS: This story works with most age groups. I have added music and clapping to energize my listeners and encourage audience participation. Whenever you want your listeners to participate, it is important to use eye contact and body language to invite them into the story. This story can work just as well without the music and audience involvement. That is the twist I put on the story; your style may call for something different. Just make sure you convey a sense of fun when you're telling it.

ABOUT THE STORY: This tale can be found in *Afro-American Folktales* by Roger D. Abrahams (Pantheon Books, 1985). Abrahams cites as his source "Folklore from Antigua, British West Indies" by John H. Johnson (*Journal of American Folklore*, 34 [1921]), pp. 40-83.

NANCY SEIDLER

This story exists in many different variations, but I have made a number of embellishments on the plot. I teach this story in my workshops to adults who work with children. I also teach it in my workshop with children, because of the repetition and the vividness of the creature's description. It is a story that's very easy to learn. Because of the humor and the embellishments I have added, it's a story that's enjoyed by both children and adults.

BETH HORNER is a former children's librarian and creative drama instructor. She has produced a six-part storytelling series for radio and worked for ten year as a professional storyteller. Her most recent appearances include the National Storytelling Festival, National Conference on Storytelling, Illinois Reading Council, National Council of Teachers of English, and the Ravinia Festival. She served for six years on the Board of Directors of the National Storytelling Association. Her recordings include *An Evening at Cedar Creek, Mothers and Other Wild Women,* and her ever-popular *Encounter With a Romance Novel.*

The Mischievous Girl & the Hideous Creature

Beth Horner

ADAPTED FROM AMERICAN FOLK HUMOR

One night there was a girl who was doing what she loved doing more than anything else: scaring her younger brother to death.

She loved to scare her younger brother to death because he annoyed her. Each evening after supper he would run to the television set and plop himself down right in front of it, so that his big head covered the entire screen. No one else could see anything! No matter how politely she asked, no matter how rudely she threatened, he would not move his big head. He annoyed her.

So, when he was concentrating very intently on a television program she would sneak, sneak, s-n-e-a-k up behind him and shout "BOO!" and watch him hit the ceiling. She loved to do that.

One night after she'd caused him to hit the ceiling approximately twelve or thirteen times, her younger brother went to bed. Her older brother went to bed. Her parents went to bed. And she went to bed. She was in her room ... all by herself ... in the dark ... when she heard a *tap, tap-tap, tap,* on the window.

She went over to the window, looked outside the window, and there on the other side of her window was a hideous-looking creature. It had long wild hair. It had two long noses. On the end of each nose was a gross wart. On the end of each wart was a long greasy piece of hair.

The creature looked at her through the window, reached out, opened up the window and said, "Do you know ... what I do ... with my long red fingernails ... and my big red lips?"

"No!" said the girl. "And I don't want to know!" She slammed down the window and jumped under the bed. She stayed there all night.

The next day, however, she forgot about the creature. She was too busy to think about it at school. She was too busy to think about it at home ... until that night at supper when she was doing a second thing she loved doing more

106

than anything else: trying to make her older brother sick to his stomach at the dinner table.

She loved to make her older brother sick to his stomach at the dinner table because he annoyed her. He'd tease her and pick on her and tease her again. He annoyed her.

That evening they were having peas for dinner. So while her parents were away from the dinner table, she reached out, took a great handful of peas, jammed them into her mouth, and began to chew … and chew … and c-h-e-w until they were green and gloppy. Not runny! Just a green, gloppy, gooey, repulsive mess.

Then she turned to her older brother and tapped him on the shoulder. When he turned toward her and said "Yeah? Whadda ya want, Pipsqueak?" she opened up her mouth very wide and said, *"Blaaah!"* clearly displaying the green, gloppy, gooey, repulsive mess. Her brother covered his mouth with his hand and ran to the bathroom … just in time. She loved to make her older brother sick to his stomach.

However, after a while, her older brother went to bed. Her younger brother went to bed. Her parents went to bed. And she went to bed. She was in her room … all by herself … in the dark … when she heard a *tap, tap-tap, tap* on the window.

She went over to the window, looked outside the window, and there on the other side of her window was a hideous-looking creature. It had long wild hair. It had two long noses. On the end of each nose was a gross wart. On the end of each wart was a long greasy piece of hair.

The creature looked at her through the window, reached out, opened up the window and said, "Do you know … what I do … with my long red fingernails … and my big red lips?"

"No!" she said. "And I thought I told you last night that I don't want to know!" She slammed down the window and jumped under the bed. She stayed there all the night.

The next day, however, she did not forget about the creature. She was uncharacteristically quiet in school. She was uncharacteristically quiet after school. She was uncharacteristically quiet at dinner … until she thought about doing a third thing she loved doing more than anything else: trying to trick her parents into saying something impolite at the dinner table and then getting money from them when they did it.

She turned to her parents and said, "I will bet you one dollar that I can make you say something impolite at the dinner table."

"Oh, that's impossible!" said her parents. "We always speak politely at our dinner table."

"Well, I'll bet I can make you do it. I'll bet you one dollar that I can make you say something impolite to me right now."

"Oh, that's ridiculous!" they said. "We would never speak impolitely to you."

"Well, I'll bet you, I'll bet you, I'll bet you!" she said.

"All right," replied her parents looking at her sweetly. "If it will make you feel good, we'll take the bet."

"One dollar," she said. "I have a riddle. Answer my riddle: Pete and Repeat were sitting on the fence. Pete fell off. Who was left?"

Her parents thought about the riddle for a moment and replied, "Repeat."

"Repeat?" she said. "OK: Pete and Repeat were sitting on the fence. Pete fell off. Who was left?"

Again her parents replied, *"Repeat."*

"Repeat?" she said. "OK: Pete and Repeat were sitting on the fence. Pete fell off—"

"Oh, *shut up!*" they said, then suddenly covered their mouths with their hands. "Ooops!" Slowly her parents reached into their pockets, pulled out one dollar and said, "Here's your dollar."

She loved tricking her parents.

However, after a while, her parents went to bed. Her older brother went to bed. Her younger brother went to bed. And she went to bed. She was in her room … all by herself … in the dark … when she heard a *tap, tap-tap, tap* at the window.

She went over to the window, looked outside her window, and there on the other side of her window was a hideous-looking creature. It had long wild hair. It had two long noses. On the end of each nose was a gross wart. On the end of each wart was a long greasy piece of hair.

The creature looked at her through the window, reached out, opened up the window, and said, "Do you know … what I do … with my long red fingernails … and my big red lips?"

"What, what, WHAT?" she replied.

This creature was beginning to annoy the girl.

She continued, "Every night you come here. You ask me the same ridiculous question. Do I know what you do with your long red fingernails and your big red lips? Well, I don't know! I don't know! *And* I don't care! So why don't you answer the question yourself? What do you do with your long red fingernails and your big red lips?"

The creature looked at the girl, smiled hideously, slowly reached out with one of its long long red fingernails, reached toward its two big big red lips and went, *"B-b-b-b-l-l-l-b-b-b-b-l-l-l!"**

And that is the end of the story of the mischievous young girl and the hideous creature.

TELLING TIPS: This story is great for whole-audience participation. When telling to a children's or school audience, I usually begin by stating: "Now I am going to teach you a story that you can tell to someone else. Listen, watch, and I will tell you when your part begins." (Pedantic, perhaps, but clear, concise directions are great when you have 500 children in front of you!) There are two participatory points in the narrative: the description of the creature, and the creature's question to the girl.

I invite the listeners to join in the creature's description the second and third time it comes around. Often, I will get them started by simply gesturing for them to fill in the last word of each sentence. For example: "...and there on the other side of her window was a hideous-looking _____ ('Creature!'). It had long wild _____. ('Hair!') It had two long _____. ('Noses!')" Children and adults alike relish the creature's description. Feel free to ham it up! Specific hand gestures and facial expressions enhance both the repetition of the description and the creature's question.

I usually invite the listeners to join in the creature's question on the third time only. This helps to build to the climax without their being bored by too much repetition.

Many listeners already know the story's punch line once they hear the creature's question. However, they always get a kick out of the story because of the added elements of the creature's description and the girl's antics on the three successive evenings. If you see recognition in their faces during the creature's first question and are worried by it, simply state, "If you know the ending already, keep it a secret and join in with me at the end of the story." They are then "in on" the secret and enjoy it even more.

---

* The sound a finger makes when it goes up and down between two big red lips—for approximately five seconds!

RAY HUNOLD

STEVE SANFIELD is an award-winning author, poet, and storyteller. In 1977, he became the first full-time Storyteller-in-Residence in the United States, under the aegis of the California Arts Council. His book, *The Adventures of High John the Conquerer,* was named a Notable Book of the Year by the American Library Association. His most recent collection, *The Feather Merchants and Other Tales of the Fools of Chelm,* was an American Booksellers Pick of the List and a Parents' Choice Honor Book. He is the founder of the Sierra Storytelling Festival held each July in Nevada City, California.

As a young boy, I spent a great deal of time with my grandfather (may his memory be a blessing). Not only was there a deep love between us, but he was the *storyteller in my life. As a child, I could not get enough of his stories. He told all kinds of stories: stories that reflected Jewish history and tradition, stories that bespoke his moral and religious values, stories that kept the sense of family alive, and stories like this one, which not only describe the reality of immigrating to America but, more importantly, would bring a smile or a laugh anytime it was told.*

What He Could Have Been

Steve Sanfield

A JEWISH STORY

In the years between 1881 and 1914, over 2½ million Jews left Russia and eastern Europe to immigrate to the United States. They came seeking freedom from pogroms and persecution. They came seeking a better life for themselves and their children. Most of them entered this country through Ellis Island, and, for a while anyway, settled on the Lower East Side of New York City.

Among them was a man named Morris Silverman. He had come from a tiny Jewish shtetl, a small Jewish village, in the Ukraine. There he had worked as a shammes, the caretaker of the synagogue, a helper of sorts to the rabbi. So naturally when he heard they were looking for a shammes at the Second Street Synagogue, he went to apply for the job.

The president of the synagogue was quite impressed with Morris Silverman's qualifications and experience. As the interview neared its end, the president said, "And, of course, you can read and write."

"Well," said Silverman, "to tell you the truth I can't. I'm an orphan, and I never got to go to school, so I never learned. I can pray, but no, I can't read or write."

"I'm sorry, Mr. Silverman," said the president. "This is the United States of America, and here a shammes has to be able to read and write."

Needless to say, Silverman did not get the job, but somehow he managed to acquire a few needles and a spool of thread. He stood on the corner of Mott Street with the needles and thread in the palm of his outstretched hand, and he sold them.

He was smart enough not to spend the money on himself. Instead he used it to buy more needles and thread, which he also sold. By the end of the week Silverman could be found every day on the corner with a wooden tray held by a leather strap around his neck selling needles and thread, a few thimbles, a pair of scissors, even some bits of cloth.

Before long he had his own pushcart and then his own store. It was then that Morris Silverman found his true calling in life, because he ended up owning the building that the store was in and the building across the street and three in the next block and three more in still another block. Morris Silverman parlayed all his natural talents and abilities into becoming one of the richest, one of the most powerful real estate men in all of New York City.

Finally the time came for his biggest deal. He needed a million dollars in cash. Where do you get a million dollars in cash? Well, if you lived in New York at that time, you'd go to the Chase Manhattan Bank—which is exactly what Silverman did.

The deal was set. Silverman went to the bank on the appointed day to get his money, and who should greet him personally but the president of the bank, John D. Rockefeller himself.

"Mr. Silverman," he said with a courtly bow, "please come in, come in," and he led him into his private office.

They seated themselves on opposite sides of a huge mahogany desk, and Rockefeller said, "Mr. Silverman, it's an honor to do business with a man like yourself. You're the epitome of the American dream. Not so long ago you came to America penniless, and through your own initiative and hard work you've become a man of power and influence. And now I'm about to loan you a million dollars."

With that Rockefeller pushed a large open checkbook and a gold fountain pen across the desk and said, "Mr. Silverman, just fill it out however you want for whatever amount you want."

Morris Silverman gazed down at the checkbook and the pen for a moment. Then he looked up and said, "Mr. Rockefeller, I must confess something to you. I never learned to read or write."

"What?" exclaimed Rockefeller. "You never learned to read or write. Why, do you know what you might have become if you knew how to read or write?"

"Yeah," shrugged Silverman, "the shammes at the Second Street Synagogue."

TELLING TIPS: Since a certain sophistication is required to understand the humor, this story does not work well with young children. I find it works best with audiences fourth grade and up. In telling the story, as much exaggeration as the storyteller is comfortable with adds to the impact of the story, particularly in the scene between Rockefeller and Silverman. Each of the two characters—through voice, gesture, body language—should be as separate as possible. It is the contrast of Rockefeller, the richest man in New York City, and Silverman, the once-poor immigrant, that gives the story its power and humor.

DAVID HOLT is an award-winning musician and storyteller. He is best known for his appearances on The Nashville Network and as host of the PBS series "Folkways" and American Public Radio's "Riverwalk." In 1984, Holt was named in *Esquire* magazine's Register of Men and Women Who Are Changing America. He had four award-winning storytelling recordings and four music recordings, including Grammy nominee *Grandfather's Greatest Hits.* A native of Garland, Texas, Holt has lived in the western North Carolina mountains for two decades.

BILL MOONEY starred for many years as Paul Martin in the ABC daytime serial "All My Children" and is a two-time Emmy nominee for that role. His one-man show of humorous frontier stories, *Half Horse, Half Alligator,* was recorded by RCA Victor and toured America and Europe for two decades. Mooney currently lives in East Brunswick, New Jersey.

In 1985 we started touring Banjo Reb and The Blue Ghost, a Civil War play we wrote and produced. While sitting around airports and making long drives between shows we worked up old folktales for fun. This one came to life somewhere between Dallas and Tampa. We've taken this old Texas tale and given Rabbit a real attitude. We've turned his talking into rhyme just to give him a cocky edge. With the addition of jaw harp for sound effects, children love to join in on this one.

Is It Deep Enough?

David Holt and Bill Mooney

AN AFRICAN-AMERICAN STORY

Ole Possum and his family loved to eat frogs. Possum hunted for them every day. But after a while, the frogs got so smart Possum couldn't catch any of them. He didn't have a thing to eat at his house. His children were awful hungry, and his wife was mad at him 'cause he wasn't catching any frogs. She kicked him out of the house and told him not to come back till he'd found some frogs to eat.

Well, Possum set off down the road wondering what he was going to do. Just then Rabbit came skipping along. He saw Possum was worried. He threw back his ears and said,

"Mornin', Possum."

"Mornin', Rabbit."

"You don't look so happy, Pappy."

"Well, the frogs have all gotten so smart I can't catch a one of 'em. I don't have a lick of food in my house. My wife is mad and my children are hungry. Rabbit, I gotta have some help. Something has got to be done."

Well, Rabbit looked off across the river for a long time. Then he scratched his right ear with his hind foot and said,

> "You go down by the river,
> Shake all over with a deathly shiver.
> Act like you're dead, just do your best.
> Don't move a muscle, and I'll do the rest."

"Thank you, Rabbit!"

So Possum moseyed on down to the river, acting all the time like he was mighty sick. The frogs heard him comin'. And they said,

"Look who's comin'. Look who's comin'. Look who's comin'."

And the little frogs said,

114

"Possum. Possum. Possum."

And the big old frogs said,

"Knee-deep. Knee-deep. Knee-deep."

And *ker-chug*—all the frogs jumped into the knee-deep water.

When Possum got to the beach he started limping. Oh, he looked mighty bad. He sat down on the sand and moaned real loud, "Oh, I'm not feelin' so good. I feel like I'm gonna die. Yessir, I'm about to give up the ghost. Start pushing up daisies. Kick the bucket. Buy the farm. Eat my lunch. Bite the big one."

Then all of the sudden, he started shaking all over. "Buuurrrr." He went through all kinds of contortions like he really was about to turn up his pretty little pink toes. Then he shook harder. "Buuurrr."

His left arm went out and he shook that arm. "Aaahhh."

He shook the other arm. "Aaahhh."

His ears went back. His eyes got wild. He jumped two or three jumps and fell flat on his back and didn't move one lick.

Well, the flies started buzzing around him. They crawled all over his face, but Possum never moved a muscle. The breeze began to tickle his nose, but he didn't twitch a hair. The sun started shining down hot on him. It got hotter and hotter. It made him sweat and the sweat made him itch, but Possum stayed as still as a stump. He just laid there like he was d-e-a-d.

Pretty soon Rabbit came runnin' through the woods and out onto the sandbar. He put his ears up high and hollered out,

"Hey, lookee here, ole Possum just passed on."

Looks to me like he's dead and gone."

And the big ole frogs in the middle of the river said,

"Don't b'lieve it. Don't b'lieve it. Don't b'lieve it."

And all the little frogs around the edge said,

"Me neither. Me neither. Me neither."

But ole Possum just laid there as still as a stump.

All the frogs came up out of the river and hopped over where ole Possum was lying.

But, just then Rabbit winked his eye and said,

> "Look at ole Possum.
> Is he alive or dead?
> Don't leave 'im layin' there.
> Bury him instead.
> Just to be safe, put him deep in the sand
> So he can never come back from the Promised Land."

So all the frogs began to dig out the sand. Dig out the sand from underneath and around ole Possum. And when they had dug a great big deep hole with ole Possum *right in the middle of it* just as still as a stump, those frogs were all tuckered out, and the big ole frogs said,

"Deep er nough. Deep er nough. Deep er nough."

And all the little frogs said,

"You said it. You said it. You said it."

Rabbit woke up, cocked his eye over the edge of the hole, and said,

> "Hey, Good Buddies,
> Just croak or shout.
> I wanna know,
> Can you jump out?"

The big frogs looked up at the top of the hole and said,

"Yes, I can. Yes, I can. Yes, I can."

And all the little frogs said,

"No sweat. No sweat. No sweat."

Then rabbit told them,

> "Now, if I was you and I had my way,
> I'd dig it deeper,
> So that lazy, no-count Possum could never get away."

So all the frogs went back to work and they dug a great big deep hole, way down inside the sand with ole Possum *right in the middle of it* just as still as a stump. And the frogs, they were gettin' pretty tired, and the big ole bullfrogs they sang out,

"Deep er nough. Deep er nough. Deep er nough."

And all the little frogs sang out too,

"You betcha. You betcha. You betcha."

Rabbit, he woke up again, cocked his eye over the edge of the hole, and asked them,

> "Hey, Good Buddies,
> Just croak or shout.
> I wanna know,
> Can you jump out?"

The big ole frogs said,

"B'lieve I can. B'lieve I can. B'lieve I can."

And the little frogs said,

"You got it. You got it. You got it."

Rabbit looked down in the hole again and said,

"Now if I was you and I had my way,
I'd dig it deeper so that lazy, no-count, frog-eatin', beady-eyed, mangy,
malcontented marsupial could never get away."

So all the frogs started to work again—throwin' out sand, throwin' out sand—until the sun was almost down and they had a great big deep hole with ole Possum lying *right in the middle of it* still as a stump. Well, the frogs were awful tired. Plum tuckered out.

The big ole bullfrogs said,

"Deep er nough. (whew) Deep er nough. (whew) Deep er nough."

And all the little frogs said,

"No more. (whew) No more. (whew) No more."

But rabbit looked down in that hole again and said,

"Hey, Good Buddies,
Can you jump out now?
If you can,
Just show me how!"

And they all tried to jump out.

Then the big ole bullfrogs said,

"Cain't do it. Caint do it. Cain't do it."

And the little frogs said,

"No way. No way. No way."

Rabbit jumped right up to the edge of that hole and looked down. Then he hollered out,

"Wake up, Possum! Get ready to eat!
You're lying in the middle of your favorite treat.
You got frogs for your chillun, and frogs for your wife.
You got enough frogs to last you for life!"

TELLING TIPS: Children enjoy making all the voices of the frogs. When we tell it, we invite the audience to croak the words with us. The teller only needs to say the first "Look who's coming'" and gesture for the audience to join in.

The scene where Possum "dies" can be great fun. We make this very animated, wild, and wacky. The kids love it. We also use the sound of the jaw harp (which children can't get enough of) to give the story added texture and create the sound of the frogs jumping.

This story works well as a tandem tale, with one person taking the part of the Possum and narrator and the other becoming Rabbit.

ABOUT THE STORY: The source for our version is the story "How Sandy Got His Meat: A Negro Tale from the Brazos Bottom" in *Treasury of American Folklore* edited by B.A. Botkin (Crown Publishers, 1944).

JON SPELMAN is a solo theater preformer, a narrative artist, a monologist, and a storyteller who travels throughout the United States with almost twenty hours of performance material for children, families, and adults, and a variety of workshops and residency activities. He has performed and taught at over 2,500 locations in the United States and at theater festivals in Sweden and Denmark. He is the recipient of a Solo Performance Fellowship from the Theater Program of the National Endowment for the Arts. For his work on television he has received three Emmys. In May of 1993, Mr. Spelman was selected to represent the United States at the First International Solo Theatre Festival in Tel Aviv, Israel.

I think my dad probably told me this story, in 1955 or 1956. One day, in 1984 or 1985, I started remembering little pieces of it. I must have heard it, or different versions of it, a number of times. The form in which it appears here is the telling shape the little pieces had fallen into by 1994. My recollections are that the story has English origins, which seems logical since my father's family was English, and that it has some kind of literary source, since my father was always reading little magazines and books he collected while rummaging through used bookstores.

The Old Giant

Jon Spelman

A STORY FROM ENGLAND

One time, there was this boy named Jack and somebody, I think it was his uncle, had told him a lot of stories about Jack the Giant Killer. And he got to thinking, "You know, my name's Jack too, so that when I get old enough, I could probably become a Giant Killer myself."

So when he was old enough, which he figured was sixth grade, he went to his dad and he said, "Hey, Dad, what do you think of my becoming a Giant Killer?"

And his dad, whose job it was to cut wood and sell it, wasn't doing very well, not bringing too much money into the house, he joked with Jack. He said, "Well, Jack, that might be a real good idea, because if you could kill some giants, you could probably be paid a lot of money and that would sure help out."

And Jack said, "Good, that's what I'll do."

And his mother said, "What are you talking about?"

And Jack said, "I'm going to quit school and become a Giant Killer."

And his mother said, "No, you're not."

He said, "Yes, I am!"

And she said, "You go to your bedroom without any supper."

And the next morning when his parents got up Jack had done something very silly. He had made a big mistake. He had run away from home. Jack got up and ran away from home. There was just a note left on his bed:

Dear Mom, Dear Dad:
    I've gone off to kill giants. I'll be back with the money.
                                    Love,
                                    Jack

Oh, his parents were so upset. And his mother yelled at his dad. She said, "It's all your fault. You told him to do it and now he's gone."

And his dad said, "I was just kidding. And don't worry: he's not going to find any giants. He'll be back."

"No he won't!" she said. And they kept arguing, but after a while they stopped, because they had to work so hard just to put enough food on the table. So presently they said, "Oh well, it can't be helped." And they gave up.

Now in the meantime, Jack, he was traveling on and traveling on and traveling on. And every time he came to a place where there were some people, in a little town or a city, he'd say, "Hi. My name's Jack. I kill giants."

And they'd say, "Yes?"

And Jack would say, "I'm here to kill your giants."

And they'd say, "Jack, we don't have any giants. Nobody has any giants."

"Oh, sure they do!" said Jack. And he'd go on to the next place and say, "I'm here to kill your giants."

And they'd say, "We don't have any."

Well, Jack was just about to give up when he came to a town and he said, "I'll kill your giants."

And they said, "Well, you're just a little late, Jack. We used to have a giant."

"Oh, you did!" said Jack. "You had a giant here? What happened to him?"

They said, "Well, we're not sure, but he was pretty old and maybe he died."

And Jack said, "Oh, no! He can't be dead. I want to kill him!"

And they said, "Well, we don't know where he is, Jack."

And Jack said, "Well, tell me about him."

And they said, "Well, his name was Old Muggle. And Muggle, he used to live up in the hills and he would come down and eat people's cattle and sheep, and some people said their children were missing. And we were really concerned about it, but then he left and everything's been fine since then.

"Now, he might not be dead, Jack. He just might have gone on to some other place."

"OK," said Jack. And he went on to some other place.

And when he got there they said, yea, they had a giant.

And when Jack asked about it, it seemed like the same one. They said his name was Old Muggle, he lived up in the hills, he ate cattle and sheep, and they were worried about their children. And Jack said, "I'll tell you what. I'll climb up that mountain there and I'll kill that giant if you'll give me a lot of money."

And they said well, they sure would.

So Jack said, "Well, how do I get to him?" And they showed him. And it was a path and it was really steep and really narrow, but Jack wasn't too scared. And he went up that path to the top of the mountain and there was nothing up there but this great big rock. Jack called out. He said, "Hello, Giant."

And there was a giant there. He stuck his heads up from behind this big rock—he had two heads—and one of the heads said, "What do you want?"

And Jack said, "Are you Old Muggle?"

"Yes. What do you want?"

"I've come to kill you."

"What for? I don't do any harm to anybody."

"Yes, you do," said Jack. "You eat their cattle and their sheep and they're worried about their children."

"So what. Are they worried about you?"

"No, because I've come to kill you."

"Yeah," said the second head. "Why don't you just try it, you stupid little brat. I'll bite your head off."

And now Jack was getting scared because that second head was really talking mean. He was quite concerned. He put a stone into a sling and he flung it around and around and around and—*whit, wham*—he threw that stone and—*whack!*—he hit the giant right in one of his heads, but he couldn't tell which one because it was getting dark. He hoped it was the mean one. But then Jack didn't hear anything for a long time.

And finally he heard "Oh *[crying sound]*, you nasty little boy. You killed my other head."

And then Jack took a chance. He figured if the head that was left was crying it was probably pretty nice, so he said, "Well, you don't need that mean old head anyway, do you?"

"No," said Muggle. "But what am I going to do with it? It's just hanging here. The least you could do is help me cut it off and bury it."

"OK," said Jack. So they cut it off and they buried it. And it really was ugly.

But the one that was left, why the more Jack looked at it, it was pretty nice. And Muggle himself seemed pretty nice, because he said, "Thanks a lot, Jack. I'm sorry that head yelled at you and I'm sorry that that's the one that eats the meat."

"Oh, you don't eat meat?" said Jack.

"No," said Muggle. "I'm a vegetarian. Whenever I eat meat I get sick to my stomach. He's the one that always wanted to have it. Hey, Jack, you probably don't want to spend the night up here on the mountain with me. You must be tired climbing all the way up here and burying the head and everything. I could carry you down if you wanted."

"Oh, that would be wonderful," said Jack. He got up into Muggle's hand and Muggle could carry him easily. And Muggle carried him down to the bottom of the mountain.

And on the way down Jack said, "If you don't eat meat, what kind of vegetables do you eat?"

And Muggle said, "Well, any kind. My very favorite kind is cabbages, but I hardly ever get cabbages or even really vegetables. Mostly I just eat the leaves off trees."

"Oh, yuck!" said Jack.

"No," said Muggle. "Particularly if you can get acorns, you know, eat oak trees with those acorns on them."

And then they were at the bottom of the mountain in the town and everybody came running out, and Jack said, "OK, I did it. Give me my money."

And they said, "What? You didn't kill a giant. He's standing right there."

"Look," said Jack, "I killed his bad head. It's the nice one that's left. Come on, give me my money."

"No!" they said. "Not only did you not kill the giant, you brought him into town. You're under arrest."

And then Muggle said, "Hey, I think you ought to give the boy something."

"Oh, sure, sure," they said. "Jack, what do you want? How much money do you want?"

"I don't want money," said Jack. "I want cabbages. You give me cabbages."

Oh, everyone was so relieved, and they ran to their houses and brought out as many cabbages as they could find, about sixty-five.

And Muggle said, "I'll carry those." And he and Jack took off walking.

And they weren't very far out of town before Jack heard, "Ah!" *[chewing and swallowing sounds]* And he looked over and Muggle had eaten every one of those sixty-five cabbages. Muggle kind of burped and he said, "I'm sorry Jack, but I haven't had cabbages in over a year."

"Oh, no. That's fine," said Jack. "That's fine. You go ahead."

"Well," said Muggle, "where are we going?"

"Well," said Jack, "I guess we're going to my house. Come on."

And they set out and they traveled on and they traveled on, and it was a long way. And part of the way, Jack, he rode up on Muggle's shoulder, holding onto his earlobe, and he'd talk to him and tell him stories and jokes. And they would laugh. And they got to like each other a lot. Muggle liked Jack and Jack liked Muggle. And Muggle even liked himself, because he said, "You know, Jack, I think with that other head gone, I might be a pretty nice person and some people might like me."

"Oh, I'm sure they would," said Jack. "I like you very much."

And then they got to Jack's house and Jack's mom and dad were very happy to see him. But his mother said, "Who's this you brought with you?"

"Oh, this is a giant, Mom."

"Yeah, I can see that, Jack. What's he doing here?"

"Well, Mom, he's going to live with us."

"Oh, no. Oh, no!" said his mother. "No. We do not have enough food to feed ourselves. We certainly can't feed a giant. They eat much too much. No, he may not stay."

But Muggle did stay. Things worked out very well. Here's how: Remember I said that Jack's daddy was a woodcutter? He cut up wood to sell it to people to burn in their fireplaces. And Muggle ate the leaves off trees. So Muggle would just go out into the forest and eat all the leaves off a tree, and then pull it up by the roots and bring it home and break it into big pieces with his hands and then into smaller pieces with just his fingertips. And then Jack's daddy just had to trim it up a little bit and carry it into town and sell it. And very often Muggle would carry it into town and sell it and everybody wanted to buy wood from a friendly giant.

So pretty soon Jack's daddy was rich. And he bought a great big place with lots of trees growing on it. And the first forty acres of trees they cleared, why, Jack's daddy planted that full of cabbages so that whenever Muggle wanted a cabbage, he just went out *[licking sound]* and ate one.

And Jack, he came to love Muggle. And Muggle loved him. And Jack's daddy liked Muggle quite a bit too. And Jack's mama said, "Well, he gives me the creeps, but he can stay."

And Muggle did stay, for a very long time. And he and Jack were very good friends. But you know, Muggle had been pretty old to start with. One day Muggle died, and Jack was very sad. But life goes on and Jack's life went on. And now Jack is about my age and he's a friend of mine. And sometimes he tells me stories about Muggle or he tells them to his sons. He has twin boys. And I was over there a while ago and Jack was telling us some stories about Muggle and then the boys said, "Hey, Daddy, you know what? We've never seen a picture of Muggle. You keep telling us these stories, but we've never seen a photograph of him. Show us one."

And Jack said, "Boys, I'm sorry. I don't have a single photograph of Muggle. Of course, we were going to take his picture the first day he was there, but he saw the camera and he said, 'I hate cameras, I hate having my picture taken. If you ever take one I'll leave.' So we never took his picture. I'm sorry, boys, I can't show you one."

And then one of the boys said this wonderful thing, I thought particularly for a storyteller to hear, he said, "Oh, you know what, Daddy? That's OK, that's OK. We don't need photographs, because stories are better than pictures." And I think so too.

And that's the story of the old giant.

TELLING TIPS: This story works best for ten- to twelve-year-olds, though adults at family concerts enjoy it, too. I usually try to tell it in a kind of off-hand manner, the way Jack himself might have told it when he was a boy; also, this Jack reminds me a bit of the Jack I have met in the Appalachian Jack tales—and they may in fact be related.

One reason I like this story is because it's about a potentially scary being who turns out to be a wonderful friend—it's a "multicultural" story without trying too hard to be one. And I like the way it affirms the value and special quality of storytelling and story listening.

Like many native American stories, this story is designed to both entertain and teach a lesson. One of the major lessons to be found in "Little Hare" is the realization that judging people by their appearance is as foolish as thinking that someone is only going to succeed because he is bigger or stronger than someone else, as both Little Hare and the monster he confronts discover.

JOSEPH BRUCHAC is a storyteller and writer. He is of Abenaki Indian and European ancestry. He lives in Greenfield Center in upstate New York. He has written *Return of the Sun; The Faithful Hunter; Hoop Snakes, Hide Behinds and Side-Hill Winders;* and (with Michael Caduto) *Keepers of the Earth.* Bruchac and his wife of thirty years, Carol, live in the Adirondack Mountains in the house where he was reared by his Abenaki grandfather.

Little Hare and the Pine Tree

Joseph Bruchac

A WINNEBAGO STORY

One day, as Little Hare was out running all around the earth, he saw a great monster coming towards him. It was Flying Ant. Flying Ant had a huge body, but his rawhide belt was bound so tight about him that his waist was very small. Flying Ant had pulled up a great spruce tree and was using it as a club. As he walked around and walked around the hills he pounded his club on the ground and sang his hunting song. Whenever he saw an animal of some kind, he would throw the tree at it, crushing the animal with its roots. Then he would pick that animal up and swallow it.

As Flying Ant came striding over the hills towards him, Little Hare laughed.

"Hey," Little Hare said, "his waist is as thin as a hair. I will blow him in two." Then Little Hare began to blow. *"Whooo, whooo."*

Flying Ant paid no attention. He threw his spruce tree club and it flattened Little Hare.

But when Flying Ant lifted up the tree, he was not pleased at what he found.

"Hungh," Flying Ant said, picking the little thing up by its ears and then throwing it away, "this is no good to eat."

When Little Hare did not come home that night, his grandmother became worried. Little Hare always came home at night, even though he ran all over the earth each day. "My grandson has been killed," she said.

When morning came, Grandmother tied her dress up above her knees and went out to look for Little Hare. She ran all over the earth looking. Then she heard the sound of Flying Ant pounding his club and singing his hunting song.

126

As soon as Flying Ant saw Grandmother, he lifted his club to throw it.

"Brother," Grandmother said, "you should not do that."

Immediately Flying Ant lowered his club.

"Old Woman," Flying Ant said, "I did not recognize you. What do you want?"

"I am afraid my grandson has been killed. I think perhaps he bothered you and you killed him."

"What kind of a grandson was it? Was it a big tasty one good to eat or a little smelly one not big enough to keep?"

"A little one, Brother."

"It may be that I did kill him," Flying Ant said. "Yesterday I killed something very little that was no good to eat. I threw it away down there in the swamp."

Grandmother went down into the swamp. There was Little Hare, flattened out and dead. She grabbed him by the ears and shook him.

"Grandson," she said in a stern voice, "you have slept too long. It is time to wake up and work."

As soon as she dropped him back on the ground he jumped up, ran in a circle and then sat there.

"Grandmother," he said, "I was sleeping soundly. Why did you wake me up?"

"You were not asleep," Grandmother said. "The big Old One who walks and walks around the hills killed you. You bothered him yesterday. I made you alive again."

"You are right," Little Hare said. "I remember now. Tomorrow I will go and see him again."

Then Little Hare went home with his grandmother. He ate and ate, and when the morning came he ate again. Then he was ready to set out. He ran all over the world until he came to the end of the earth. There the tall pine trees grew. Little Hare went to the tallest of all the pines. He ran around the tree four times and then he placed tobacco at its base.

"Pine Tree," he said, "I wish to use you. Allow me to pull you from the ground. I need you to help me. There is a big Old One who crushes all the plants and animals. I will set you back here again when I am done."

Little Hare grabbed hold of the great pine. As soon as he did so, he began to grow until he was the same height as the big tree. He pulled and the big pine came out easily by its roots. Then Little Hare went back to the hills where Flying Ant walked around and walked around. When Flying Ant saw Little Hare he began to pound his club on the ground and sing his song. Little Hare did the same and they danced towards each other, singing and pounding the earth. But Little Hare danced faster than Flying Ant. The earth shook as Little Hare pounded it with the great pine tree. As Little Hare danced closer and closer, Flying Ant became afraid. He lifted up his club and shouted, but Little Hare was too quick for him. Little Hare lifted the great pine up and struck the monster. His blow was so strong that it broke Flying Ant into many pieces. Each piece became a winged ant and flew away.

"So it will be from now on," Little Hare said. "No longer will ants be huge monsters. They will always be small."

And so it has been to this day.

Then Little Hare carried the great pine tree back to the place where it had been growing.

"Thank you, Pine Tree," Little Hare said.

Then he set it back carefully into the earth. And if you do not believe my story, just go to that hill. You will see that tree. It still grows there to this day.

TELLING TIPS: People need to remember that silence in a story is just as important as sound. The moments of silence in telling are guideposts that help you into the narrative that is being given. When I tell a story, it's like taking a walk through the forest. Sometimes you just have to listen to the story and follow along as you walk through it. Rather than memorizing it word for word, let the story tell itself to you. See the story in front of you, and walk through it.

ABOUT THE STORY: Another version of this story, as told by the Winnebago elder Chash-chunk-a (Peter Sampson), may be found in Natalie Curtis's *The Indians' Book* (Harper & Bros., 1923; reprinted by Dover Publications, Inc., 1968). My thanks to White Rabbit, a Winnebago veteran of the Vietnam War, who first told me this story twenty years ago in Madison, Wisconsin.

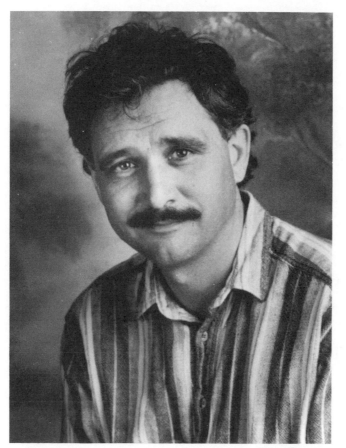

JIM MAY has been featured at storytelling festivals throughout the United States and Europe. In 1989, he was awarded a Chicago Emmy Award for his performance in a television version of "A Bell for Shorty," an original story that appeared on WTTW-TV. He is a sought-after keynote and conference speaker and has told stories in hundreds of schools, from the elementary to the university level. He lives in a restored barn in Harvard, Illinois, with his wife, Nancy Seidler. His book, *The Farm on Nippersink Creek*, published in 1994 by August House, is a collection of stories based on his childhood in the rural Midwest.

This is the kind of tale that my father and his horse-trading friends would relish. This version most closely resembles one that I heard when I was telling stories one evening at a community center in Versailles, Missouri. A local friend of mine got use of a little hall and I helped put up folding chairs for an after-supper round of storytelling. When I was done telling my own stories about growing up in an Illinois farm community, and the small crowd was breaking up, an old farmer came to the front and told me his version of this traditional story. He still had his work clothes on, so he apparently had come right from chores. I loved the story immediately and was most grateful for his telling it to me in his own dry, kitchen-table storytelling style.

The Dead Mule

Jim May

A STORY FROM THE AMERICAN MIDWEST

There was an old farmer who had a place down off the road there by the creek. All his life he worked mule teams on that bottom land and he got along real well. Even when the tractors came out after the war, he said he'd just as soon farm the way he always had.

Well, he had the prettiest pair of white mules you ever saw. They were dead ringers, couldn't tell one from the other. Both were white as snow and stood about fourteen hands high. He always kept them in good shape, too. He was as proud as he could be of those two mules, and would drive them in parades and keep them just so.

One of those mules was older than the other and just keeled over dead one day. The farmer was heartbroken and told all of the horse-traders in that part of the country that he was looking for a mule that matched his white Jenny. Now the traders started looking around because that was how they made a living. They'd find a single mule over in one county, buy it at a good price, and try to sell to someone who was looking to have a matched team. They all knew it would take some time because this farmer was particular and he had loved that old mule of his so.

Finally word got back that there was a trader who had found a nice, gentle, hard-working white mule that would make a good team for that farmer. He went right over to the trader's place to look the mule over. To his great relief and joy, it was a fine specimen, indeed, fourteen hands high and white as the driven snow. The mule seemed healthy enough, was nice and fat, and had a good grass shine to its coat, like it had spent some time in a good pasture.

"Is the mule for sale?" inquired the farmer.

"Oh," said the trader, "I don't need to sell it, but I suppose I could."

One of the first rules of horse trading is that neither party can show too much enthusiasm for the stock.

"Well, she's not much to look at, but I could give you seventy-five dollars," offered the farmer.

"Heck," replied the trader, "I'd be better off working her around here, than take a price like that," he lied.

After considerable dickering the farmer and the trader struck a deal for a hundred dollars. The farmer gave the trader ten dollars and said that he would sell a load of calves by the end of the week and return with the rest of the money.

Friday rolled around, and that farmer was in his pickup truck, ninety dollars in his pocket, on the way to pick up his mule. He pulled into the trader's barnyard and stopped. The dealer came out of the barn and walked over to the truck. He leaned against the old pickup there, and the old men talked for a while about the weather and crop prices and so forth. Finally the trader said, "Your mule's dead."

"Dead? What happened?" the farmer inquired, his spirits deflated.

"Don't know. Must 'ave gotten the shippin' fever or somethin' at the sale barn. I came out to the barn this mornin' and there she was, deader than a doornail. I'll give ya your money back."

"I believe I'd like to see the mule." said the farmer.

"Suit yourself."

The two men walked around behind the barn and there it was. The mule lay in the barnyard with flies buzzing all around it. It had a pretty good bloat to it since the weather had been warm, and those four skinny legs were just sticking right up into the air. It wasn't a pretty sight.

That old farmer's shoulders just kind of slumped when he saw that fine mule in that condition; for he was first and foremost a lover of fine livestock. He had been looking forward to having a team to work with again, a team that would be admired by his friends in the community.

Finally, after a good long silence, the farmer seemed to perk up just a little and he said to the trader, "I believe I'll take the mule."

Now there was never a horse-trader alive who would turn down money, so the trader said, "Suit yourself."

The farmer took nine ten-dollar bills out of his pocket and counted them into the trader's palm.

The farmer had a hand winch on the old pickup. He tied a couple of ropes to the mule and cranked the carcass right up into the bed of that

131

truck, flipped up the tailgate, shook hands with the trader, and drove away.

The horse-trader leaned against the fence and watched the truck make its way down the driveway. The mule's four legs were sticking up over the wooden rack, and whenever the pickup hit a bump those four legs would kind of jostle and rock back and forth.

Standing there watching this, the trader just shook his head and said to himself, "I guess I've seen everything now."

That trader went on the road to trade a string of horses, and was away for almost an entire season. When he did finally drive into town, he went into the coffee shop one morning and ran across the man who had bought the unfortunate mule. There were several farmers at the table talking about the dry weather, and how the price of corn and hogs was climbing pretty good, and such things as farmers tend to discuss. Finally the group had pretty well broken up and just the farmer and the trader were left.

Well, that trader had been wondering for some time about the mule, so he thought he might like to satisfy his curiosity right then and there. He leaned across the table and inquired of the old farmer, "Say, I've been wondering just a little. What the heck did you do with that dead mule?"

"Oh, the mule. Well, it worked out all right, I guess. I raffled him off at a buck a chance, made two hundred dollars."

"You raffled off a dead mule!"

"That's right," answered the farmer, calmly.

"Didn't you have a lot of fellas mad at you when they found out he was dead?"

"No, just the guy that won, and I gave him his dollar back."

TELLING TIPS: I think this story should be told in a dry, understated style. When I was growing up in rural Illinois I heard many stories of this ilk told by my father's horse-trading friends. The scene might be a barn or stable with a couple of the men sitting on hay bales, while another would be standing, maybe absent-mindedly whittling or trimming his fingernails with a small pocket-knife. The narrator would be speaking in an almost halfhearted tone but nevertheless telling the story with a good bit of precision. The punchline would be delivered without a speck of drama or body movement but would sometimes be received by explosive laughter.

JACKIE TORRENCE has performed at Lincoln Center, the Kennedy Center, Wolftrap, Colonial Williamsburg, the Chicago Blues Festival, the International Children's Festival, and the National Storytelling Festival. She has won numerous awards and commissions. She has recorded nine audiotapes, and her collection of stories, *The Importance of Pot Liquor,* was published by August House in 1994.

"The Golden Arm" is an old standby that works with audiences of all ages and sizes. I especially enjoy telling jump tales like this one to children, because they make no effort to mask their reactions to the building suspense. Jump tales can serve many purposes in storytelling. If told effectively, they are a good way to establish trust with your audience. They know you're taking them somewhere they're not quite sure they want to go, but if you're driving carefully, they'll always come along for the ride.

The Golden Arm

Jackie Torrence

A STORY FROM ENGLAND

Now once there lived a man and his wife. The man was an ordinary man. After supper every night he would take a seat in front of the fireplace and watch the smoke of the fire disappear beneath the chimney. He would light his pipe and watch the smoke rings curl before him.

Now the unusual person in this family was the wife. After she finished washing the dishes and straightening the house or whatever it was that she did after supper, she would settle down with her husband before the fire. She would take into her right hand a very soft cloth. Then she would place her hand before her chest and rub that cloth across her arm and hand, for you see her left arm and hand were made of solid gold. Every night she would polish and shine.

One night as she polished and shined the golden arm she said to her husband, "If anything should happen to me I want you to promise me that you will bury me with my golden arm. Will you promise me that?"

And her husband thought, *Huh? What? What does that mean?* And without much thought, he said, "Yes, I promise."

Well, years and years went by and one day the woman passed away. The night before they buried her, her husband started to think about it.

"I can't let them bury that gold. Why if I had that golden arm I could buy myself a brand new house. If I had the gold from that golden arm I could buy myself a brand new suit of clothes. If I had the gold from the golden arm I could buy myself a wagon and ten white horses."

So he went to the place and he cut off the golden arm. And they buried his wife without it.

The next night he stood in front of the fireplace holding the golden arm, talking to himself, "Ha, ha, ha … I've got the gold from the golden arm. I shall buy myself a brand new house. I shall buy myself a wagon and twenty white horses. I shall buy myself a brand new suit of clothes. Ha, ha, ha!"

And just then he looked up through the window, and the sky that had been so bright and blue with stars was now dark, dark, dark. And all of a sudden the wind started to blow harder, and harder, and harder. And over the sound of the wind he heard, "Who's got my golden arm?"

"Oh," said he, "who is that?"

After a minute, he laughed at himself and said, "It's just my imagination. There's nobody there."

But he went over to the window just to be sure. And the sky grew darker and darker, and the wind blew harder and harder, and the voice was louder and louder. "Who's got my golden arm?"

"Oh," he said, "who knows that I have this arm? I must hide it. I must hide my golden arm."

So he looked all around the house, and there was only one place, a closet. He reached toward the wall where there hung a key to the closet. He pulled the key from the wall, ran over to the closet door, opened it and just before he stepped inside he looked back at the window. And the sky was darker and darker, and the wind blew harder and harder, but this time the voice was just at the front door. *"Who's got my golden arm?"*

He locked the front door and ran inside the closet.

"Oh," he said, "I'm safe. Nobody will ever take this golden arm away from me now."

But then he realized that inside the closet it was dark, dark, dark. And all around the house the wind blew harder, and harder, and harder, and the door that had been locked now opened all by itself *[creaking sound]*. And he could hear the voice coming across the room.

"Who's got my ... YOU'VE GOT MY GOLDEN ARM!"

And the ghost of his wife grabbed that golden arm, turned around, ran through the house, and leaped through the window. And nobody's ever seen that ghost or the golden arm again.

TELLING TIPS: This is a good story to tell with children because it is the sort of story they love to tell among themselves. Like any jump tale, its success lies in its pacing. I lower my voice as I near the end of the story, causing my listeners to lean forward. Their body language will cue you when they're hooked in, and you can easily improvise until they're ready for the "jump." With young listeners, I try to inject as much humor as possible so as not to frighten them too much.

ABOUT THE STORY: This story is, of course, widely known and exists in countless versions. Some printed versions can be found in the following works: Joseph Jacobs'

English Folk and Fairy Tales (G.P. Putnam's Sons, 1898); Phyllis Fenner's *Ghosts, Ghosts, Ghosts* (Franklin Watts, 1952); and Maria Leach's *The Thing at the Foot of the Bed and Other Scary Stories* (World Publishing Co., 1959).

BARBARA MCBRIDE-SMITH is a full-time school librarian. She also travels extensively across the United States as a storyteller and workshop presenter. She has been featured at the National Storytelling Festival in Jonesborough, Tennessee. One reviewer reported, "Oklahoman Barbara McBride-Smith is entertainer, educator, comedian, storyteller, and historian all rolled into one package. Her performance is an experience not to be missed." (*New Directions for Women*, January 1991). She has recorded four audiocassette tapes featuring her unique approach to ancient mythology.

This story is the result of frustration. For more than a year, I had been trying to put together a tellable version of Hercules' twelve labors. Finally, a friend said to me, "You're laboring as hard as Hercules. You can tell this story in less than five minutes, and it'll be a lot funnier than your current five-hour rendition." So, I took good advice and poetic license and came up with this modern Megahertz version of an ancient myth. Learning it requires some memory work, but, like poetry, it says a lot with a few carefully chosen words. Read it aloud several times and you'll start to feel the rhythm of the words and phrases. If you tell it with rapid-fire delivery, careful enunciation, and deliberate pauses, your audience will be amazed and delighted.

The Twelve Labors of Hercules

Barbara McBride-Smith

A STORY FROM ANCIENT GREECE

Two things you need to know about Hercules.

Number one: He was very impulsive. If he thought of something, he just did it, before anybody could even say, "Hercules, that is the stupidest thing you have ever ... Hercules? Oh, Hercules, why did you go and do that?"

Number two: He was very strong.

Now you take those two characteristics, put them together, and you've got a guy who spent most of his life in trouble.

Hercules would get into a scrape and then have to do community service to get out of it. Next thing he knew, he was into another scrape. The Twelve Labors are what he did to get out of an especially big heap of trouble he got into.

One of those labors was to clean the Augean stables in a single day. Let me ask: Did you ever have a little bitty dog that made a mess on the floor? Remember cleaning it up? You had to pick up the mess, get rid of it, wash the floor, rinse the floor, and spray the floor with deodorant. Then you had to look your little bitty dog in the eye and say, "Noooo! Bad dog! Not on the floor!" And of course, the first chance your little bitty dog got, he came back to the very same spot and made another mess. Dogs are creatures of habit.

So are cows. The Augean stables were full of cows. Thousands of cows. Those cows were huge. Each one weighed several metric tons. And their stables had never been cleaned ... not ever. Are you gettin' my drift here? It was a mess, and Hercules was hip-deep in it.

Well, if I went into all the details of this one labor of Hercules, I could spend a whole hour telling you about it. And there would still be eleven labors to go. So here's the subcompact version. It goes fast. Pay attention.

The way I see it, you've got:

nine animals,
one monster,
a few golden apples,
and one pair of underwear!

More specifically, you've got:

one feline,
one equine,
one porcine,
three bovine,
one canine,
one serpentine,
the birds,
the apples,
the deer,
and one pair of underwear!

You've gotta:

clean one,
chase one,
capture two,
kill two,
and that leaves six to fetch.

Are you having trouble following this? Well, I guarantee that you are a lot smarter than Hercules was, so just imagine what he was up against.

Quick summary now. Here's what Hercules had to remember:

Try to capture the big old hog,
Bring back from Hades the three-headed dog,
Fetch two of the three bovine herds,
Chase away the big ugly birds.
Kill the many-headed snake,
Clean up after the other beefsteak,
The big deer lives,
Big lion has to die,
Don't use the golden apples to make a nice pie.
You must put a stop to the man-eating mares,
And don't forget the underwear!

I'm all out of time now. Gotta go. But that's the story of the Twelve Labors of Hercules.

TELLING TIPS: Unless your listeners have a strong background in classical mythology, they may not understand the cryptic references to Hercules' twelve labors. Therefore, I most often tell this story when I know I can combine it with a "teaching opportunity."

As a professional storyteller, I believe that a good story needs no explanation. As an educator, though, I believe that storytelling can be a powerful teaching tool.

Before or after telling this story, I ask my listeners: "Can you name or describe any of the famous labors of the strongman Hercules?" Responses are often sparse and sometimes mingled with feats belonging to Samson or Goliath or a current movie hero. Using a chalkboard, an overhead projector, or a large piece of butcher paper, I make a list or a web of Herculean tasks they can recall. Then, anecdotal style, I fill in the missing labors.

Next, I demonstrate how each labor, while a full-length story of its own, can be condensed to a few carefully chosen words and phrases. This can be developed into a writing lesson when time permits. Now I'm ready to display the print version of the story and ask the listeners to identify the twelve labors. Suddenly the story makes sense. It's even funny!

Remember the mnemonic devices we all used to learn the number of days in each month, the letters of the alphabet, and those tricky rules for spelling? Perhaps this teaching tale can serve a similar function. You can say with pride, "The Twelve Labors of Hercules? Of course, it's Greek to me!"

ABOUT THE STORY: If you, the teller, aren't familiar with these adventures yourself, do your homework. The following provide good reading: *Hercules* by Bernard Evslin (William Morrow, 1984); *Greek Gods and Heroes* by Robert Graves (Doubleday, 1960); *The Adventures of Hercules* by I.M. Richardson (Troll, 1983); and *The Amazing Adventures of Hercules* by Claudia Zeff (Usborne, 1982).

Note: Hercules is the Roman name for this hero. To the Greeks, he was known as Heracles, named in honor of the Olympian goddess, Hera.

ROBIN MOORE had been a storyteller since 1981 and has presented more than 3,000 programs at schools, museums, conferences, festivals, and on radio and television. Before becoming a full-time professional storyteller, Robin served as a combat soldier in Vietnam, earned a journalism degree from Penn State, and worked as a newspaper reporter and magazine editor. He is the author of the bestselling *Awakening the Hidden Storyteller,* as well as three award-winning historical novels for children, *The Bread Sister of Sinking Creek, Maggie Among the Seneca,* and *Up the Frozen River.* He has also written two collections of tales from the Pennsylvania Mountains: *When the Moon Is Full* and *The Cherry Tree Buck.* He is the owner of Groundhog Press, a small independent publishing house which produces books and tapes celebrating the oral tradition.

I first heard this story from my father. He told it to me nearly forty years ago, when I was a boy growing up in the mountains of central Pennsylvania. The simple magic of this tale has stayed with me all these years. And now, as I tell the same story to my own children, I understand more than ever how important it is to preserve and protect these old stories. They tell us of a time when the natural world was the only world we knew, when the natural laws and the natural rhythms of life were the only ones that mattered. Like Turtle, maybe we too can learn to escape from the wolves.

How the Turtle Cracked His Shell

Robin Moore

A CHEROKEE STORY

Nowadays, if you pick up Turtle and look him over carefully, you'll see that his shell is covered with cracks.

But it wasn't always that way.

In the old days, back in the days when the animals could talk, the turtle's shell was smooth and shiny like a mirror.

That was in the days when Turtle and Possum used to spend their days together, enjoying the fruits of creation.

One day Possum was up in a persimmon tree, picking the delicious, sticky fruit and throwing the persimmons, one by one, down to Turtle, who waited on the ground.

Every time that possum would toss down one of those persimmons, that turtle would open his jaws and—

"Glump!"

—he'd swallow one of those persimmons.

It was while that was going on that a big wolf came loping out into the clearing. He saw Possum tossing down those persimmons and decided to get some for himself.

Wolf sat down right next to Turtle.

Every time that Possum would toss down one of those persimmons, Wolf reached out with his huge jaws and—

"Glump!"

—he'd swallow one of those persimmons.

Turtle knew he didn't have a chance of getting any of those persimmons as long as that wolf was around.

Of course, Possum tried to help. He tossed a couple of persimmons right down to Turtle. But Wolf reached out and nipped those persimmons right out of the air before Turtle could even get near them.

If that had happened to you or me, we'd probably be pretty perturbed.

But not Turtle. Instead, he just sat there, calmly watching as Wolf devoured that sticky fruit. Slowly, Turtle began to hatch himself a plan.

Turtle called up to Possum in that lazy, slack-jawed, leathery-necked, tortoise kind of way, saying,

"I'll tell ya what, Brother Possum, you just aren't bein' fair to Brother Wolf here. Yer tossin' him down nuthin' but small ones. A big wolf like him deserves somethin' better. Toss him down a really big one." And he winked.

"That's right," Wolf said, in a voice grown hoarse from howling at the moon. "Do what Turtle says. Toss me down one of those really big ones."

Possum smiled and climbed high up into the tree, where the big sticky persimmons grow. He plucked a huge, sticky persimmon and tossed it right down to Wolf.

Wolf opened his greedy jaws and—

"GLUMP!"

—he swallowed that persimmon.

That was, he tried to swallow it. Instead, that persimmon got caught in his throat. Wolf coughed and choked and gasped for air. Then he fell over stiff, with his feet sticking up in the air.

Turtle glanced up at Possum.

"That'll teach those wolves to fool with me," he said.

And he and Possum walked off, in search of other trees and other fruits.

At that moment, Wolf's fellow wolves came running through that clearing. They pulled Wolf to his feet and slapped him on the back and with a great gasp, Wolf coughed up that persimmon.

As soon as he caught his breath, Wolf snarled.

"How humiliating," he said to himself, "to have to have my fellow wolves save me from a turtle."

He sat with his paws together in a bunch. He lifted his snout to the sky and started singing that song he's been singing ever since, the one that sounds like:

"Owwwmmmgoona get himmm …

"Owmmmgoona get himmm …"

So he went out and got him.

As you can imagine, it wasn't that hard for Wolf to track Turtle down and carry him back to his wolf den up on the side of the hill.

As Wolf dropped Turtle on the ground in the center of those wolves, Turtle stretched out his leathery neck and looked around.

All the other wolves were there, both males and females, young and old. The whole pack was assembled for the feast. They had a huge fire going on the ground outside their den. And on that fire was a clay pot, filled with boiling water.

If that were happening to you or me, we would probably be pretty scared.

But not Turtle. He just lay there, chewing his tongue and blinking his sleepy eyes at the wolves.

"Now listen here, Turtle," the wolf said. "You see that pot of boiling water over there? I'm gonna take you and throw you in that pot and boil you up and eat ya!"

Turtle just looked up at Wolf.

"Oh, yeah? Well, I'll tell ya what: You throw me in that pot, I'm just gonna kick it to pieces!"

"Hoooooooooooo!" Wolf said, "I didn't think of that! Well, all right, I'll throw you in the fire and roast you up!"

Turtle just looked up at Wolf.

"Oh yeah? Well, I'll tell ya what: You throw me in that fire, I'm just gonna roll all around with my shell and stamp it out."

"Hoooooooooooo!" Wolf said, "I didn't think of that. All right, I don't even care about eatin' ya. I'm gonna take you and throw you in the river!"

Now you and I know the turtle's a pretty good swimmer, right? Well, the wolves didn't know that.

Turtle just looked up at Wolf and said, "Oh, yeah? Well, I'll tell ya what: You could put me in that pot; you could put me in that fire; but whatever you do, please don't throw me in that river!"

"That's exactly what I'm gonna do!" the Wolf hollered.

He grabbed that turtle and threw him through the air.

It was a good throw. That turtle sailed through the air and landed in the deep water in the middle of the river. And he swam away, laughing.

"Hoooooooooooooooo!" the Wolf said, "I didn't think of that!"

And that should be the end of the story, except for one thing:

While the turtle was flying through the air, just before he hit the water, he struck a great big rock in the center of the river and it cracked the poor turtle's shell into thirteen tiny pieces.

When Turtle crawled out on the opposite bank, he pulled himself up in the river weeds.

"Aw ...," he moaned, "my achin' back!"

He glanced over his shoulder and Turtle gasped at what he saw:

The beautiful shell he had been so proud of was destroyed.

Turtle lay down in the sun and let the sun shine on him and heal him up.

But it didn't heal him completely.

To this day, if you look really close at the Turtle's shell, you can still see those thirteen tiny pieces.

And you can still see those cracks from hitting that big old rock in the center of the river.

TELLING TIPS: One of the neat things about this story is audience participation. When the possum first tosses the persimmon down to the turtle, I actually use my hands in front of my face to mime the turtle catching the persimmon in his mouth. So I start with my hands open, and then when the line comes up, "When Possum tossed down that persimmon, Turtle opened his jaws and—'*Glump!*'—and swallowed the persimmon." Then I address the audience saying, "Do you want to help me do that? Well, get your jaws ready." They move their hands to be like a jaw and then we all do it together. Each time the possum tosses the persimmon down, whether it's to the turtle or the wolf, we use that gesture.

The other thing that is fun about this story is hamming up the characterizations of the wolf and the turtle. Of course, there isn't just one right way to them, but my own way is to have the turtle be very laconic and laid back. The wolf is forceful and sometimes hysterical. The greater the contrast between the turtle and the wolf, the more your audience will enjoy it. Everyone in the audience, young and old, gets a big kick out of seeing how handily Turtle puts Wolf in his place.

The other thing to remember when you are telling a story like this: you need to be carefully prepared. The key to all spontaneity is careful preparation. If you have your characterizations and sequence of events clearly in mind, then you are free to have fun with the story. You can really ham up the parts that work and move on through the parts that could bog you down.

ABOUT THE STORY: My father learned this story from Cordon Bell, who wrote a collection of Cherokee Indian legends called *John Rattling Gourd of Big Cove.* Mr. Bell rescued Turtle's story from an article in the 1897 report of the American Bureau of Ethnology by anthropologist James Mooney. The story was told to Dr. Mooney by John Axe and Swimmer, two Native American men who were the last of the traditionally trained storytellers of the eastern Cherokee. Now Turtle's story is reaching new generations of listeners. I hope you enjoy it as much as my family has.

ED NUTE

JAY O'CALLAHAN's most recent performances have been at the Abbey Theatre for the Yeats International Theatre Festival in Dublin and the Glistening Water Festival in New Zealand. Jay has also performed at the National Theatre Complex in London, in Niger, Africa, The Hague, in Boston with the Boston Symphony Orchestra, and at Lincoln Center in New York. In 1991, the National Endowment for the Arts awarded Jay a fellowship for a series of pieces called "The Pill Hill Stories." Jay has been creating and performing stories for over fifteen years. He lives in Marshfield, Massachusetts, with his wife, Linda, and their children, Ted and Laura.

In 1963, my ship, the USS Cimarron, *went to Kyoto, Japan. I was intrigued by the zen gardens, the tea houses, and the sense of hospitality. Right then I began telling stories of Japan.*

There are scores of stories of where the salt in the sea comes from; every nation by the sea has one. I've told this story for long years and added tiny rhythms and touches. I like this version because it captures a sense of Japan and, while others give the ending away with their title, this one keeps the listener guessing until the very end.

The Magic Mortar

Jay O'Callahan

A STORY FROM JAPAN

The day before New Year's, a young man was standing in his shack and he said to his wife, "I don't have any rice. I'm sorry. Nothing for New Year's."

She said, "Borrow some from your older brother, he's rich."

"You know my brother, he's cruel. But I'll try."

He got his courage up. He went all the way down to the river and he got in his boat and he rowed over to his brother's island. His brother had built a wonderful palace on the island. The younger brother went right in and said, "Lend me some rice for New Year's. I'll pay you right back."

The older brother looked at him.

"I'm a busy man, I don't have any time, I don't have any rice."

Then he dismissed him with his fingertips.

The younger brother felt crushed. He rowed back to the mainland. He began to walk like an old man. His shoulders were bent. His back was bent.

A really old man was watching. The old man finally said, "Come over here, young man, come over here. What's the trouble?"

"I'll tell you the trouble. I've got one brother in the world. I asked him for some rice. He lied to me—said he didn't have it. The world is so cruel."

"Ah, it's not as bad as you make out. Here. I'll give you a rice cake with honey on it. Now, you see there's a break in the wall there. You go through there and you'll see a little statue of the Buddhah. You'll find some little men. Now you give them this rice cake with the bead of honey if they give you a mortar and pestle."

The young man took the rice cake with the bead of honey. He went between the break in the wall. There was the statue of the Buddhah and there were tiny little men—twenty or thirty of them, tiny little fellows, a couple of inches high—and they were trying to lift a log into a hole. The brother said, "Here, I'll help you. Oh, I didn't mean to step on you."

"Well, you did."

He picked up a little fellow and said, "I'm so sorry. Look at the size of you."

"Look at the size of you," the little fellow said. "What have you got?"

"I've got a rice cake."

"May I have it?"

"No, you can't have it unless you give me something. What will you give me?"

He put him down and all those little men put their heads together and they made whispering sounds.

"We'll give you bags of gold."

They began to pull these bags of gold out of the earth.

The younger brother said, "I don't want the gold. What else have you got?"

They put their heads together and whispered.

"We've got a magic mortar. You can have that."

"All right!"

They took out a tiny magic mortar. He bent down and picked it up.

"How does it work?"

"Give it back."

The little man took it and said, "When you want something, you turn it to the right. You say what you want and it will come out. The pestle will keep turning. When you want it to stop, turn it to the left and say, 'Stop.'"

"All right. Thank you very much."

With that the brother gave them the rice cake.

The young man went home and burst into the shack. His wife said, "Where's the rice?"

"Never mind, I've got a rice maker."

All of the sudden he realized he didn't know if it worked.

"Get on the other side of the table."

He took the pestle and began to turn it to the right. He said, "Rice, rice, let us have rice. Rice, rice, let us have rice. Rice, rice."

And the rice began … *pop, pop, pop, pop, pop, pop, pop, pop*. The rice popped out. It popped all over the place for hours. He gathered it up in all the bags and then he took the pestle, turned it to the left and said, "Stop!" And the rice stopped.

He said, "It's almost New Year's. Let's have some wine and celebrate."

So he turned the magic pestle to the right.

"Wine, wine, let us have wine. Wine, wine."

Wine began to pour out. He tasted it.

"Too dry, but not bad, not bad. Ha! Ha!"

They collected the wine for hours. He turned it to the left.

"Stop!"

And it stopped. They had wine enough for a year.

"It's almost midnight," the young man said. "Let's have a mansion."

"Don't be greedy," his wife said.

"I'm not being greedy. I want to have a party. We can't have a party in a shack like this. We'll have a mansion. We'll have a party today."

And he turned the pestle to the right.

"Mansion, mansion, let us have a mansion. Mansion, mansion—"

Crack! The crack was the sound of a great wall being made. Soon he could see the furniture being made. Next he ran to the window, and he could see one of those wonderful Japanese bridges. His property kept stretching to his neighbors, so he turned the pestle to the left and said, "Stop!"

That day all of his neighbors came to his party. They were all invited. They loved the young man and were glad for him. They were curious, but no one said anything. They were too polite. Except the children. Children are children. They said, "Yesterday nothing. Today everything. Poof. Wonder where he got it."

But nobody asked him.

The older brother heard and he came and he burst right in.

"Yesterday you were bothering me for rice, today you've got all this. Where'd you get it?"

The young man was too smart to say anything.

"I'm busy with the guests."

He kept being busy, but the older brother was going to find out what happened. The older brother watched the younger brother, and late in the party the younger brother wanted to give a present to the children, so he went into the kitchen and took out the magic mortar. He didn't know he was being watched. The young man turned the pestle to the right and said, "Bean candy, bean candy, let us have bean candy. Bean candy, bean candy, let us have bean candy."

The bean candies began to pour out. The older brother slipped back to the party.

When everyone left, the older brother said, "I've got a chill. I feel, I feel poorly. Could I stay?"

"Of course, you can stay, you're my brother. I'll get the tatami mat." He set down the tatami mat and covered the older brother. "Good night."

149

At three in the morning, the older brother made his way into the dark kitchen and found the magic mortar on the shelf. He had it. Ha! Ha! He would make himself the most powerful man in Japan.

The older brother ran down to the sea, got into his boat, begin to row to his island. The wind was up and the waves were rough. He got hungry and tired. He reached in and all he had were some old rice cakes—so dull. What he needed was some salt, so he took out the magic mortar and he turned the pestle and said, "Salt, salt, let us have salt."

The salt poured out and he sprinkled it on the rice cakes and ate them.

He kept rowing, and the boat was getting heavier and heavier. It was filling with salt. He picked up the magic mortar and said, "Stop making the salt. Stop making it." He didn't know how to stop it. The salt kept pouring out, and finally a wave struck the boat and the boat went down to the bottom of the sea and so did the magic mortar. And to this day the pestle is still turning to the right, and the salt is still pouring out.

And that's where the salt comes from in the sea.

TELLING TIPS: I enjoy making sounds for the tiny men and having a clear rhythm when I say "Rice, rice, let us have rice." The same rhythm returns whenever the magic mortar is used. I suggest using a distinct voice for each character. Walk around being each character. Get a sense of the character's body and outlook on life. The older brother is clearly selfish. He cares nothing for his brother. Find a voice that expresses that selfishness. Visualize each scene. Have a clear sense of place. If you're clear about each place, then your listeners will see it clearly. I imagine I'm actually holding the magic mortar and turning the pestle. The gesture helps me actually see the mortar. I heard or read this story a long time ago and made it my own by adding small touches over the years.

ABOUT THE STORY: Variants of this story appear in Yoshiko Uchida's *The Magic Listening Cap: More Folk Tales from Japan* (Harcourt, Brace, 1955) and Florence Sakade's *Japanese Children's Stories* (Tuttle, 1952). Variants also come from Denmark (*The Talking Tree* by Augusta Baker [Lippincott, 1955]); Great Britain (*Tattercoats and Other Folktales* by Winifred Finlay [Harvey House, 1976]); Norway (*Norwegian Folk Tales* collected in the nineteenth century by Peter Christian Asbjornsen and Jorden Moe [Pantheon Books, 1982]); and many other seafaring nations.

JOYCE ANN HANDCOCK

Tall tales are unique. It may be the only entertainment form that cuts through the whole socioeconomic spectrum as well as all ethnic groups. I have told tall tales to inner-city groups, native Americans, the very rich, academics, from kindergartens to retirement centers, and the laughter comes just as strongly from one group as from another. With the tall tale, you never have to worry about appropriateness. They are enjoyed by everyone everywhere.

CHUCK LARKIN has been a featured teller at over forty festivals, including three performances at the National Storytelling Festival in Jonesborough, Tennessee. He is a folk storyteller who tells tall tales, Celtic legends, ghost stories, and anything else under the sun that's outrageous. Chuck also enhances his performances with the banjo, bones, and musical saw.

The Electricity Elixir

Chuck Larkin

A STORY FROM THE AMERICAN SOUTH

I was raised on a farm so far out in the woods that the sun never came up 'till half past twelve in the afternoon. In the thirties, the Grand Old Opry radio program was broadcast from Nashville, Tennessee, on Saturday night. It was Wednesday afternoon before that program got out to our farm so we could listen.

I never will forget the first time my folks took me into town, into Pocomoke. What a day! Pocomoke was so small if you stood on a hill overlooking Pocomoke you could overlook Pocomoke. The last digit in the zip code was a fraction. The Power Company was a Sears Roebuck Diehard battery.

That first day I was brought to town, sakes alive, I had never seen people! I had never been through the woods. I was only knee high to a grasshopper. There I was, looking at the people. That day, I learned a great lesson of life. People-watching was even more fun than baiting a line with a piece of corn and chicken fishing off the back steps.

If you never tried this, take and run the fishing line through a small hole in a kernel of corn. Bless your heart but that's fun! I mean chickens will flat out give you a tussle.

In those days we had fun! Sailing bucket lids. Making balloons out of onion sacks. Trying to remove hubcaps from moving cars. I'll tell you the truth, there's more to country life then observing grass grow.

That day I remember standing and watching this traveling medicine man. He had a flat-bed wagon with an electricity machine sitting up on top.

Now you need to understand, no one had seen electricity then, on the farm or in town. People had heard about electricity and they were afraid of it. It's the truth. No one wanted an electric pole near their house because of all the strange illnesses it would bring. And when the first electricity was wired into houses no one would leave anything plugged in. They were afraid that stuff would leak out and ruin the floor.

There I stood, when all at once the medicine man began to talk about the wondrous healing qualities of electricity. I remember his words exact.

"I am proud to announce to you, the audience, the availability, for the first time, of Electricity Elixir from this electricity machine. Mothers, fathers, do your children have worms? Are your children occasionally fidgety or sleepy? Once in awhile is their behavior peevish, or unpleasant? Now or then do they pick their nose, grind their teeth or play the fool?

"Friends, if your little ones at home display any of these abnormal behavior episodes unaccompanied or in any combination, these are symptoms of worms! For your precious piece of mind, pick up a bottle of Dr. Parker's Electricity Elixir. Yes, that's the brand name, soon to be a household word.

"Ladies and gentlemen, we know Electricity Elixir kills worms, regulates the body's systems, improves a child's character, restores everybody's frame of mind while maintaining a healthy temperament. This concoction of Electricity Elixir may be used either as a tonic for the inside or an instant cooling, comforting liniment on the outside.

"I know you are thinking, will it cure everything? My friends, frankly, we don't know! When used all over the body as a liniment, you feel as if you have received a massage. When just rubbed on the back and spine, your vertebrae will self-align as if a chiropractor had giving you healing adjustments.

"In my hometown, when our neighbors have taken this Electricity Elixir as a tonic we have observed amazing symptom-redress. Both heart dropsy and night flotations have been arrested and you are put into a looking-forwards mood.

"I can tell you the Electricity Elixir cures hoarseness, restores personality, stimulates the appetite, and long-time married couples begin kissing again. You do have to be cautious. The Electricity Elixir needs to be taken in moderation. Our friends and neighbors, after their initial sampling, felt themselves grow younger everyday. They got carried away and consumed an excessive amount of this Electricity Elixir. Last month their names showed up in the birth notices."

After his oration, the medicine man pointed to a man on crutches and offered him a sample. I looked at the man when he walked up on a crutch with a busted leg in one of those old-time casts that came up to his hips. He drank a sample glass of that there Electricity Elixir the medicine man poured from that electricity machine, busted off that cast, shook his leg once or twice and walked, and then he did a little buck and wing dancing. A lady came over in a wheelchair and was introduced to the medicine man, and she drank a glass of that there Electricity Elixir and stood up and walked, and I admit she was a bit shaky, but she walked!

Next was an old World War One veteran who said he was passing through town and wanted to try that cure for his war wound. I could see where he had done had his right hand shot off in the war. He climbed up on that wagon, drank a glass of Electricity Elixir and we all stood transfixed in disbelief, gaping in amazement as a new hand grew up out of his sleeve, right before our eyes, and seeing is believing.

That was the end of the free samples, but after that every farmer there was pulling rumpled-up dollar bills out of his bib overalls and buying bottles of that there Electricity Elixir.

I was only six years old but I knew right then that if I ever took sick I was going to use an Electricity Elixir cure.

Well, it was about seven years later I took sick for the first time. I thought I was going to die I was so sick. I mean, I was awful sick. It was a ghastly experience. I had fallen in love for the first time and oh, don't that make you sick. Every time it happens it makes you sick. I still think that some day they will find lovesickness comes from a virus and find a better cure than getting married.

I was so sick, I really, really, really thought I was going to die. I couldn't talk about it because nobody runs around saying, "I'm in love, I'm in love," like some fool.

What was worse, I was in love with an older woman. That's no big deal now, but in the old days that was serious. Even more sickening, I was in love with a married woman. You all don't even know what that signifies, because today it just means you have to wait for a couple of years. But when I was young, people stayed married forever! What's worse and worse and worse—I am still embarrassed to even to tell you now—I was in love with my schoolteacher. Being in love with your schoolteacher is a poisonous scourge that dethrones reason, fills you with misery, shame, helplessness, hopelessness, and pitches you into the pits of degradation and despair.

Then suddenly I remembered the Electricity Elixir cure!

I had a problem. We still did not have electricity on our farm nor in town, and the man with the Electricity Elixir machine had gone on.

Well, I thought and remembered electricity comes from nature and in a storm there is plenty flying around in the lightning bolts. I just needed to catch me a lightning bolt like Ben Franklin had done with his kite. I didn't have a kite, but I did manage to live another three weeks until one of the summer lightning storms came in. No rain, just heat-lightning, snap, crackling and popping all through the sky.

I went out behind the barn where I wouldn't look like a silly fool, and for two hours I ran around trying to catch a lightning bolt. I got so bedraggled, dried out and parched, my tongue was hanging down around my knees.

Suddenly I seen a bolt heading towards me. I ducked my mouth under and I caught that lightning bolt!

DON'T EVER DO THAT!

That lightning bolt threw me twenty-two feet through the air, ripped all the clothes off my body, took my shoes off, turned them inside out, criss-crossed them and stuck them back on my feet! Swallowing a lightning bolt is like drinking liquid fire!

You may not believe this, but for the next three weeks I ate all of my food raw! The food was cooked well-done by the time it hit my stomach! That electricity burned all the way down through my body and turned my toenails red, white, and blue!

I was a little skinny fellow until I swallowed that lightning bolt and that thing blew me up and I have never been able to get down to average size. Oh, I still wake up at night thinking about that pain. Oh, yes, it hurt, a whole lot. It was pain, pain pain. But, I will tell you something. It was twenty-four years before I ever fell in love again.

And that's a true story.

TELLING TIPS: Tall tales and their first cousins, urban legends, are most effective when told as personal experiences. The advantage to doing this type of material is that you can elongate or shorten the story on the spot to fill the amount of time you're given. Tall tales are by nature segmented stories; that is, they are stories made up of little pieces that can stand by themselves. If you've ever been on the banquet circuit, where the audience's attention is diverted by the movement of waiters, you know the need for a story filled with independent segments that can be linked together. You're also able to do what Scheherazade did in *The Arabian Nights* and tell a story within a story.

ABOUT THE STORY: Most tall tales combine several hyperbolic one-liners with a traditional story and original creations in the folk process. "The Electricity Elixir" contains many old and new small town one-liners. For example, swallowing a lightning bolt is a very old notion. I heard it in Monterey, Tennessee, in the 1970s, but I'm sure it was told by Congressman Davy Crockett, a famous tall tale teller from Tennessee.

New material comes forth onstage. I remember the day in a school years ago when I said, "The lightning bolt burned down through my body and my toes turned red, white, and blue." That resulted in a huge laugh. And that's the folk process.

In Tennessee, I collected the line, "It was so hot in the middle of the day, I saw the shade crawl underneath a tree to cool off." When I ask people, "Have you ever seen that?," a lot of them say no. Then I ask them if they've never seen the shade go under a tree in the middle of the day. Recently I encountered the same image in a twelfth-century Sanskrit manuscript.

Tall tales can be found woven into legends around the world. I have collected a whole series of tall-tale chicken stories. A couple of the best were given to me by some opera singers who heard them in a bar in Germany. So while tall tales seem uniquely American, they have first and second cousins all over the world.

CATHERINE EMORY-BRICKER

This is my version of a story given me by Erin Garvey of Charlottesville, Virginia. She was a Peace Corps teacher in Cameroon, Africa, in 1976 at the Lycee de Mokolo. An eighth-grader passed this story in as part of an assignment to write down folktales they'd heard at home.

Erin passed some of these stories on to me a few years later, and "Panther and Rabbit" was one of my favorites.

MICHAEL PARENT grew up in Maine and tells stories that reflect his growing up in a bilingual French Canadian family. The past seventeen years he has performed throughout the United States and Europe, including four appearances at the National Storytelling Festival in Jonesborough, Tennessee. He now lives in Charlottesville, Virginia.

Panther and Rabbit

Michael Parent

A STORY FROM FRENCH CAMEROON

A long, long time ago, there lived in the jungle a strong, graceful animal named Panther. He thought he was the handsomest creature in the whole jungle.

In the same jungle, there lived Rabbit, who was not very strong, and not considered at all handsome. Whenever Rabbit crossed Panther's path, things went badly for Rabbit. So he stayed out of Panther's way and bided his time.

One day the king made an important announcement and his messengers rode throughout the kingdom. "The king's youngest daughter is now of marrying age," they proclaimed. "All eligible males may report to the palace tomorrow. The king will be speaking to those who would wish to marry his daughter and become Prince of the Realm!"

This exciting news spread quickly. When word reached Panther, he thought to himself, "Aha! Who could possibly be a better Prince of the Realm than me? I'm strong, graceful, and of course very handsome. I'll be a great prince!"

Rabbit also heard the announcement and he thought, "Hmm, why not me? I could be a good prince. And I've always liked the princess."

The next morning, many young males set out for the palace with high hopes. Panther, a swift runner, arrived before any of the others and strode past the guards and into the palace. He walked into the throne room and approached the king as though he, Panther, owned the palace. "Your Majesty," he announced, "here I am. There's no need to talk to anyone else. I'm strong, graceful, and, as you can see, very handsome. I'll make a fine Prince of the Realm."

The king had ruled fairly and firmly for many years. "Panther, your name, like all the others, will be written on the list of candidates. In two days you, like the others, will return and I will let you know what I have decided."

"That's fine, Your Majesty," Panther said. "No problem. I'll be back in two days." As Panther descended the palace steps, he saw Rabbit waiting his turn in line. He stopped, pointed at Rabbit, and began to giggle and chortle. Rabbit said nothing, but thought, "Some day it will be *my* day," and awaited his turn.

When the guards swung the doors open to allow Rabbit into the throne room, he bowed deeply and spoke slowly. "Your Majesty, it's clear that I'm not the most powerful, and certainly not the most handsome, animal in the jungle. But I can say that if I were to be chosen, I would treat your daughter with kindness and respect. I'm also a good thinker and would be helpful to you in ruling the kingdom."

"Very well, Rabbit," the king said, "I'll put your name on the list. Return in two days and I'll let you know what I've decided."

As Rabbit left the throne room, he turned to the king. "Your Majesty, could I perhaps ask you a question?"

"Well, yes, Rabbit. What is it?"

"Whose name is at the top of the list?"

"Panther's name. Why do you ask?"

"Panther? Oh, really?" Rabbit said and chuckled under his breath.

"Rabbit, what is the meaning of this?" said the king.

"Oh, Your Majesty, it's really nothing. If you don't know, perhaps I should not be the one to tell you. I really must go now."

Rabbit then felt large hands gripping his shoulders. The palace guards lifted him, placed him in front of the throne, and said, "His Royal Majesty has asked you a question!"

"I'm sorry, Your Highness. It's just that Panther is ... well, Panther is in fact my riding horse."

"Did I hear you correctly, Rabbit?" said the astonished king.

"You did, Your Majesty. Whenever I need to go someplace quickly, I just whistle for Panther, hop on his back, and we go," replied Rabbit.

"And he had the nerve to stroll in here as though he were the ... Well, this is quite a piece of news, Rabbit."

"Well, Your Highness, you asked, and I told you. Good day." And Rabbit skipped home along the jungle paths.

Two days later, when Panther ambled confidently into the palace, the king glared at him.

"Your Majesty, what seems to be the problem?"

"Panther, you have a lot of nerve to step forward as a candidate."

"What do you mean, Your Highness?"

"You'd better have a talk with your friend Rabbit."

"Oh, so that's it. Rabbit has spoken badly of me, has he? Well, I'll fetch him right away and we can straighten out this whole matter, Your Majesty."

And Panther dashed furiously toward Rabbit's house. He burst through the door and into the house to find Rabbit lying quite helplessly on his couch.

"Rabbit, you scoundrel, what did you say to the king?"

"Panther, Panther, please calm down. I had a talk with the king, certainly, just as you did. Many things were said. But what exactly are you talking about?"

"I don't know what you said, but it surely has hurt my chances to become Prince. So now, you worthless clump of fur ..."

"Panther, please, let's be reasonable. As soon as my back heals, we'll simply go to the palace and speak to the king."

"What is wrong with your back?"

"Oh, clumsy me, I wrenched it this morning and I just cannot move a muscle. I'm sure I'll be fine in three or four days."

Panther could barely contain his fury.

"We are *not* going to wait three or four days! We will go to the palace *now!*"

"Panther, I told you I can't move. Now, if you can't wait a few days, I really don't know what to do."

"We are going to the palace *now,* if I have to drag you every step of the way."

"Panther, relax. If you do drag me to the palace, I'll be shredded, bloody, and bruised when we arrive. It surely won't help your chances to become Prince if you're seen as a bully."

At this, Panther began pacing the floor and racking his brain. Rabbit groaned in pain and watched Panther for a while. Then he spoke up.

"Panther, I have a bit of an idea. On second thought, it's probably not a very good idea. You probably wouldn't like it."

"Probably not! What is it?"

"Well, Panther, I was thinking ... You're big and strong, right?"

"Of course I am! So what!?"

"So you must have a very powerful back, right?"

"Of course, you stupid Rabbit, every part of me is powerful!"

"And I'm just a scrawny nothing of a rabbit, right?"

"Of course you are. You are even less than nothing. *So what?*"

"Well, Panther, if you gave me a ride on your back to the palace, that wouldn't be much strain for a powerful ..."

"That's it! Why didn't I think of that?"

And Panther hoisted Rabbit onto his back and off they dashed toward the palace. Rabbit rode quite comfortably, waving to his jungle friends, who, of course, could not believe their eyes. As Panther and Rabbit approached the palace, the guards' jaws dropped as they swung the gates open. Panther rushed to the throne and addressed the king.

"Your Royal Highness, I want this whole matter settled right now!"

"The matter is most certainly settled, Panther," said the king. "Guards, remove this Panther from my sight. Rabbit, kindly approach the throne."

Rabbit jumped off Panther's back. Panther was dragged away, confused and screaming. Rabbit stood before the king. His Royal Highness leaned over to Rabbit and whispered:

"I don't know how you did that, Rabbit. But anyone who can manage such a thing can likely become a very good Prince of the Realm."

"Thank you, Your Majesty," Rabbit replied. "I had a feeling that today might be *my* day."

TELLING TIPS: Since this story depends so much on dialogue, I think it's important to have distinct voices for the main characters. They need not be highly dramatic, but clearly distinguishable one from the other. A simple approach to this would be to give the Rabbit a slightly high-pitched voice, and the Panther a smart-aleck, cocky kind of voice.

DONALD DAVIS grew up in a family of traditional storytellers who have lived on the same western North
Carolina land since 1781. After twenty years' service as a
United Methodist minister, Davis became a full-time
professional storyteller, now giving more than 300 performances a year. He has served as guest host of
American Public Radio's "Good Evening" and appeared
on CNN and "Nightline." He is the author of six books,
including the award-winning *Listening for the Crack of
Dawn*, which is currently being produced as a feature
film. He lives on Ocracoke Island, North Carolina.

*As I was growing up,
one of the most common adventures I heard about Jack
involved the various ways and
times when he was employed as
a giant killer. Sometimes, if the
time for the story was short,
Jack would dispatch one giant,
get his due reward, and the
story would be over. At other
times, episodes could be strung
together until Jack might kill
half a dozen giants before the
story came to an end. There
was not one story of Jack
killing giants; rather, this was
a whole set of stories. The feeling was always that the giant
was somehow not human, or so
evil that the disposal was
roundly applauded. Here is a
story of a time Jack had to do
away with some giants in
order to get on toward his fortune.*

The Time Jack Got the Silver Sword

Donald Davis

A STORY FROM THE APPALACHIAN MOUNTAINS

One time Jack and Tom and Will and their mama and daddy were living in a little house that belonged to a big farmer. They had lived there a pretty long time, and Jack and his daddy and his brothers worked for the farmer on shares. They did manage to eat pretty well, but Jack thought that if they would load up and move on out toward the west, they might could get their own land and then make them a farm of their own.

Jack's daddy and his brothers weren't much in favor of this. They just wanted to stay right where they were and keep on at tenant farming. Jack's mama thought he was right, though, and as time went on she persuaded the others that this was actually the right thing for them all to do.

One day they told the farmer that they were going to leave, and in the next week they packed up everything they had in a big old wagon that the farmer gave them. Then they got all their other things ready to head on out to look for a place of their own.

When the day came on which they had decided to leave, they hooked up their two old mules to the wagon, loaded up their last food and clothes, and headed out to the west.

Now, Jack and his family didn't exactly know where they were going. They had just heard that you could claim land if you went west and worked it, and that is what they planned to do. They traveled on for a few days and met several people who told them that the good land was a little hard to get to.

The trouble, everybody told them, was that the good land lay on the other side of a big tract that belonged to the king. It wouldn't be so hard to get over there if you could cut across the king's land. But, since the king didn't like people cutting across his land, it was going to take about two weeks to go all the way around.

One day Jack and his family were talking about this with some people they met at a little store where they had stopped to buy some food. Finally, Jack's daddy asked a question to the store owner. "Couldn't we," he said, "couldn't we maybe just ask the king if we could just go across his land for a little shortcut? It's not like we were going to stay there or even hunt any of his animals. We wouldn't bother anything. Don't you think the king would let us do that?"

Then the whole truth came out.

"The real trouble is not the king," the store owner told them. "If you could get to where the king lives, I'm sure he would tell you just to go on through.

"The trouble is *giants*. There are three big, old, ugly, fourteen-foot-tall giants that have just taken over the king's land and are living up there. They kill and eat everything that moves, and that would include you if you cut across there and got caught.

"The only reason that they haven't killed and eaten the king and his family is that they live in a big house behind a high rock wall, and the giants are so big and heavy that they can't pull themselves up over the wall to get inside. Why, the king and his family are just like in prison up there. They can't come out from behind that wall or they would be eaten up in a minute!

"Now, you stay away from there ... go around!"

And so Jack and all his family kept going, way around the outside of the king's land. They surely didn't want to tangle with any fourteen-foot-tall, man-eating giants!

Everything went along quite well for about the next week. Then, though, they all started getting anxious to get on to set up their new home. And, after all, they hadn't seen or even heard any sign of those giants they were supposed to be afraid of.

Tom and Will came up with an idea. "Let's just take a little shortcut each day. Let's cut across a corner and go quiet and fast. We're never going to get on to our new land like this.

"We haven't even seen any giants. I think that man at the store just made that all up to scare us. Come on, let's cut across ... we'll never get there if we don't."

After a day or two of begging, the whole family decided to get along with it.

Early one morning they turned their mules and wagon off the path they had been following, and started to cut right across the king's land, heading straight for the west. They traveled all day. Then when it started to get dark, they weren't even halfway across to where they were supposed to come out.

Jack's daddy pulled the wagon with the mules into a little low laurel thicket at the base of a big rock cliff, and there they made plans for the night.

"We can't afford to take a chance on building a fire," he said. "Whoever might be out here would see us for sure. We better just eat some cold beans, and we'll get on out of here in the morning.

"And," he went on, "we'd better set up a lookout for the night."

Jack's daddy took the three boys up to the top of the hill above where he had hidden the mules and the wagon, and they picked out a big maple tree to hide up in to keep watch.

"I'll take the first turn," he said. "That'll be the most dangerous time. We'll switch off about every three hours. Tom and then Will. Jack will be the last in the morning. There's not likely to be much trouble when the light's coming back in the morning.

"Whoever is up here better keep the gun with him. Now you boys go back and sleep where your mama is until time for Tom's turn."

The three boys went back down to the wagon while Jack's daddy set up for the first watch.

Nothing at all happened through that first watch, and so Jack's daddy came on down to sleep at the wagon while Tom went up to keep his watch. Tom sat up in that tree and didn't see anything either. He came down to sleep after his time was up, and then Will went on up there. Of course, Will didn't see or hear a thing; and when it was time for Jack to take the last watch, there was only about an hour to go before it would start to get daylight.

They all thought things were probably safe by now, but they still sent Jack on up there so he could have a turn at keeping watch just like the others had.

Jack climbed way up in the same big maple tree where his brothers had been for their turns. He sat there, holding his daddy's gun across his lap, and didn't hear a sound but the wind in the trees while the dark gradually faded and the light of day slipped into the woods. He thought that he'd wait just a few more minutes and then he'd go on back down to the camp where the others were.

About then, though, Jack thought he heard something coming from way down below in the woods. He got real still and strained his ears to listen. Sure enough, he could hear somebody talking and feet shuffling along through the leaves and brush on the ground.

As the voices got louder, Jack looked toward the direction of the sound. Then he saw who it was. Coming up through the woods right toward the tree where he was hiding walked *three* giants that must each one be at least fourteen feet tall.

As soon as Jack could see them, he could also tell what they were carrying. One of them had two cows slung over his shoulders. It looked like he had wrung their necks like chickens and had just slung them over his shoulders to carry them.

The second one had what looked to Jack like a handful of garden tools. He had spades and turning forks and big saws. Then Jack realized that what he was seeing was not a bundle of tools, but a set of knives and forks and spoons just big enough for these giants to eat with.

The last giant was carrying a big, black iron cooking pot. He had it upside down over his head so it was resting on his shoulders by the rim and was covering his head completely up. He couldn't see a thing about where he was going, and he kept running into trees over and over again. He kept telling the first two that it was time for them to take a turn at carrying the pot … it was giving him a headache!

"Well, there," Jack thought, "they may be giants, but from what I have seen so far, they are also mighty *dumb!* Maybe I don't have to be so scared of them after all."

The giants came right on up to under the very tree where Jack was perched. Then they threw their loads down on the ground and sat down and started talking to one another.

"I shore am hongry!" the first one said.

Then the second one said, "I shore am hongry!"

After that the third one said, "I don't know about you'all, but I shore am hongry!"

Jack thought, "They are dumb! If I'm careful, I don't think they really are much to worry about."

About then it was all the way daylight, and Jack could really get a good look at what these big boys looked like.

The youngest one had a head full of black hair and a long, black beard that flopped against his chest when he talked. The middle one was as red-headed as he could be. He was either clean-shaven or else his beard just never had come in to begin with. The oldest one was bald as a turnip, but he did have a droopy, gray-looking moustache which hung down around his mouth.

They were such a funny-looking bunch that Jack had a hard time not laughing right out loud just looking at them.

While he was watching them from his perch up in the tree, the giants had started to cook the cows for their breakfast.

They carried water from a little creek, filled up the pot, and then built a fire and started boiling the two cows whole—hair, hide, teeth, horns, hooves,

166

eyeballs, and all. Jack couldn't believe that they were going to eat such as that! They boiled those two cows until the meat started to fall apart.

By now Jack had seen about all he wanted to see. Besides, he figured if he could slip out of here and get on down to where his family was, they could slip on out of there while the giants were eating. It was so daylight that he was starting to worry that his daddy would come up here looking for him and might walk right into the middle of these giants.

The only trouble was that every time he started to ease down out of the tree, the limbs started cracking and leaves would fall. He figured he needed to get the giants distracted, and then he could slip on down.

Jack had brought his slingshot in his pocket along with a handful of sharp-edged flint rocks he had picked up the day before. He always kept his slingshot with him in case he needed a weapon. He loaded up a rock and got ready.

The biggest one of the giants took one of those giant forks and jabbed a big piece of meat with it. While he was holding the meat over the pot and blowing on it to cool it off, Jack pulled back and shot at the chunk of meat. It fell back into the pot and splashed boiling juice all over that big old giant. He was storming mad and thought for sure that one of his brothers had caused it.

"I don't know who did that, or how," the giant said to his brothers, "but you better not do it again or you'll be sorry for sure!" The other two said that they didn't do it, but he didn't believe them at all. He jabbed another hunk of that cow and started to put it in his mouth.

Jack pulled back with another rock and shot the old giant smack in the back of the hand. The giant jerked so hard that he stabbed that fork right into his own cheek.

"Now, quit it!" he hollered at his brothers.

"We didn't do nothing!" both of them fussed right back at him.

"Well, I reckon you did!" the big one went on. "Somehow you'all like to have caused me to put my eye out! Now, don't mess with me again or I'll crack both of your heads!"

The two brothers just sat there and looked dumb.

The big old giant put down the fork and picked up the big, shovel-sized spoon. He ladled up a big spoonful of the hot juice. Jack didn't even want to think about what he thought he saw floating in it. The giant blew on the spoon of cow soup once or twice.

As he lifted it toward his mouth, Jack was loaded again. He let loose with a flint rock and knocked that spoonful of hot broth right in the old giant's face.

This time the giant didn't even fuss. He just slung the spoon out into the woods and jumped right on his brothers. They were fighting and scratching and biting to beat the band, and while they were scrapping it out, old Jack was slipping down out of that tree so he could get on out of there in a hurry.

In the midst of all of that ruckus, those giants couldn't see or hear a thing besides their own fighting, and Jack made it all the way down to the bottom of the tree. He was ready to step down to the ground and beat it out of there when the last limb he stepped on broke with a loud *crack*. Those giants stopped their fighting and looked straight at Jack. He couldn't do a thing but look back at them. He was purely scared to death.

"Look, there's a little boy!" the first giant said.

Then the middle giant said, "Look, there's a little boy!"

"Hey look, you'all," the third giant said, "there's a little boy!"

When Jack heard all three giants say the same thing over and over, he remembered how dumb they were, and he wasn't so scared anymore.

He looked right at the giants and said, "You can call me a little boy if you want to, *little men,* but there are a lot of things I can do that you can't do!"

"What can you do that I can't do?" the oldest giant asked Jack.

"If you're so smart, *you* figure it out!" he answered.

The giants were so dumb that instead of jumping on Jack, they did, in fact, sit there and try to figure out something that Jack might do that they couldn't do.

They mumbled to one another for a few minutes, then went over to Jack and picked him up.

"We've got it figured out, Jack! We know exactly what you can do that we can't do. Come on with us … you're going to get us into the king's castle lands!"

Jack didn't know what they were talking about. He also didn't want to go with them. But he didn't have any choice about that since they had already picked him up, and the biggest one had him under his ugly arm.

Jack knew that his daddy and Tom and Will would come up to the lookout tree any time now to see why he hadn't come back to the camp. He also knew that they would not find a thing to tell them that he was alive and, so far, well. He couldn't imagine what they would think when they found nothing but a big cooking pot full of cow bones left under the maple tree.

The giants seemed to be getting pretty excited about wherever they were taking Jack because they went faster and faster as they carried him through the woods. They passed him back and forth whenever the one who was carrying him got tired, and a time or two they almost made a little game out of throwing Jack around.

"Watch out!" Jack hollered when they almost dropped him on one toss. "If you kill me, you won't know whether I can do it or not." (He didn't have any idea what "it" was, but his warning to the giants seemed to work.)

Finally, they came up over a big hill, and up ahead Jack began to see something strange showing up through the trees.

At first he thought it was a low rock cliff, but then as they got closer he could see that it was actually a man-made rock wall. The wall was about twenty to thirty feet high and was so long that it just faded out of sight in the woods long before Jack could see either the end of it or where it made a turn.

"Here we are," the biggest giant said.

"Well, here we are," said the middle giant.

Jack knew what was coming next. The youngest giant said, "Hey, boys, here we are."

They carried Jack on along the wall until they came close to a place where a huge wooden gate was closed fast. Then they walked back down from the gate a little way until they came to the spot where the wall seemed to be the shortest.

"Here we are, little boy," the oldest of the giants said to Jack. Of course the other two went on and also said the same thing, but Jack was getting a little tired of hearing everything three times by now, so he didn't pay any attention to it.

"We've been wanting to get into the king's castle lands for a long time now, but we're so big and strong we can't get up over this wall." The biggest of the giants was doing all the talking now. "We are awful glad that you told us you could do stuff we can't do or we never would have figgered this out.

"Now, little boy, what we are going to do is to *throw* you over this wall. When you come down on the other side, you run up to that big old gate up there and open it up and let us get in."

The oldest of the giants now handed Jack over to his younger brothers to do the throwing. They got hold of Jack by his arms and legs and swung him back and forth a few times to warm up. Then they let go, and Jack went sailing up through the air like a little rock, just flying over that wall like there was nothing to him at all.

What neither Jack nor the giants could see from the ground was how wide the wall was. When Jack got up to flying through the air, he saw that the wall was a good twenty feet thick. It was so wide that the top was almost like a road, except that there was grass growing up all over it.

That thick wall just may have saved Jack's life because, instead of flying all the way over it and then having to fall all the way down to the ground, Jack happened to land right on top of the wall in the middle of some high grass. He looked down at the giants and waved to them to show them how well he had landed.

All three of the big old giants cheered for Jack, and even he was right proud of himself.

"Now, little boy, get down on the other side and go on up to the gate. We will wait for you right up there on the outside."

Every so far along the inside of the big wall there was either a ramp or a set of stair steps going down to the inside ground, so it was no problem at all for Jack to go on down to the ground. He didn't know exactly what he was going to do next, so he walked up toward the gate where the giants were just to get a look at what held it shut.

When he got there, he saw a sort of big tunnel through the wall, with the gate right outside of it. The gate was held shut by a big beam which was slipped down into some brackets on the doors. All you needed to do to open it was just to lift up that beam, and the doors would be free to open.

The giants on the outside already were hollering through the gate to Jack before he even got there. "Come on, little boy, open the gate. Let us get on in there right now!"

Jack knew that no matter what he decided to do, opening the gate was not going to be part of his plan.

He got up to the gate and started banging around on it and rattling some of the hardware that was there on the inside. He also started huffing and snorting like he was trying mighty hard to lift or move something heavy. The giants got real quiet as they listened and tried to imagine what Jack must be doing.

Finally Jack hollered out to the giants, "Well, boys, I'm not having any luck in letting you'all in. I see exactly how to open the gate, but the latch is rusted shut because it's been closed up for so long and I can't bust it loose.

"You'all wait right here, and I will go scout around some and see if I can find something that I can knock it loose with." The old giants all agreed and sat down to wait on the outside.

Jack was not sure where he was or what he was going to do, but at least he was safe from the giants for a little while. He started following the road that led in from the gate to see where he was and who or what he could find.

In no time at all, Jack rounded a curve in the road, and there in front of him was the biggest house he had ever seen. It just had to be the king's castle house.

Jack walked up to the castle house and was just amazed by the size of it. It needed a lot of work, though, and Jack reckoned that being shut up in here because of those giants—even having a lot of gold—wouldn't do a king much good. He walked up on the front porch.

It was still fairly early in the morning, and it seemed like everybody was still asleep, as Jack didn't hear a sound coming from anywhere. He thought he would just walk around a little bit and check things out.

When he came to the front door, it was standing wide open, and Jack began to wonder if anybody actually lived there or not. He didn't stop to think that with a big wall around everything, there wasn't any point in even closing the door at night.

Jack walked on in and found himself inside a big hall that was bigger than any house he had ever been in before. There were all kinds of furniture and old stuff just everywhere.

While Jack was looking around, he saw something on the wall that he got real interested in. It was a great big, long silver sword that looked just as sharp as it could be.

Jack thought, "If I had that sword, I could go back down there and maybe take those giants on a little bit."

He tried to pick the sword up from where it was hanging on the wall, but it was so heavy that he couldn't budge it. Then he saw the sign that was hanging on the wall beside the sword.

It said, "Whoever is strong enough to drink the draught is strong enough to heft the sword." Jack looked all around there but didn't see anything to drink, so he figured that it was just some old saying of some kind from a long time ago.

"Too bad," Jack thought, and then he started exploring around the castle house some more.

Every door was standing wide open, and so Jack could either see or just wander around through all the rooms as much as he wanted to.

He went on to one big room where he heard some snoring, and there, right in the bed with his crown hanging on the bedpost, was the old king himself. In the next room the queen was asleep. Jack thought it sure was a waste of rooms to have the king and queen taking up two whole rooms for nothing but sleeping.

He wandered down the hall and into another room. All of a sudden he looked over the bed and saw a girl sleeping in there. Jack didn't know that he had stumbled onto the only daughter of the old king himself.

She was so pretty that when Jack saw her he had to grab onto the wall to keep from passing right out on the floor. Every time he looked at her he about lost his breath, but he just couldn't keep from looking again. Why, he never did know that girls could be made this pretty, and she was not even awake.

Then Jack saw a glass bottle on a shelf on the wall. The bottle was dark colored and had a cork in the top, and over it there was a sign on the wall. The sign said, "Whoever is strong enough to give in to love, is strong enough to drink the draught."

Jack wasn't sure just what this meant, but after what looking at this girl had done to him, he needed something to drink.

He picked up the glass bottle and pulled the cork out of it. When he did, smoke came out with a sound like it was fuming around on the inside. Still, Jack turned it up to take a drink.

When he did, what came out of the bottle was the most wonderful-tasting liquid he'd ever had. It was sweet and pure and smooth and clear, and it tickled as it ran across his tongue. Jack drank the whole bottle without stopping and wondered why nobody else had drunk from the bottle, as good as it tasted to him.

This time when he looked back at the sleeping king's daughter, he didn't get dizzy. He just knew now, though, that it was time to go get rid of those giants so these people could get back to living the way they were supposed to.

Jack went marching back out through the big hall of the house, and, as he passed that silver sword, he reached out and just grabbed the handle.

When he did, the sword came right off the wall into his hand, and this time it felt as light as a feather. Why, it was about seven feet long, and still Jack could swing it around his head until it made the air whistle. He started out the door with the sword and headed down the road to where the giants were.

Jack did a little thinking on his way back to the big gate. He figured that with this sword he could take on any one of the three giants, but he began to realize that trying to take on all three at one time might be a little too much for him. So he started trying to come up with a plan.

Jack had noticed a little low tunnel down close to where he had first come off of the wall, and when he checked it out he saw what it was.

About fifty yards down the wall from the big gate there was a little late-night tunnel for people in the old days who got shut out of the castle walls after the gates were closed for the night. It was a low tunnel, not big enough for somebody to ride a horse through, and narrow enough that it would just take one soldier to guard it. Jack thought that it was probably just big enough for the giants to be able to crawl through, one at a time, on their knees. Now he knew what to do.

He walked back up to where they were waiting for him on the other side of the big gate. Jack didn't say anything about having the big silver sword. He just told the giants that he was back to try to get them inside the castle land.

While the giants listened, Jack told them that he just couldn't find anything that could help him get the gate opened, but that he had found another way they could get through the wall. He told them that there was a little crawly-tunnel right down the wall from where they were, and that if they would come on down there he would show them exactly how to get in.

The giants were really anxious to get inside by now, and they followed the sound of Jack's voice as he led them down the wall to the late-night tunnel.

Old Jack actually crawled most of the way through the low tunnel until the three giants could see him from the outside. Then he told them that if they would crawl through the low tunnel one at a time, he would have a real surprise waiting for them on the inside.

Those giants all wanted in there so badly that they had to fight for a little while before they could decide which one got to crawl through the passageway first. Finally, the big old one with the black hair won out, and he started in through the hole.

Jack could both see him coming and tell which one it was because he could just see the top of his dirty black hair as he scrunched on his belly to get in through the late-night crawly-hole.

Jack picked up the seven-foot-long silver sword, and, when that black-headed giant's head came popping out of that hole, you can just guess what happened to it!

The other two giants wanted to know why the first one was not crawling on through the hole. Jack hollered out to them that he was stuck and they would have to push him on through. They did, and then Jack could see the bald-headed one coming next.

In no time there was not a giant in the king's whole land who had not lost his head to that old silver sword.

About that time Jack heard horses coming, and, when he looked up, here came the king and all his men riding down there on their horses. They had seen that the silver sword was gone when they got up in the morning and were out looking for the man powerful enough to handle it.

Whey they saw that it was little old Jack, then they knew that it was the power of the love draught and not his own natural strength that had done away with the giants. So they loaded Jack up and took him right back up there to the castle house where that beautiful king's daughter was just having her breakfast.

When she saw Jack, she told her daddy that he was just the boy she had been dreaming about the night before; and by noon, it was agreed that Jack was going to stay on there and marry her.

Jack was so excited about all of this that he almost forgot to go back and hunt up his mama and daddy and Tom and Will. But he did remember after a while, and he went back through the woods with some of the king's men and found them.

They were awful upset about Jack being gone, but when they saw him and then heard about the whole story, they were glad to stop and settle right there on the king's land, and some people say that they are living right on there to this very day.

TELLING TIPS: When I heard traditional stories in my childhood, I experienced them visually, seeing a series of pictures that together told the story. Later I used those pictures as visual guides to remember and retell the same stories.

Rather than organizing with words or memorizing the script, try organizing the story in picture blocks. Then tell each picture in your own words. Using a visual base makes a traditional story vibrate.

Another thing to take some time with is the setting. If listeners can't see where the story is happening, they can't follow the plot. Too often, "once upon a time" and "everywhere" translates into "no time" and "nowhere." Be sure you have a clear picture of the story's characters, setting, and time period.

ANDREW SEMEL

MILBRE BURCH has performed from Maui to Martha's Vineyard. She has produced seven tapes and published stories in magazines, in *XANADU 2*, and in *Best-Loved Stories Told at the National Storytelling Festival*. Two of her poems will appear in the upcoming anthology, *Snow White, Blood Red 3*. She lives with her husband and daughter in Pasadena, California.

In 1986, when I told stories at the Children's Hospital in St. Louis, Missouri, "Little Burnt Face" seemed a good bet. Just before I began, one last patient was wheeled into the dayroom. She had pale skin and a few golden curls. The rest of her head was bald. She was being treated for cancer. When I got to the part where the girl's hair grows back, I happened to look at this child and her face was radiant. I knew that was the moment for which I had learned this story.

The memory of this little girl followed me home, and I told a friend about her. My friend said, "I hope that child lives long enough to see her hair grow back." For the first time I understood. While she was listening to the story, she was living through that day. Sometimes that's all we get. And sometimes that's enough.

Little Burnt Face

Milbre Burch

A MICMAC STORY

Once there was a brave warrior named Strong Wind. He had such powerful magic that he could make himself invisible. So he could walk among his enemies and they would not know he was there. He could listen to their battle plans and they would not know he heard. He could defeat them in war and they would not know how. Strong Wind.

Now a man like that gets to be famous. And many young women wanted to marry him. Those who did would go down to the lake to the tent where he lived with his sister, and call his sister out. Together the women would step along the edge of the water until, just at sunset, Strong Wind's sister would say, "Here he comes. Can you see my brother?"

And the women who wanted to marry him would look, and see nothing. Strong Wind was invisible. But they wanted to marry him so badly, they would lie. One might say, "Yes, I see him." Another might say, "I think I see him."

And either way, Strong Wind's sister knew those girls were lying. So she said, "Look again. Tell me what he uses to pull his sled along the ground."

Again the girls would look. Again they would see nothing. Again they would lie. One might say, "A strong pole." Another might say, "A piece of rawhide." But either way, Strong Wind's sister sent those lying girls home without a husband.

Now, not far from this place there was a village. And in the village there was a chief. His wife had died many years ago, but he had three daughters. Of the three, the youngest was very beautiful and she had a gentle heart. And her sisters were jealous of her. Little by little they stole from her her clothing until she had nothing but rags to wear. Then they took away her earrings, necklaces and bracelets until she had no fine jewelry at all. One time they cut off her long, black, beautiful hair and singed the edges so that her hair was burnt and rough and stood on end. Once because their jealousy would not die, they took

176

hot coals and burnt her face, and they told their father she had done it herself. But through all of this she kept her gentle heart.

Now there came a day when the two older girls decided they wanted Strong Wind for their husband. Since they couldn't agree who should go first, they went together, arguing the whole way. Roughly they called Strong Wind's sister out. She looked first at one girl and then at the other, asking "What is it you want?"

They said, "We want Strong Wind for our husband."

"I see. Then you walk here and you walk here." Together the women walked along the edge of the lake until just at sunset, Strong Wind's sister pointed and said, "Here he comes. Can you see my brother?"

First the one girl looked. Then the other girl looked. And of course they saw nothing. Strong Wind was invisible. But they saw each other out of the corners of their eyes and neither wanted to be the second one to speak. So they said together, "Yes, I see him! Oh, I saw him first!"

The warrior's sister said, "Then you can tell me what he uses to pull his sled along the ground."

Again the women looked; again they saw each together; again they lied with one voice. "Rawhide! Surely, it's rawhide!"

And Strong Wind's sister laughed in their faces and sent them home without a husband.

A short time later, their little sister—the one with the scarred face and the gentle heart—decided that she would seek Strong Wind for her husband. Because she had no fine clothes to wear, she left the village dressed in rags, her burnt hair standing on end. And her sisters stood at the edge of the village and cried out, "Silly girl, ugly girl, scar-faced girl! Strong Wind will never take you for his wife!"

And so when she reached the tent she stood outside, her eyes to the ground, and never said a word. When Strong Wind's sister came out of the tent, she was surprised to find a girl standing there. And a strange-looking girl it was.

"What is it you want?" she asked.

Without looking up, the scar-faced girl said, "I want Strong Wind for my husband."

For a long time Strong Wind's sister looked at this girl, and then she took her hand and said, "Come with me."

Together the women walked along the edge of the lake until just at sunset. Strong Wind's sister pointed and said, "There. Can you see my brother?"

For the first time the scar-faced girl raised her eyes up, and then she lowered them again, saying, "No, I see nothing."

And Strong Wind's sister smiled because she knew that this girl was telling the truth. "Look again. Tell me what he uses to pull his sled along the ground."

Again the girl looked, and this time she gasped because Strong Wind had made himself visible to her. "Why, he's a magic person. He uses a rainbow to pull his sled."

"Yes, he does," said Strong Wind's sister. "Look one more time. Tell what his bowstring is made of."

The scar-faced girl was almost afraid to look. But she raised her eyes up and said, "His bowstring is made of the Milky Way."

"It is indeed," said Strong Wind's sister, and she took this girl by her hands and led her back to the tent. There she took away from her her ragged clothes and gave her a new dress to wear. Then she took water and bathed this girl's face, and when she was done, the scars were gone. And then she took a comb and combed this girl's hair and as she did, it grew longer and blacker and more beautiful. At last she gave her earrings and necklaces and bracelets to wear so that when Strong Wind came into the tent, he found a lovely girl with a gentle heart, and he made her his wife. After that she went everywhere with him and helped him with his magic.

But he did not forget her sisters. And he sought them out to punish them. This time they saw him coming: "Ah!" And he turned them into trees. He turned them into aspen trees. And even to this day when the wind blows through the aspen trees, the leaves quiver and shake. For they remember the power of Strong Wind, and their cruelty to their sister.

TELLING TIPS: Whatever the source of the tale, make the story your own. Put the story on, try on several versions and see what fits you best. Turn the collar down; roll up the sleeves. Live with it. Commit to getting to know it (and its context) better. Wear the story awhile, till you get comfortable in it. And if the two of you really are "a fit," both teller and tale will grow from the experience.

ABOUT THE STORY: Several printed sources have contributed to my version of this legend: "Little Burnt Face" from *Red Indian Fairy Book* by Frances Jenkins Olcott (Houghton Mifflin Co., 1917) and reprinted in *The Arbuthnot Anthology of Children's Literature* (Scott, Foresman & Co., 1976); "Little Burnt Face" in *The Talking Stones* edited by Dorothy de Wit (Greenwillow Books, 1979); and "The Indian Cinderella" from *Canadian Wonder Tales* by Cyrus Macmillan (John Lane, 1918) and reprinted in *North American Legends* edited by Virginia Haviland (William Collins Publishers, 1979).

And of course, tellers will want to take a look at a resource that was not available when I started telling the story: *The Rough-Face Girl* by Rafe Martin (Putnam, 1992).

ALBERT J. WINN

PENINNAH SCHRAM has been telling stories professionally since 1970. She has written four books, including *Jewish Stories One Generation Tells Another* and *Tales of Elijah the Prophet.* She is Associate Professor of Speech and Drama at Stern College of Yeshiva University. She travels across the United States and other countries, appearing at major conferences and festivals as a featured storyteller, including the National Storytelling Festival in Jonesborough, Tennessee. She is the Founding Director of the Jewish Storytelling Center in New York City.

Cumulative tales like this one are great fun to tell because they involve reasoning and sifting on the part of the listener and an opportunity for dialogue between the storyteller and the audience. This type of tale flourishes in the folklore of every nation. I have told this story often, both to young audiences and to elders. Children as young as four or five answer as wisely as the older people. The "why" behind their answers vary, but they always reveal something fascinating about themselves.

The Magic Pomegranate

Peninnah Schram

A JEWISH STORY

Once there were three brothers who loved adventure. One day they decided to go on a journey, each one to a different country, and to meet again on a certain day ten years later. Each brother was to bring back with him an unusual gift.

The oldest brother decided to go to the East. When he arrived in a certain Eastern town, he was fascinated by what he saw there; magicians, dancing girls, jugglers, and acrobats were everywhere. As the brother was watching the entertainments, he saw one magician hold up a magic glass through which he could see to the distant corners of the kingdom.

"Ah!" thought the oldest brother, "I would like to have that glass, for that would certainly be an unusual object to share with my brothers." He asked the magician, "Tell me, how much is that glass? I should like to buy it from you." At first the magician would not part with his magic glass, but after much pleading by the older brother, and some bargaining, they agreed upon a price and the magician sold the glass to the oldest brother.

The second brother traveled to a country in the West. Wherever he went, he kept his eyes open, and his mind as well. He was always on the lookout for the most unusual gift he could bring back to his brothers.

One day, he was attracted by the cries of an old carpet seller, who called out, "Carpets for sale! Beautiful! Wonderful! Carpets here!" The brother approached the carpet seller and began to examine his carpets, when suddenly he saw the carpet at the bottom of the pile begin to move. It seemed to be moving by itself! "What kind of carpet is this one?" he asked, pointing to the bottom one, which was quite visible by then.

The old merchant motioned for him to bend down and whispered in his ear, "This is a magic carpet. Buy it, and it will take you anywhere you want to go—and quickly too!" The second brother and the carpet seller finally settled upon a price, and the brother took the magic carpet with him, satisfied that he had a most unusual gift.

The youngest brother went South, and when he arrived in a certain country, he traveled far and wide to see what he could find to bring back to his brothers.

Now, this was a country noted for its many forests. One day, the youngest brother was walking in a grove of trees, when he noticed something strange—a tree that was of a different shape from the hundreds of other trees around it. It was covered with orange-red blossoms, and it was so beautiful!

As the younger brother came closer, he saw that there was only one red pomegranate on the tree.

"This is strange indeed," thought the young man. "A pomegranate tree with only one pomegranate." He approached the tree slowly, laughing to himself and thinking of the story he would tell his brothers about the pomegranate tree full of blossoms with only one fruit on it. As he reached for the pomegranate, it fell into his hand even before he could pluck it from the branch. As soon as that happened, another pomegranate burst from one of the blossoms. When the brother saw this, he looked at the pomegranate in his hand and said to himself, "This must be a magic pomegranate. It was the only one on the tree, and yet as soon as it fell into my hands when I was about to reach for it, a new pomegranate appeared suddenly. But what kind of magic does it perform, I wonder?"

The youngest brother examined the pomegranate, marveling at its beauty. "The shape is so perfect," he thought, "crowned with the crown of King Solomon." He walked away from the tree looking at his mysterious new treasure. When he looked back to see the pomegranate tree once more, it was no longer there. It had disappeared. "Now I know this is a magic pomegranate, and so this is what I will bring to my brothers."

Ten years passed, and when the three brothers met as they had planned, they embraced with delight. They eagerly showed each other the unusual objects they had brought back from their journeys.

The oldest brother said, "Let me look through my glass and see what I can see." When he held up the glass, he saw, in a far-off kingdom, a young princess lying ill in bed, near death.

"Quickly, dear brothers, get on my magic carpet and we'll fly there," said the second brother. In what seemed like seconds, the three brothers arrived at the far-off kingdom.

In the royal palace of this kingdom, the king, whose daughter lay ill, was grief-stricken. He had sent for every doctor in the country to cure the princess; but they had all failed and there was no hope left for the princess. Finally, the king had sent a messenger throughout the country saying, "Whoever can save my daughter, the princess, will have her hand in marriage, and half the kingdom!"

As if in a dream, the youngest brother heard a voice whisper inside him, "The pomegranate!" The youngest brother approached the king and asked, "May I try to cure the princess?" The king agreed and led the young man to the princess's chambers.

When the young man saw the princess, he approached quietly and sat by her side. Then he took the pomegranate from his pocket, cut it open with gentle care, carefully cut each kernel from its place, and then fed the juicy red kernels to the princess. In a few moments, the princess felt stronger, and the color returned to her cheeks. Soon, she sat up in bed, fully restored to health.

The king was overjoyed. He hugged his daughter and, turning to the three young men, he announced, "The man who saved my daughter will marry her."

The three brothers began to quarrel, each one claiming to be the one who should marry the princess.

The oldest brother said, "If it were not for my magic glass, we would never have known the princess was ill in the first place. So, since I discovered this first, I deserve to marry the princess."

"But, brothers, it was because of my magic carpet that we could arrive so quickly," argued the second brother. "Otherwise, the princess would have died. I deserve to marry the princess."

Then the youngest brother said, "It was my magic pomegranate that actually healed the princess. I deserve to marry her."

Since the three brothers could not decide which one should marry the princess, the king tried to decide. He looked at the three clever young men, but he could not decide who deserved to marry his daughter.

The king finally turned to the princess, who was known not only for her beauty but also for her wisdom, and asked, "Who do you think deserves to marry you, my daughter?"

The princess answered simply, "I will ask each of them a question." She turned to the oldest brother and asked, "Has your magic glass changed in any way since you arrived in this kingdom?"

"No," replied the oldest brother. "My glass is the same as always, and I can look through it and see to every corner of this kingdom."

The princess then asked the second brother, "Has your magic carpet changed in any way since you arrived in this kingdom?" And the second brother answered, "No, my carpet is the same, and I can fly anywhere on it, as always."

Turning to the youngest brother, the princess asked, "Has your magic pomegranate changed in any way since you arrived in this kingdom?" And the youngest brother answered, "Yes, princess, my pomegranate is no longer whole, for I gave you a portion of it."

The princess turned to the three young men and said, "I will marry the youngest brother because he performed the greatest good deed—because he gave up something of his own."

The brothers and the king all understood the wisdom of the princess. A lavish wedding was arranged for the princess and the youngest brother.

And the king appointed the princess and all three brothers to become his royal advisers.

TELLING TIPS: Since this is a cumulative tale, there is a natural place for the story to stop (just after the king asks the princess to choose) and ask the audience to respond to the question, "If you were that wise princess, who would you choose to marry you?" Ask several members of the audience, but follow up their answers with *"Why* would you choose that brother?" The reasoning behind the answer is more important than just the answer.

Another way to get the audience involved: When the second brother gets to the marketplace and asks about the moving carpet, the merchant says, "Buy this carpet, for it is a ..." At this point I turn to the audience and nod so as to indicate that they can help me fill in the word—and they always do—"a magic carpet" or "a flying carpet." And often I add, "Oh, you were there!" Then I continue with the story.

At the end of the story, I add, "And they lived ..." and with a sweeping gesture for the audience to join me, they continue with "happily ever after."

ABOUT THE STORY: "The Magic Pomegranate" and the many Jewish versions of it are uniquely Jewish, because the kernel of these stories is the talmudic teaching that the greatest *mitzvah* (good deed) is performed by the person who gives of himself or herself—or who gives up something of his or her own.

I started telling the tale after I first read it as "Who Cured the Princess?" in Dov Noy's book, *Folktales of Israel* (University of Chicago Press, 1963), but I changed various elements in the story. Two other Jewish versions are a Yemenite tale entitled "The Mute Princess" in *Elijah's Violin & Other Jewish Fairy Tales* by Howard Schwartz (Harper & Row, 1983) and "The King's Daughter and the Choice of Her Heart" in *The Golden Feather: Twenty Folktales Narrated by Greek Jews,* collected by Moshe Attias and edited and annotated by Dov Noy (IFA Publication Society, 1976). There are about 20 IFA (Israel Folktale Archives) versions from Morocco, Libya, Tunisia, Egypt, Yemen, and Poland. Tale Type 653 in Aarne-Thompson is a close version of this tale, but the IFA listing of 635 *C, with three versions from Iraq to Yemen, is the epitome of this telling.

We do a lot of school assembly programs, and this is always a fun one for school audiences of all ages. So get out the jingle bells and any other Christmas props you may have.

THE FOLKTELLERS (Connie Regan-Blake and Barbara Freeman) have captivated audiences nationwide for over eighteen years. They have twice been featured in *School Library Journal* and are three-time recipients of the American Library Association's Notable Recording Award. In 1986, Connie and Barbara opened their original two-act play, *Mountain Sweet Talk*, which enjoyed a successful eight-year theater run in Asheville, North Carolina. They can be seen and heard on their highly entertaining videos: *Storytelling: Tales and Techniques* (workshop) and *Pennies, Pets & Peanut Butter* (performance for children grades 1-4).

Santa Visits the Moes

The Folktellers

A STORY FROM THE APPALACHIAN MOUNTAINS

One night before Christmas, the Moe family had all gotten into bed and Mrs. Moe turned to Mr. Moe and said, "Mr. Moe, there's too much light in this room. It's like Grand Central Station. Could you please blow out the candle?"

He said, "Why, certainly dear."

He walked over to the candle and picked it up, but he had a problem. You see, he could only blow air by putting his lower lip over his upper lip. So when he blew, all the air hit the ceiling and it missed the candle altogether. He took a deep breath and *[inhale/blowing sounds]* blew, and all the air hit the ceiling.

"Oh, I'll just do it myself dear," said Mrs. Moe.

So she got out of bed, and walked over to the candle, but she had a problem too. She could only form her mouth by putting her upper lip over her lower lip. So when she blew, all the air hit the floor and missed the candle altogether. She took a deep breath *[inhale/ blowing sounds]*, but no success.

Oh, what were they going to do? She said she would never get to sleep with all the light. "I don't want to wake up the children," she said, "but let's just call little Anne."

"Anne!" they called out.

Anne rubbed her eyes, put on her little housecoat, came down the steps, and said, "Is it Christmas yet?"

"No, dear," they said. "We need your help, honey. We can't seem to blow out this candle. Would you please blow it out for us so we can get to bed?"

"Why certainly!" she said. And she yawned a little. She walked over to the candle, but she had a problem too. She could only blow air out of the left side of her mouth. So when she blew, all the air hit the left wall and missed the candle altogether. And she took a deep breath *[inhale/blowing sounds]*.

"Oh, no, let's call John. John! John!"

Well, John woke up, put on his nightcap and houseshoes, came stumbling down the steps, and said, "What's going on?"

They said, "John, honey, we can't get to sleep with this candlelight. Would you please blow it out?"

He walked over to the candle, but he had a problem. He could only blow air out of the right side of his mouth. So every time he blew, the air hit the right wall and missed the candle altogether. He went [inhale/blowing sounds] out of the side of his mouth.

Oh, they were so sad. "What are we ever going to do?"

Just then they heard bells ringing.

"HO! HO! HO!"

It was Santa Claus!

And then Santa spoke up and he said, "Oh folks, what are you doing up? You're all supposed to be in bed so that I can put out your presents!"

Mrs. Moe said, "Oh, Santa, you see there's too much light in the room. We can't get to sleep."

Santa said, "Oh, I'll be glad to help."

And he walked over to the candle, formed his mouth like you always do when you blow out a candle, and in one [puff] blew out the candle.

They were so thankful. "Oh thank you, Santa. Thank you! Thank you!"

And Santa said, "Off to bed with you now!"

And little John and little Anne went upstairs to bed, and Mr. and Mrs. Moe thanked Santa one more time. Mrs. Moe got back into bed. Mr. Moe was helping Santa when, all of a sudden, Santa said, "Well, I suppose I'll go up this dark chimney and make my way to the rest of the world."

"Oh, Santa," said Mr. Moe, "it is awfully dark. Here, let me help you."

And he went over and lit the candle, and he held it up so that Santa could see his way up the dark chimney.

"Oh, that's very kind of you! HO! HO! HO! Merry Christmas! And to all a good night!"

And he was gone.

Then Mr. Moe turned and put the candle back onto the table. And Mrs. Moe said, "Mr. Moe, could you please blow out that candle."

And so it went all night long. [blowing sounds/huffing sounds] Until Mr. Moe got under the candle and Mrs. Moe got over it. And then little Anne got to the right and then little John got to the left of it and all together in one [puff] they blew out the candle.

TELLING TIPS: In the telling of this story have some little jingle bells as one of your props and ring them. You will also need candles and matches. When told in tandem (as we do), one takes the part of Santa and the other takes the part of the Moe family.

ABOUT THE STORY: This story is our adaptation of an old mountain joke, "The Twist Mouth Family." Another version, "The Snooks Family"—featuring a policeman instead of Santa Claus—is found in *Juba This and Juba That,* edited by Virginia A. Tashjian (Little, Brown & Co., 1969).

JANICE BUCKNER

"The Talking Skull" is a story about storytelling. A popular tale from west Africa, it poignantly shows how speech can cause trouble when words are carelessly spoken. My retelling adds a touch of poetry to the traditional plot line.

HEATHER FOREST's unique minstrel style of storytelling blends original music, folk guitar, poetry, prose, and the sung and spoken word. She has toured her repertoire of world folktales for the past twenty years to theaters, major storytelling festivals (including the National Storytelling Festival), and conferences throughout the United States. She has recorded six albums of storytelling, the latest being a musical collection of Aesop's fables, *The Animals Could Talk,* published with a libretto by August House. Ms. Forest's books include *The Baker's Dozen: A Colonial American Tale,* published by Harcourt Brace Jovanovich, and *The Woman Who Flummoxed the Fairies: An Old Tale From Scotland,* which was a Junior Library Guild Selection and a Pick of the List for 1990 by *American Bookseller* magazine. Her newest book, *Wonder Tales from Around the World,* is soon to be published by August House.

The Talking Skull

Heather Forest

A STORY FROM WEST AFRICA

There was once a man who was walking in search of food. He came upon a whitened skull lying on the ground in the hot sunlight. He approached the skull and wondered out loud, "What brought you here?"

The skull's jaw began to creak and move. The curious man moved closer to the skull and heard it say,

> Woe is me, Misery!
> I cannot shed a tear.
> Woe is me, Misery!
> My mouth has brought me here.

The man was amazed! "A talking skull!" he exclaimed. He almost forgot his hunger for a moment. He was curious and asked, "How could your mouth bring you here?"

Then the skull spoke again and said, *"I will show you. First, walk a distance in the direction my nose points and you will find some calabashes filled with millet to eat."*

The man walked and walked and came to some calabashes filled with grain. He was so happy to find food. He ran back to the skull and said, "Thank you! If I had not found these calabashes, I too might be a skeleton soon!"

The skull replied, *"Do not tell anyone about me or you will be sorry."*

The man ran to the village. He showed the food. Everyone was glad to see the grain. The king demanded that the man come to his hut. "Where did you find this food?" he asked.

Forgetting the warning of the skull, the man said, "A talking skull told me where to find the calabashes filled with millet."

"You are lying," said the king. "Perhaps you have stolen this food. There cannot be a talking skull."

"I will take you to it," boasted the man. "Then you will see that what I say is true."

"If you are lying we will cut off your head," said the king.

The man led the king and several warriors to the place where he had seen the skull. "There it is," he said.

The skull's dark eye sockets stared like small caves. Its jaw hung open. The man leaned close to the skull and said, "Now tell everyone where to find the food."

The skull sat white and silent in the sun.

"Please," said the man, a bit nervous under the glare of the king's eye, "tell everyone what you told me!"

But the skull sat like a hard dry stone.

The man threw himself on the ground and begged, "Show them I am not a liar! Tell them! Tell them! Where is the food?"

But the only sounds they heard were birds and insects.

The king was outraged and commanded, "Kill him. Cut off his head, for he has lied."

And they cut off the man's head and left him there.

In time two whitened skulls were lying next to each other on the ground in the hot sun. The first skull turned to the second and finally said,

> *Woe is me! Misery!*
> *What I said was true.*
> *It was my mouth that brought me here, my friend.*
> *Your mouth has brought you too!*

TELLING TIPS: Creating a supernatural voice for the speaking skull offers the storyteller an opportunity to experiment vocally. Since the talking skull is a magical element, stylistically, its voice possibilities are unlimited. The skull's lines can be spoken or sung in any unusual tonality. For added sound texture, the voice of the skull can be accompanied rhythmically, with percussion or rattle. As the tale is told, clearly differentiate this supernatural voice from your own narrative voice.

ABOUT THE STORY: This story has been documented in Nigeria, Cameroon, and other parts of west Africa. Commentary about the Nigerian version can be found in *Afro-American Folktales: Selected and Retold* by Roger D. Abrahams (Pantheon Books, 1985). Another printed version can be found as "Now You Know" in Loreto Todd's book, *The Tortoise and Other Trickster Tales From Cameroon* (Schocken Books, 1979).

ED STIVENDER is known for his unique renditions of fairy tales with a comic twist and his comic portrayal of St. Francis telling updated Bible stories in "The Kingdom of Heaven is Like a Party." He is in demand at colleges and religion conferences alike. He has appeared at the Walnut Street Theater Stage Five, the International Children's Festival at the Annenberg, The Philadelphia Folk Festival, as well as comedy clubs, schools, and churches. His television credits include the Christopher's Story laboratory and a featured spot on H.W. Wilson's American Storytellers Series. Four audiocassettes are also available. A collection of his coming-of-age stories, *Raised Catholic (Can You Tell?),* is available in book form and on audiocassette from August House. Ed currently lives in Germantown, Philadelphia.

As one who is more concerned about the schtick than the moral of the story, I've always loved the rhythms of Joel Chandler Harris's Uncle Remus tales. Jackie Torrence's renderings of these classic tales made me aware of their performance possibilities. I was attracted to the Tar Baby story because of its chorus: "Br'er Fox and Br'er Bear, they lay low." The substitution of the Honey Bunny relieved me of the fear of offending the African-American community while including a rich memory of my youth—when my Aunt Fran would bake a cake in the shape of an Easter bunny.

Honey Bunny

Ed Stivender

AN AFRICAN-AMERICAN STORY

Well, you don't have to call me Mister Fox. Well, you don't have to call me Brother Fox. You don't have to call me Br'er Fox. You can just call me Fox. 'Cause I'm the slyest fox that ever there lived. And there's one thing I love more than anything else, and that's rabbit. I'll eat rabbit baked, I'll eat rabbit flaked, I'll eat rabbit boiled, I'll eat rabbit broiled, I'll eat rabbit any way I can get it ... You might say I got the "rabbit habit."

You like rabbit? It's a little bit sweeter than snake. And there's one particular rabbit I've been trying to catch over these oh so many years, a fellow by the name of Br'er Rabbit. And I'd like to tell you what happened last Easter Sunday, when I got up early and I baked a cake.

You see I knew he was coming so I baked a cake. And I made that cake in the shape of a little Easter bunny—a little girl Easter bunny. And I covered that Easter bunny all in honey, nice sticky honey—I called it my "honey bunny." I put a little bow in her hair and I put her out on the road where I knew Mr. Br'er Rabbit would be coming any minute, and I hid back in the bushes waitin'. I lay low. And sure enough hippity, hoppity, hippity, hoppity, hippity, hoppity, down the road comes Mr. Br'er Rabbit and he sees that Honey Bunny. He walks up to the honey bunny and says, "Good morning, Miss Honey Bunny."

Well, Miss Honey Bunny, she don't say nothing. And me, I lay low.

"I said to you 'Good morning, Miss Honey Bunny,'" said Br'er Rabbit to the Honey Bunny.

Well, Miss Honey Bunny, she don't say nothing. And me, I lay low.

Did you ever say hello to someone and they didn't say hello back? You feel kind of offended. You feel kind of hurt. Well, that's how Mr. Br'er Rabbit felt. He said to Miss Honey Bunny, "What's the matter, Miss Honey Bunny, are you stuck up?"

Well, Miss Honey Bunny, she don't say nothing. And me, I lay low.

Well, Mr. Br'er Rabbit, he figures he's going to teach Miss Honey Bunny a lesson. And so he rears his forepaw back. He's going to whop her up alongside the head, which no boy should do to no girl, and—*shlurp*—he sticks in the honey. "Let me go, let me go."

Well, Miss Honey Bunny, she don't say nothing. And me, I lay low.

Well, Mr. Br'er Rabbit takes out his other forepaw, gonna get her up on the other side of the head and—*shlurp*—"Let me go. Let me go."

Miss Honey Bunny, she don't say nothing. And me, I lay low.

Well, Mr. Br'er Rabbit, he takes one of his hind paws, gonna kick her on the side and—*shlurp*—"Let me go. Let me go."

Miss Honey Bunny, she don't say nothing. And me, I lay low.

Well, Mr. Br'er Rabbit has one hind paw left. He's gonna kick her on the other side and—*shlurp*—"Let me go. Let me go."

Miss Honey Bunny, she don't say nothing. And me, I lay low.

Well, Mr. Br'er Rabbit only has one thing left. And that's his head. Well, he has not been using his head to any great advantage this morning, so he rears his head back, gonna butt her head like Andre the Giant on Hulk Hogan and—*shlurp*—"Let me go. Let me go."

Miss Honey Bunny, she don't say nothing. And me, I lay low.

Well, I take pity on that rabbit. And I come out from behind the bushes and I walk over and I begin to peel that rabbit off the Honey Bunny first by the ears, then by his paws and then his hind paws. And then I say, "Oh, Rabbit, I finally caught you. I wonder how I shall kill you before I eat you. Perhaps I shall throw you in the pond and drown you."

And Br'er Rabbit, he goes, "Whew!"

I say, "What do you mean, 'Whew'?"

"Well, you can drown me, Br'er Fox, but I thought for sure you were going to throw me in those sticker bushes."

"Well, maybe I won't drown you. Maybe what I'll do is take you and put you in a pot of boiling oil."

And Br'er Rabbit goes, "Whew."

I say, "What you mean 'Whew'?"

"Well, you can put me in boiling oil, Br'er Fox. But I thought for sure you're going to throw me in them sticker bushes."

"Well, maybe I won't boil you alive. Maybe what I'll do is skin you alive."

And Br'er Rabbit goes, "Whew."

I say, "What you mean 'Whew'?"

He said, "Well, you can skin me alive, Br'er Fox. But I thought for sure you were going to throw me in them sticker bushes."

Well, I got to thinkin' that maybe this rabbit wasn't as tender as I thought he was and if I threw him into the sticker bushes I could kind of tenderize him. So I whirled him around my head and I threw that rabbit into them sticker bushes and I walked over to them sticker bushes to look and see my tenderized rabbit, but I couldn't see any rabbit in there.

I looked as close as I could without getting my nose sticker-bushed, and I realized there wasn't any rabbit in them sticker bushes. All of a sudden I hear, "Yoohoo!" I look up on the other side of them sticker bushes up on the hill, and there's Br'er Rabbit, doing a dance and mocking me.

"Hoo, hoo, Br'er Fox, I fooled you. I love the sticker bushes. I was born and bred in the sticker bushes. April Fool's."

Well, I'm going to catch that rabbit one of these days, and when I do, I'm going to cook him and maybe I'll invite you over to dinner. Do you like rabbit? It's a little bit sweeter than snake.

TELLING TIPS: My first concern in telling this story was the appropriateness of telling in dialect. In my approach to the dialect, I stand (in the first line) behind the coattails of another white performer, the Comic J.J. Johnson ("You don't have to call me *Mister* Johnson"). I felt that imitating him would be a way around the shock that might come to sensitive ears of a white man doing a black dialect story.

My goal is to fit into the ampersand between Amos & Andy. Your goal should be to find your own way into the story so that it feels comfortable and the dialect issue doesn't get in the way of the story.

You will see I have disposed of Br'er Bear in my version and changed the narration to first person, using my voice and position to cue the audience to character changes. The Fox's voice is throaty and breathy, and Rabbit's is in my higher range, though not falsetto.

I play two simple chords on the banjo—C and B flat—behind the text when I do it, but it can be done with no accompaniment.

After the capture, I hold the rabbit by the ears at eye level for the quick take on "What do you mean, 'Whew'?" Each time the question is more frantic. I always act out the hands, feet, and head being stuck.

I always give the kids the last word. "Do you like rabbit? It's a little bit sweeter than _____."

Putting it at Eastertime also lets me bring in the April Fool's joke.

ABOUT THE STORY: This is the only story I tell in which I make an ethical comment to the audience: "—which no boy should do to no girl." On one level, the story is about physical abuse that backfires. However, the tale is more about the Islamic code of conduct than anything else. The reason Br'er Rabbit is upset is the bunny's refusal (incapacity) to return his greeting of peace. Find a Muslim and ask him or her about this. Have them point out other such motifs in the texts of traditional African material.

PAUL SKEEHAN

Several years ago, I was researching stories that would appeal specifically to students in grades three through six, when I came across "The Wise Judge." I started working on it and put together the version you read here. It is a story that always "works." Kids love the fact that it appears to be going in a particular direction—and then doesn't. They especially love the double-whammy at the end.

SUSAN KLEIN has been featured at over thirty storytelling festivals nationwide, including the National Storytelling Festival. She resides on Martha's Vineyard in Massachusetts where she was born and reared. She has been heard on numerous radio programs and was guest host and storyteller for Minnesota Public Radio's "Good Evening." Susan has recorded five cassette packages, including *Through A Ruby Window: A Martha's Vineyard Childhood.* Recently, ABC News' "Nightline" produced and aired a thirty-minute special on the Festival of Storytelling on Martha's Vineyard, which Susan founded in 1988 and still directs annually the last weekend of June.

The Wise Judge

Susan Klein

A STORY FROM JAPAN

Once there was a baker who worked long hours through each night to prepare his wares for market. One morning, the market was filled with very hungry people. It took him only two hours to sell his big basket full of fried dough to his customers.

He was exhausted! He climbed a hill just beyond the marketplace and sat next to a huge stone to count his money. When he found he had taken in two hundred dollars for his morning's work, he was even more exhausted just thinking about it.

So, he put the money in the basket, put the basket on the stone and went to sleep.

When he woke up, he was stunned to find that the money was gone. Leaving his empty basket on the stone, he ran back to the other vendors shouting, "There's a thief in the marketplace; a thief in the marketplace!"

The other vendors gathered round, holding tight their money pouches, and listened to the baker's story.

He said, "I sold everything so fast today and was exhausted when I climbed the hill! I counted two hundred dollars, put the money in my breadbasket, put the basket on the stone, and went to sleep. When I awoke, the money was gone! There's a thief in the marketplace!"

Not one of the salesmen liked the sound of that. They all started yelling at once, some waving their arms in the air.

"If a thief strikes once, chances are he'll strike again," they thought.

No one wanted to be the next victim. Everyone seemed to have an idea about what to do. Talking all at once, no one heard anything anyone else said. Finally, one voice rose higher than the rest. Everyone stopped shouting to listen to someone say, "Why not ask the Wise Judge? He knows *everything!*"

"Wonderful, *wonderful,* WONDERFUL idea!" shouted the baker, as he ran through the city toward the house of the Wise Judge.

When the excited baker was granted an audience, he bowed low and said, "Please listen to this tale of woe, Your Excellency. I was in the marketplace today as I am every day. I sold all my fried dough and climbed the hill to count my money. I was exhausted. So I put the two hundred dollars in the basket, put the basket on a large stone, and went to sleep. When I awoke, the money was gone! There's a thief in the marketplace!"

The Wise Judge leaned back on his cushions, closed his eyes and asked the baker to repeat his story. When the baker was finished, the Wise Judge lay there in silence. With his eyes still closed, he slowly moved one long finger along the ridge of his nose across his forehead to his hair line and back again.

"Tell me again," he said.

When the baker had told his story a third time, the Wise Judge stood up, eyes wide and said, "You sold everything you had brought to the marketplace. You climbed the hill. You counted your money to find you had two hundred dollars. You put the money in the basket. You put the basket on the stone. You went to sleep. When you awoke, the money was gone. Is that all correct?"

"Exactly!" said the baker.

"Then let us go to the place where you left the basket," pronounced the Wise Judge, swooping out the door.

The baker followed the old one to the marketplace and then led the way up the hill. The vendors all bowed low as the Wise Judge passed, showing him the honor that one so highly respected deserves. Then they all grabbed their money pouches and followed the two up the hill. While they climbed, they talked loudly about the shortsightedness of the thief to forget such a great and wise judge lived nearby who would surely discover his identity before the sun set.

When they reached the top of the hill, the basket was still sitting on the stone. The Wise Judge called for silence in a most dramatic fashion, as was his style.

When the crowd quieted, he said, "The baker sold all he had in the marketplace this morning. He came here to count his money. He had two hundred dollars, which he put in this basket. He put the basket on the stone and went to sleep. When he woke up the money was gone. There is a thief in the marketplace!"

Everyone was excited and forgot to remain quiet.

"SILENCE!" shouted the Wise Judge, flinging his arms straight up into the air. "I have thought about this the entire way here, and the answer is simple.

If the baker put his money in the basket, put the basket on the stone and slept, awakening to find the money gone, then I say the stone is the thief. It is abundantly clear. So let us arrest the stone in haste!"

It took only a split second for the crowd to gasp in disbelief. It took only a split second more for the crowd to yell "Charlatan!" and "Fool!" at the top of their voices. One moment they had hung on his every word; the next they turned on him and were about to head down the hill, never to listen to his nonsense again.

The Wise Judge shouted "SILENCE!" once more. This time his eyebrows peaked like sharp mountains beneath his brow.

"How dare you question my proclamation! Have you no upbringing at all to show such disrespect?"

That did it. Knowing what they had done would reflect on their families, the crowd in one motion, fell to their knees loudly asking forgiveness.

"For the public display of disrespect you have shown, you will each spend three days in jail."

"You can't *do* that!" they wailed, thinking that of course he could, but three days in jail meant three days with an empty money pouch!

"Of course I *can* and I just *did!*" said the Wise Judge, fury swirling in his eyes.

They bowed lower, begging his indulgence for what now seemed to be *thoughtless* disrespect.

He relented at last.

"I believe you are sincere," he said. "Instead of three days in jail you will each pay a fine of twenty dollars to be collected by the baker who began all this foolishness."

Piercing the baker with his gaze, he instructed him to fetch a pail of hot water.

When the baker returned, all the merchants from the marketplace were in line mumbling about the baker's misfortune causing their own and waiting to pay the fine. They hoped to do it quickly so as to return as soon as possible to their places of business.

The Wise Judge said, "I am still annoyed with all of you. Therefore, I wish to have no part in this transaction. The baker and I will stand here and the bucket will collect your fines. Simply toss your twenty dollars into the bucket one at a time. When you do so, you are free to go."

The baker and the Wise Judge stood near the bucket. When the first merchant in line dropped his twenty dollars into the bucket, he bowed low to the Wise Judge and went on his way. The second man did the same.

But when the third man threw his twenty dollars into the bucket, the Wise Judge seized him saying, "You are the man who stole the baker's money! For all the disturbance you have caused today, you will spend a long time in jail!"

The Wise Judge, as usual, was right. But, how did he recognize the thief?

TELLING TIPS: For children in grades three and up, this story can be used as a springboard for introducing or exercising any number of students' skills, including attention span lengthening, story line sequencing, predicting outcomes, deductive reasoning, and creative writing.

Introduce the story with a suggestion to listen well as the audience will be asked to help solve the mystery. This is a great way to encourage poor listeners to attempt a deeper attentiveness as well as to challenge those who will automatically give their full attention.

Asking the final question of the story, "How did the Wise Judge recognize the thief?" will elicit a wide variety of answers. Let the students know at this point that all answers will be honored and taken seriously. This encourages the students with low self-esteem or a lack of experience in problem-solving to give it a try.

Sometimes the answer (see * below if you need assistance figuring it out) will be derived because the students will present a chain of answers that feed one off the other to bring out the truth. You may need to give them a hint or two, or say "You're getting warmer," to facilitate the direction of the thinking so that the answers can stay somewhat on track. For instance, if the "guesses" get too far afield, bring them back with a direct task such as "Let's pay attention to two obvious things that make absolutely no sense. There's where the clues are."

Those two things are:

1. A supposedly wise judge says something as stupid as "The stone is the thief."
2. The judge makes the merchants throw their money in a bucket of hot water.

When asked, the students can usually come up with the accurate answers readily.

Once that's established—on their own or with prodding if necessary—the students will generally figure it out.

The second investigation can begin there, asking "why then would the Wise Judge blame the stone for the theft?" Getting to the answer on this one is usually easier as they have gotten into the investigative mode and can see that the Wise Judge was truly wise as he created a scenario of nonsense to force the thief to produce the greasy money, in spite of allowing the populace to think him foolish for a short while.

End the session by asking the audience if they think the first two suspects in line received their twenty dollars back, and then by thanking them for the cooperative effort of thinking together as a problem-solving body.

A few exercises (other than the one above) that can be initiated by this story follow:

1. After telling this story, instead of group discussion, have each listener do his/her own deductive thinking as a silent writing assignment in class.
2. Break up into small groups, each with a moderator to facilitate the flow of ideas, to ferret out the answers. Each group reports orally or in writing.
3. If the full group reasons together, have the full group listen to the student who gave the correct answer, synopsize the sequence of his/her clue connections that lead to the right answer.

4. Have the student (individually or in small groups) create stories in a similar genre that have a built-in mystery.

5. Research the 398.2 (Folklore and Fairy Tales) section of the library for similar tales from Japan or other cultures.

6. Assign parts and dramatize the story above.

ABOUT THE STORY: There are many different versions of this story. I chose a version from Japan. However, there is a good version from China found in *Myths and Folk Tales from Around the World* by Robert R. Potter and H. Alan Robinson (Globe Book Co., 1980). A Russian version is an old Kirghiz tale from the steppes of southwestern Asia found in the fourth revised edition *The Arbuthnot Anthology of Children's Literature* revised by Zena Sutherland (Lothrop, Lee & Shepard, 1976).

*The baker's hands would be greasy because he sold fried dough, which would make any money he handled greasy as well. Being asked to drop twenty dollars in a bucket of hot water, the baker's money would release the grease which would float to the top, incriminating the thief.

BILL MOONEY starred for many years as Paul Martin in the ABC daytime serial "All My Children" and is a two-time Emmy nominee for that role. His one-man show of humorous frontier stories, *Half Horse, Half Alligator,* was recorded by RCA Victor and toured America and Europe for two decades. Mooney currently lives in East Brunswick, New Jersey.

This story comes from a number of different sources. While it is not a true story, it is based upon actual accounts of shipwrecks and rescue efforts. The wild storms that pound the Atlantic coast have always been a source of great interest to me. They have caused more damage, including shipwrecks, than most folks care to remember. I have taken events from several of these storms and combined them, then added a few twists of my own. If you would care to look over some of my source materi-al, I highly recommend Karl Baarslag's Coast Guard to the Rescue *(Holt, Rinehart and Winston, Inc., 1973), and* Ghosts, Gales and Gold *by Edward Rowe Snow (Dodd, Mead & Co.). They are both filled with wonderful tales of the sea.*

The Wreck of the Sea Rover

Bill Mooney

AN ORIGINAL STORY OF THE EASTERN SEABOARD

Long before ships were powered by steam or diesel or atomic energy, huge sheets of canvas scooped up the wind and sent beautiful sailing vessels skimming over the seven seas to all the ports of call.

It's mid-February, more than a hundred years ago.

A sleek three-masted schooner called the *Sea Rover* has picked up a cargo of sugar in Cuba. Now she's sailing full-tilt up the Atlantic coast, all sheets to the wind, bound for New York harbor and a berth at Hoboken.

The *Sea Rover* is carrying a crew of ten, plus her captain—Captain William Brennan. Captain Brennan is sick, as sick as he has ever been in his life.

By the time the *Sea Rover* reaches the southern tip of New Jersey, out from Cape May, a storm—a fierce Nor'easter—begins to move in rapidly behind her, and she is trying desperately to outrun it.

Shortly after midnight, a mate knocks at Captain Brennan's door.

"'Scuse me, Cap'n. 'Scuse me, sir, but we're pickin' up a light from shore. Thought you oughta know."

"Where are we?"

"Oh, about mid-way up the Jersey coast, sir. Almost home."

I don't know—maybe it's his illness—or maybe just bad judgment—but he mistakes the light on shore for the beacon at Barnegat Lighthouse. He orders a change in course. Then he goes back to the cabin he shares with his wife, Nelle, and their little eighteen-month-old daughter, Geneva. Geneva is lying asleep in her crib and has no idea her father has just made such a terrible mistake.

Captain Brennan's change in course heads the *Sea Rover* straight for the hard beach at Long Branch.

Now it's about three in the morning. The wind has picked up considerably. The storm is near gale force and the seas are quite high.

A surfman is out patroling the beach at Long Branch. Suddenly he looks up and sees, looming out of the storm, a three-masted schooner heading straight for the beach. He waves his lantern back and forth ... back and forth ... trying to warn her. But no one on the ship sees it. And the *Sea Rover* crashes into the beach ... hard ... about two hundred yards from shore.

The surfman lights a Coston flare so the ship's crew will know they've been seen. Then he runs for help. Meanwhile, the sea begins to destroy the *Sea Rover*.

The crash brings all hands on deck. They douse the sail and prepare to abandon ship. But it's difficult. Freezing spray coats everything with ice. A crewman slips off the deck, falls into the boiling sea and is not seen again. Captain Brennan's cabin starts filling with water. He wraps baby Geneva in blankets and oilskins and takes her and his wife out on deck.

The seas keep smashing at the *Sea Rover*. They soon make short work of the jolly boat and then, a few minutes later, the longboat as well. No way off now.

Hundreds of people have gathered on shore. They can see the ship's crew clinging to the rigging. They look like insects caught in an icy web. The lifesaving crew knows they have to get these men off the ship as soon as they possibly can.

Shortly after daybreak, the gale reaches Force Ten. The seas are enormous— too high for the lifesaving crew to launch a surfboat out to the *Sea Rover*. So they drag a Lyle gun and some breeches buoys down to the shore.

A Lyle gun is really a small cannon. They load it with a seventeen-pound shot that has a thin line tied to it. They point the gun at the *Sea Rover* and fire. The shot goes up ... up ... and out ... toward the ship. But the wind catches it and it falls short. They load the gun again, and again the shot line goes up ... out ... out ... and this time it falls fair near the main mast.

The sailors know what to do. They grab the shot line and start hauling on it, hauling out something that looks like a long loop of clothesline attached to a great big pulley.

It takes the sailors two hours to drag this whip line and tail block out to the ship and then haul it up the main mast. It's hard treacherous work. Ice is coating everything. Finally, they manage to wrestle the tail block up, up the mast, and there they lash it, high above the breakers.

Now it's the surfmen's turn. They use this endless loop of rope, this whip line, to pull a heavier rope, a hawser, out to the wreck. They pull and pull and pull. It's back-breaking work. They have to fight not only the wind and the cold and the stinging sand, but worst of all, the huge seas that keep throwing the hawser back at them.

Finally, they get the hawser out to the ship. And, once again, the sailors grab hold of it and climb the icy mast, hauling this heavy rope behind them. They tie the hawser five feet above where the tail block is lashed. Once it's tied, the surfmen on shore flip their end of the hawser over a large tripod, pull the rope taut, and stake it to the ground. Now, their makeshift suspension bridge is ready. Maybe … just maybe … the crew can make it safely to shore.

But the storm is intensifying. The seas are now so high and furious they start smothering the wreck, knocking the sailors' feet out of the rigging, dragging them out almost horizontally. Not a moment too soon to put the breeches buoy to work.

A breeches buoy looks like a great big pair of canvas kneepants sewn into an oversized life ring. It hangs suspended from another big pulley that runs along the hawser. It's pulled back and forth, from shore to ship then back to shore again, by means of the whip line. The breeches buoy is big enough for two people to get into and be hauled to safety by the surfmen.

Geneva and her mother go first. Geneva is snugly wrapped in blankets and oilskins. Then she's strapped to her mother. A signal from the wreck and the surfmen haul away. The storm tosses and bounces the buoy as if it were a toy on a string. The sea leaps and tries to snatch them from below. As they get closer, and closer, the people on shore start to cheer and applaud. But the cheers freeze in their throats as the breeches buoy suddenly stops a hundred yards from shore.

The pulley has jammed … jammed with ice that's collected on the hawser. The surfmen pull, they *pull,* but it wouldn't budge. Halfway! Halfway between ship and shore. Halfway between life and death! Captain Brennan and his crew look on in horror. They can't do a thing. And the buoy won't budge.

The head of the lifesaving crew says, "All right, men, I want you to start running up the beach and pull on this line with all your might and main. Either we break the ice or we break the line."

It's a desperate measure. But something has to be done. They pray the line will break between the breeches buoy and the ship. Then Geneva and her mother can be dragged to shore. But if the line breaks between the buoy and the shore … Geneva and her mother are doomed.

They pull, *pull,* PULL … and the whip line stretches, stretches, and … snaps … between the buoy and the wreck! "We've got 'em, boys! We've got 'em! They're saved!" And everyone starts to cheer again.

But … hold it … *hold it!* … all this strain of pulling on the whip line has yanked the ropes out of the pulley! The breeches buoy carrying Geneva and Nelle Brennan to safety … the breeches buoy falls into the waves below.

"They're in the water! They're in the water! Pull, boys, *pull!* PULL!"

The surfmen start pulling again as hard as they can. They pull Geneva, her mother, still in the breeches buoy, pull them the hundred yards through the crashing waves, pull them to shore.

Captain Brennan ... maybe it's his illness ... maybe he just can't hold onto the icy rigging any longer ... or maybe it simply takes the fight out of him to see his wife and baby fall into the sea ... I don't know, but whatever it is, it allows the wind to lift him up out of the rigging and blow him to his death in the sea below.

Geneva's mother, by the time they get her to shore, is dead. They see the bundle strapped to her. They peel back the oilskins. Unwrap the blankets. And this little child ... little eighteen-month old Geneva ... she's alive. They quickly wrap her back up and run her to a heated shack nearby.

Meanwhile, the surfmen don't give up. Shot line after shot line is fired out to the *Sea Rover*. They rig up several other breeches buoys. They manage to get four more people off the ship before the storm finally destroys her. Those still left on board are lost to the sea.

Now, you might think that's the end of the story, but it's not.

Geneva is adopted by some folks in Trenton and grows up to be a fine young woman.

But every year on the anniversary of the wreck of the *Sea Rover*, on the exact spot where Geneva and her mother were pulled from the sea, a pale woman with wet matted hair is seen walking on the beach. She seems to be looking for something. She moans the most piteous moans and seems to cry uncontrollably. Then she calls, "Geneva ...! Geneva ...!"

If the onlookers get too near, the apparition disappears. When they move away again, she reappears and calls once more, "Geneva ...! Geneva ...!"

Finally, a minister from Atlantic Highlands, who had heard about this poor woman's ghost, comes down to Long Branch to put her soul to rest. He decides to hold a commital service on the twenty-fifth anniversary of the wreck of the *Sea Rover*. But he does an even cleverer thing. He learns where baby Geneva is now living, although she's no longer a baby, and he arranges for her to be at the service.

After it's over, Geneva walks to the water's edge and whispers, "Rest easy, Mama. Please, rest easy. I'm fine. Really I am. I'm married now, Mama, and I have a little baby. A little baby girl. I named her Nelle, Mama, after you. I love you, Mama. Please rest easy now. Please. Rest. I'm fine. I'll always love you. Goodbye, Mama."

And Nelle Brennan did rest easy. Her ghost was never seen again.

And Geneva? Well, she and little Nelle lived happily the rest of their days.

TELLING TIPS: I have placed this tale in the present tense to give it more of a sense of immediacy. The pacing is measured and deliberate. It should be told as if you were watching the action taking place. Let yourself be caught up in the desperation of the shore patrol to get the seamen off the *Sea Rover*. See the waves breaking over the ship. See the ice freezing on the lines. Feel the stinging sand. Feel the force of the wind. If you feel it and see it, the audience will feel it and see it. This story is appropriate for fourth grade and up.

There have been a lot of stories about Jack and his beanstalk. Most of the ones that I heard had Jack being a thief and stealing from the giant and finally killing him. This Jack story has a different slant, one that results in a slightly different psychological ending, without taking away from the deeper meaning of a young boy's quest to obtain manhood.

BOBBY NORFOLK, a three-time Emmy Award winner, began his career as a National Park Service Ranger presenting first-person historical narratives for tours at the Gateway Arch in St. Louis. He founded, in the mid-1970s, The Bobby Norfolk Comedy Revue, opening for such entertainers as Roberta Flack, B.B. King and Lou Rawls. He toured Missouri with the Imaginary Theatre Company. An accomplished writer and director, Bobby blends new stories with old favorites as he travels around the world performing in concert and workshops.

Jack and the Magic Beans

Bobby Norfolk

A STORY FROM ENGLAND

Once upon a time there was a little boy named Jack. He was living with his mother and they were very poor. Finally Jack's mother said, "Jack, I think you're going to have to go sell the cow so we can get some food to eat."

And so reluctantly Jack took the cow and started off to town. Halfway down the road Jack ran into an old man. The old man said, "Jack, if you give me that cow I will give you some magic beans."

Jack said, "Oh, magic beans! Oh boy!"

So Jack gave the cow away and took the magic beans. He ran back home and said, "Mom, Mom, Mom, I'm back home. I'm back home."

His mother said, "Jack, how did you get to the market so quickly?"

"I didn't go to the market."

"Well, where are the groceries you were supposed to get?"

"I didn't get any groceries."

"Then where is the money?"

"I don't have any money either."

She said, "Then what do you have, Jack?"

He said, "I have five magic beans."

She said, "What? Magic beans? You foolish boy!" She grabbed those beans out of Jack's hand and spanked him. Then she said, "Now you go to bed!" And she took those beans and hurled them out of the window.

That night it began to rain and the beans took root. They began to push from the ground. They grew higher and higher and higher, until they split the clouds.

The next morning Jack awakened and saw a shadow in his window. He ran to the window.

"Ah, a beanstalk!"

Jack put on his clothes and jumped on the beanstalk. He climbed higher and higher and higher, until he got through the clouds. There was a huge land up there. The grass was as tall as young saplings. Jack began to roam through the large blades of grass until finally he saw a huge castle.

He saw this big castle. The door was so tall Jack couldn't reach the doorknob. But he saw the airspace underneath the door. So he got down on his belly and crawled under the door. He stood up and he was in a huge room. Jack then crept through the room. He started smelling something: *[sniff-sniff-sniff]* "Ummm, food!" said Jack.

He followed the aroma of the food until finally he came to a large dining room. He jumped up and grabbed the tablecloth and started scaling it. He climbed higher and higher and higher, just like the beanstalk. Jack then arrived on top of the table, and the food smelled so delicious. Jack ran over to a big bowl of green peas. He tasted them—*slurp, slurp*—and ran over to the corn and grabbed a big kernel out of the bowl—*munch, munch.* He then ran over to the mashed potatoes—*nibble, nibble, burp.*

"Needs a little salt."

Then he ran over to the fried chicken and grabbed a piece of chicken—*nibble, nibble, burp*—and tasted that.

All of a sudden Jack started hearing this sound: BOOM! BOOM! BOOM!

Then Jack panicked. He ran behind the biscuits. He didn't feel safe there, so he ran behind the mashed potatoes. Then he ran behind the green peas. It was the giant's wife entering the room. When she saw Jack running across the table, she said, "What is that roach doing on my table!"

She took her big shoe off to smack Jack upside the head. She moved the mashed potatoes and Jack said, *[screaming]* "Please don't hit me."

She said, "Oh, I wouldn't hit you. I've always wanted a little boy."

She picked Jack up and his feet were kicking out from underneath the giant's hand. All of a sudden there was another sound: BOOM! BOOM! BOOM! BOOM! She said, "Oh, that's my husband."

She then put Jack inside her apron pocket. Well, the big giant came in.

> "FE, FI, FO, TOY,
> I smell the blood of an English boy.
> Be he live or be he dead,
> I'll beat him up and slap his head!"

She said, "Aw, that's nothing but the fried chicken you're smellin', fool. Sit down and eat."

"Oh, sorry about that, wife."

The giant sat down and he ate his meal. Jack slipped out of the woman's apron, jumped back down to the floor and ran into another room—*boodagie, boogadie, boodagie.*

As he was running into this other room, he happened to see a hen, and this hen was sitting on top of a golden egg. He said, "Oh, a hen that lays a golden egg."

He went over to the hen and the hen said, "Yes, Jack. My owner was the old man who gave you those magic beans. He meant for you to come up here and rescue me. So if you can take me back down to the earth, I am yours."

Jack took the hen and he took the golden egg and stuffed it in his pocket and he ran back to the beanstalk. He climbed down, down, down to the ground. He ran into the house. "Mother! Mother! Mother! Look what I have. I have a hen that lays golden eggs!"

He took that egg out and laid it on the table. His mother was so very happy.

But then the hen said, "Jack, there's one more thing you have to get up there. It's a magic harp that the giant stole from the old man too."

And Jack said, *"[gulp!]* Well, OK. I guess if I have to do it, I have to do it. Mother, please, don't fret for me, OK?"

His mother said, "OK, Jack. But please be very careful."

So Jack slipped back off and went up the beanstalk higher and higher and higher and higher, until he got back to Giantland. Then Jack went through the large stand of grass. He finally came to the castle, crawled under the door space, and went back into the house. At this point the giant was taking a nap. Jack went into one room, went into another room, until finally he saw the magic harp. He touched that harp and the harp yelled out, "Aaahhh! Who are you?"

"Shh! Be quiet! I'm trying to take you away and save you."

The harp was not as intelligent as the hen, and the harp started yelling, "Help! Help! Thief! Thief!"

Jack tried to muffle the harp, "Mmmm!" And the harp bit his hand. "Ouch!" said Jack.

That woke the giant up. "Hey, boy, who are you?"

Jack panicked. He grabbed that harp as tightly as he could and ran as fast as he could to the door—*boogadie, boogadie, boogadie.* He slid under the door space. The giant was right behind him. BOOM! BOOM! BOOM!

Jack ran back through the forest made of grass, jumped back on the beanstalk, and went down, down, down the beanstalk as fast as he could. His mother was waiting at the base of the beanstalk. She saw him coming down. "Oh, Jack, you're back!" She looked up higher. "Aaahhh, what is that thing you're bringing down here, boy?"

"Mother, that's the giant. Please get the axe, get the axe!"

Jack's mother ran, got the axe. Jack took the axe and started chopping away at that beanstalk—*chickaboom, chickaboom, chickaboom.* All of the sudden the giant started to swing—"Whoa, Nelly!"—and the beanstalk started to swing the other way—*"Whoa, Nelly!"*—and the beanstalk fell backward—"Ahhhh, look out below!"—BOOM!

The giant bounced off the ground and went back up into the clouds and couldn't get back down. The clouds started to roll away and the big giant was shaking his fist at Jack. "Jack, one day I'll get you for this."

Jack said, "Good luck, Giant!"

Jack and his mother now had a hen that laid golden eggs, and they had a magical harp that they finally taught some intelligence to.

And they lived happily ever after.

TELLING TIPS: This story is so familiar that you can make it fresh by telling it "free style." Use whatever colloquial style suits you. This version reflects the style that works for me. Sometimes I modernize it by placing modern objects into the story (for example, Jack's mother may look in the refrigerator and see they are out of food). I vary the colloquialisms, slang, and catchphrases I use according to the age and general makeup of my audience. The most important thing is to have fun with the story.

The original version, of course, has Jack stealing the giant's objects, killing the giant, and making a widow out of the giant's wife. I added a slant to the story by making the giant's possessions actually the stolen property of the old man who gave Jack the magic beans. The hen attests to this in the story when Jack stumbles upon her. Within the story are the universal character traits of teamwork and cooperation, self-esteem, humanity, respect, honesty, and manhood achieved.

OLAN MILLS STUDIOS

Sweet Harmony Chapel is a powerful story based on truth. I tell it as though it were true because I like to walk in the valley where it takes place and see the people and be part of what went on there. The people of that community went through a life-changing experience, and this story shows the beauty in their hearts.

GWENDA LEDBETTER grew up on Virginia's Eastern Shore where storytelling was part of the conversation. Trained as a teacher, she worked first as a storyteller at Pack Library in Asheville, North Carolina, where she was seen on WLOS-TV as the "Storylady." She's been featured at the National Storytelling Festival in Jonesborough, Tennessee. Gwen has taught at the National Institute and has served on the Consulting Committee of the *National Journal* as a reviewer. Her most recent tape, *In Sound and Sight of the Sea,* tells of growing up on the Eastern Shore.

Sweet Harmony Chapel

Gwenda LedBetter

AN ADAPTATION OF A STORY BY C. HODGE MATHES

Galax Cove was a small mountain town tucked into the folds and ridges of what is now the Tennessee side of Thunderhead Mountain. If you wanted to go there (and you really had to want to because nobody just passed through) you'd have to cross a beautiful mountain stream called the Powderhorn, about twelve times. Four of those times, you could get over on pole bridges, logs laid side by side. The rest of the time, you'd have to depend on wagon, horseback or rock hopping. None of these would be a problem unless it was right after the spring thaws when the water came rushing down the Powderhorn like a great white waterfall.

The first thing you'd see of Galax Cove would be Nate Walker's tub mill, over to your right. Up the road a ways was the Free Will Baptist church—there by the river for necessary reasons. There was a Methodist church in town, too—up on higher ground. There were about forty houses and a general store. When you got to Huse McKinney's back pasture fence, you'd find yourself staring at Thunderhead Mountain and you'd know you had come to the end of Galax Cove.

This story has to do with the ministers of the two churches. Ike Gallaher was the Baptist minister. He was a tall skinny man who always wore black and walked around town with his hands clasped behind his back and his eyes peeled for sin. Wes Shelton, the Methodist minister, was what you call an "itinerant." He came into town once a month on the back of his mare, Mag'alene. Wes said he called her Mag'alene because he had to get "seven demons out of that rascal before I could ride her."

Now, with two churches in that little community, you'd think it would be bursting with brotherly love, but that was not the case. When Wes Shelton came riding into town, he came to deliver his people from the Baptist. Not Baal! Ike Gallaher was constantly thundering out against the preaching of "that

Methodist feller." The two of them preached more against each other than they did *for* anything, and they were so passionate about it that the two churches bristled at each other like fortresses. Then came the spring of the Big Tide.

It was what they called a "forward" spring in Galax that year. It got warm early and everything was bursting into being. The dogwood was turning the mountainsides into a fairyland. Wildflowers sprang up right under your feet. Folks got all their planting done; corn and sweet potato slips were both in the ground, and tobacco was under those canvas sheets, gleaming in the morning light. What with the warm weather and all the plantin' done, there was a lot of finger twiddlin' going on. Ike Gallaher noted this on his daily rounds and he had it norated that there'd be meetin' come candle-lightin' time, first Sunday in May.

People in the mountains loved meetin', or revival as it is also known. Especially in the spring. They said it was better than a dose of salts gettin' rid of that winter bile. When first Sunday came, people filled the church down by the river. Women sat on one side and men on the other. The little children sat on quilts up front. There were four kerosene lamps hung high on the walls, casting great dark shadows. They made Ike Gallaher look more like a big black bird than ever. When he started waving his arms around, warming to his task, the children watched him with their mouths agape, expecting him to take off right over their heads and fly out the door.

Now, some of the Methodists were sitting in the back rows. They had come out of love of meetin' and to see what Brother Gallaher was goin' to say ag'in' 'em this year. They came seekin' and went away having found, as the saying goes. Ike Gallaher gave it to them as he believed it to be.

"Friends. Neighbors. Now, the Good Lord didn't have to save us but he did it of his own free will. And it says it right here in the Good Book how he done it. Says John the Baptist led the Son of Man inter the water. He baptized him and then he led him outen the water. It don't say nothin' about no sprinklin' or pourin'. Now, some folks around here is leadin' people into mighty slippery places. When they gets to heaven the Judge'll say, 'Depart from me. I never knowed ye!'"

Well, the whole Tobe McIntosh family, who had been Methodist all their days, converted to Baptist there on the spot! Nobody knew afterwards how Wes Shelton heard about it but hear it he did. He came into town on the following Saturday with all the mare power Mag'alene'd give him. It was almost sundown when he got to Nate Walker's tub mill. Some men were standing around talking and Wes Shelton inclined his head.

"Evenin' gen'lemen. How's she grindin'?"

"Purty slow, Brother Shelton," Nate answered. "Purty slow. Hasn't rained in two or three weeks. Hardly get a turn ground out. Reckon you'll be preachin' tomorrer."

"Lord willin'."

Then Nate couldn't resist.

"Reckon ye heared the Baptist been havin' meetin'."

"Yes. I heared and I aims to speak to that tomorrer morning!"

As he turned to head up the hill towards his sister Rachel's place, it was hard to tell where the most sparks were comin' from—Mag'alene's hooves or Wes Shelton's eyes.

Well, it got bruited around that Wes Shelton was in town and was going to answer back the Baptist, and the next morning there wasn't an empty seat to be found in the Methodist chapel—and half of 'em were filled with Baptists! Even Granddad Peterson, the senior deacon and leading pillar of the Baptist church, declared, "This rheumatism in my knee's so bad, I don't believe I can make it to big church. I'll just stop off and see what that Methodist feller has to say."

Folks said Wes Shelton looked mighty old and tired that morning. In his day, he could have out-rode, out-boxed, and out-fought any man in town, and he was still strong though he had seven decades to him. But that May morning, he looked like an old feedsack with all the feed let out of it. However, when he stood up, folks said it seemed like he grew three times his natural size. He came to the plain pine table that served as pulpit, opened the Bible, and eyeballed the people.

"Brethren. Sisters. I aims to speak to you from the ol' book of Genesis where God said to Noah, 'The end of all flesh is come before me for the earth is filled with violence. Behold! I shall bring the flood of waters upon the earth and destroy all flesh.' Now, some folks around here have been trustin' in the waters of the Powderhorn to save their guilty souls. Let me tell you, the flood of God's wrath is comin' down the Powderhorn and it's a-comin' soon!"

It was a mighty sober bunch of people that came out of the Methodist chapel when meetin' was over. The Methodists were shakin' their heads like they "knowed it all the time." The Baptists were hoppin' mad. Granddad Peterson lifted pebbles with his cane and sent 'em flying.

"I reckon—huh!—the Lord God knows more about—huh!—who's goin' to get drowned than certain folks—huh!—who call themselves a prophet!—huh!"

But before he entered his house, he cast a weather eye skyward and noted a white rill of a cloud right over Thunderhead Mountain. And he thought he heard the faint rumble of thunder.

After church, everyone went home for Sunday dinner. Ike Gallaher was crossing the footbridge over the Powderhorn toward his son Link's house. He was still full of the fire he'd delivered to his diminished congregation. Hearing the sound of a horse behind him, he turned and stared straight into the face of Wes Shelton. The two men had just finished denouncing each other in the pulpit. It was too quick to pull up the mask that all of us wear, and the look that passed between them was so full of hate, you could have stood on it.

Nobody knew it in Galax Cove, but out in the Caribbean, a storm was gathering. About six o'clock, a great black cloud filled the sky all over the valley. The wind began to shriek and scream, tearing up trees and sending branches sailing through the air. The thunder bounced like cannonballs off the mountains. Lightning split the dark sky, lighting up the whole valley. It flashed back and forth between Leconte and Thunderhead all night long. When the rain came it was a deluge, hard and sharp as knives.

Monday night, Tobe McIntosh was standing on Granddad's porch.

"Reckon it's lessenin', Granddad?"

Granddad shook his head.

"Nope. I looked at the almanac and we're in for a heap of fallin' weather. I can't help thinkin' about what that Methodist feller said."

Granddad and the almanac were both right. It rained all Monday night. All day Tuesday and Tuesday night. By Wednesday morning, Nate Walker's tub mill was swept downriver, for the Powderhorn had become a flood tide. Its water was an angry brown with yellow foam. Great rocks grinding one on the other were being carried by the force of the water. All the bridges were gone, for the Powderhorn had eaten up its banks and overflowed them. Trees with chickens in them, and boards from people's barns and houses flowed downstream. The roar of the floodwaters was so strong, no one could be heard yelling from one side to the other. Galax Cove was split right in half.

Wednesday night, Big Davy Holder went out to survey the storm damage and check on the floodwaters. He saw where a smaller river was branching off from the main flood and cutting up behind Link Gallaher's place. He yelled and waved to Link, who was standing on his porch.

"Hey, Link! It's cuttin' up behind your house!"

Link couldn't make out what Davy was saying so he just waved back.

Thursday morning, when Link looked out the back door, he found the whole back yard of his house full of water. Ike had stayed on after Sunday dinner because of the storm. The two men wrenched off the kitchen door and put Link's wife Celie and the little girl, Beulah, on it. Then, half wading, half swimming, they pushed it before them towards the higher ground of the orchard. Afterwards—no one knew how it happened—but suddenly everyone was floundering in the water. Link grabbed a white oak with one hand and Celie with the other and got her on dry ground. Ike made a grab for Beulah, who was holding onto the door for dear life, and missed her about a hand's breadth. He would have plunged in after her, but Link grabbed his father and Celie cried,

"We're goin' to head her off, Pop. Link's got a pole."

The old man went down on his knees and prayed,

"Oh, Lord, save that baby or take me, one!"

When they tried to reach the door with the pole, it was too far away and they watched helplessly as the little girl and the door were carried closer and closer to the main flood tide.

On the opposite bank, some men had been running, watching the tragedy. Suddenly a man in a big felt hat ran through the rest and dove into the Powderhorn. There were many strong swimmers in Galax Cove, but no man in his right mind would try to swim in a flood tide. Everyone stared as the man disappeared in the torrent, then appeared and with great strong strokes headed toward the little girl.

Ike cried, "God's sent an angel!"

Well, the angel caught up with the door just as Beulah's fingers started slipping. The swimmer pushed her up on the door and pushed it toward the rock where Link had jumped. The impact of the door on the rock sent the little girl up into her father's arms and his cry of joy could be heard clear across that raging river.

When Link tried to reach out to the swimmer with his pole to help him, it was too late. His strength was gone and the flood tide took him over, a-tossing him on the waves like a rag doll. One wave turned his head so his face could be seen. Davy Holder cried out,

"It's Brother Wes Shelton and he's drowning right before our eyes!"

They found his body three days after that, caught in some bushes beside the Powderhorn. The water was still up and the bridges were out, and there was no way to get a Methodist minister to do the funeral. So, the people went to Ike Gallaher. They say it was the biggest funeral in Galax Cove. The church was full and folks were standing out in the yard. It had finally stopped raining and the sun was shining in the windows of the church. You could hear bees buzzing and Rachel Shelton sniffing but even that stopped when Ike Gallaher stood up to speak. He stood behind the plain pine box for what seemed an uncommonly long time.

Then he slowly lifted his head and said,

"Friends. Neighbors. I feel mighty strange standing here, in the very spot where the one afore me preached to you a many a Sunday. Him and me walked different paths and we said hard things ag'in' each other. You all know how on Thursday my grandbaby, Beulah, was near taken in the flood. But maybe you don't know that I prayed for an angel to save her. Well, that angel came and plunged into the flood tide. I watched him swim like no man I ever saw and send that baby right up into her daddy's arms. When they told me that the angel was my brother Wes Shelton, it just about broke my ol' heart in two.

"Chances are it won't be too long before I'll be heading through those Pearly Gates myself. When I get to heaven, I'm going to ask for a peek at my Savior and a few words with Martha, my wife, and then, oh, friends, I'm going to walk them streets until I find my brother Wes Shelton and I'm going to take him by the hand and ask him to introduce me to God Almighty."

They never did rebuild the Baptist church, which was swept away in the flood tide. From then on, they just had the one meeting house in Galax Cove. They called it SWEET HARMONY CHAPEL and it's the only church I know of in the Appalachian Mountains with a Methodist chancel in front of the altar and a baptismal font right beside the pulpit steps.

TELLING TIPS: It will help to have seen a mountain valley like Galax Cove so you can have it around you as you tell this story. It starts out with warmth and humor. I use a higher voice for Ike Gallaher; a deeper one for Wes Shelton. If you use a voice change, be sure the voice fits how you see the two men. The pace of the story picks up when the storms comes, accelerates with the floodwaters, and slows down with Davy Holder's "It's Brother Wes Shelton ..." Then the pace is slow and steady until Ike's funeral speech and the heart-warming ending.

Mr. Mathes says this story was based on truth. That truth shines every time you tell it.

ABOUT THE STORY: My telling is based on a short story called "Harmony Chapel" by C. Hodge Mathes, originally published in 1923 in the periodical *Everybody's First in Fiction* and reprinted in a collection of Mr. Mathes's work entitled *Tall Tales from Old Smokey* (Kentucke Imprints and Appalachian Consortium Press, 1975).

DAVID HOLT is an award-winning musician and storyteller. He is best known for his appearances on The Nashville Network and as host of the PBS series "Folkways" and American Public Radio's "Riverwalk." From 1975 through 1981 he founded and directed the Appalachian Music Program at Warren Wilson College. In 1984, Holt was named in *Esquire* magazine's Register of Men and Women Who Are Changing America. He has four award-winning storytelling recordings and four music recordings, including Grammy nominee *Grandfather's Greatest Hits.* He performs over 300 concerts a year throughout the United States. A native of Garland, Texas, Holt has lived in the western North Carolina mountains for two decades.

In 1971 I was on a music tour of the Far East for the U.S. State Department. We spent several days in Chiang Mai, Thailand, performing and meeting the people. At this time the Thai people were afraid the Vietnamese were going to overrun their country and everyone was on edge. I heard this simple yet powerful story from a young boy who was our unofficial guide around Chiang Mai. He said, "The story gives us courage."

The song in this tale is a melody the children in Thailand use to taunt one another. Since that time this story has found a life of its own in the storytelling community.

I am glad to see it is being told.

The Freedom Bird

David Holt

A STORY FROM THAILAND

Once a long time ago a hunter was walking through the woods. Far off in the forest he heard the faint sound of a bird singing a very strange song:

[Audience repeats: Nah, nah, nah, nah, nah, nah, nah]

The hunter walked and walked until at last he came to a tree with a beautiful golden bird sitting in the top.

He said, "Why does such a beautiful bird like you have such an ugly song?"

The bird looked down at the hunter and sang:

"Nah, nah, nah, nah, nah, nah, nah."

[Audience repeats: Nah, nah, nah, nah, nah, nah, nah]

The hunter said, "If you don't stop singing, I'm going to shoot you with my bow and arrow!"

The bird just looked down and sang again in a mocking voice:

"Nah, nah, nah, nah, nah, nah, nah."

[Audience repeats: Nah, nah, nah, nah, nah, nah, nah]

The hunter put an arrow in his bow and shot … and he missed. The golden bird sang again:

"Nah, nah, nah, nah, nah, nah, nah."

[Audience repeats: Nah, nah, nah, nah, nah, nah, nah]

The hunter put another arrow in his bow and shot again. The arrow went right through the bird's heart. As the bird began to fall, the hunter rushed under the tree and caught it in his sack. He pulled the sack tight and started to walk home. But from down inside the bag, he heard the muffled singing of the bird:

[Storyteller keeps mouth closed and hums]

"Nah, nah, nah, nah, nah, nah, nah."

[Audience mimics and repeats: Nah, nah, nah, nah, nah, nah, nah]

The hunter took the bird home, pulled it out of the sack, put it on the chopping block and plucked all the feathers from it. When he turned around to get a knife to cut the bird up, he heard over on the chopping block:

[Teller and audience fold their arms and shiver when they sing this line]

"Brr, brr, brr, brr, brr, brr, brr."

[Audience repeats: Brr, brr, brr, brr, brr, brr, brr]

The hunter took the knife and cut the bird up into a hundred small pieces, and then scraped them into a large pot full of water and put it on the stove to boil. When the water began to boil, he heard from down inside the pot, the bird singing:

[Teller and audience make a gurgling sound when they sing the song]

"Burgh, burgh, burgh, burgh, burgh, burgh, burgh."

[Audience repeats: Burgh, burgh, burgh, burgh, burgh, burgh, burgh]

Now the hunter was starting to get mad. He took the pot outside and put it on the ground and found himself a shovel and started to dig a deep, deep hole. When the hole was way over his head, he climbed out and poured all the parts of the bird into the hole and covered it with dirt. And as he turned to go back into the house, he heard from deep down in the ground the bird singing:

[Teller and audience sing with hand over mouth to give muffled sound]

"Nah, nah, nah, nah, nah, nah, nah."

[Audience repeats: Nah, nah, nah, nah, nah, nah, nah]

Now the hunter was furious. He grabbed his shovel and dug up every piece of the bird and put them in a little wooden box, and tied a large rock across the box with some rope. He went down to the river and threw the box as far as he could out into the water. It splashed and went straight to the bottom. He stood on the bank waiting to hear the sound of the bird. He heard nothing, so he went home.

At the bottom of the river, the water loosened the rope around the box. The rock fell off and the box floated to the top of the water. It drifted along the river for three days. On the third day, the box floated by some children who were playing on the banks of the river. They saw this beautiful wooden box passing by and they wanted to know what was in it. They waded into the water and brought the box to shore.

When they opened it, out flew a hundred golden birds all singing in a full voice:

"Nah, nah, nah, nah, nah, nah, nah."

[Audience repeats: Nah, nah, nah, nah, nah, nah, nah]

About a year later, the very same hunter was walking through the woods. And far off in the distance, he heard the strange sound of the bird singing. He walked and walked until at last he came to the same tree where he had first seen the strange bird. But this time when he looked up in the tree, instead of seeing one bird, he saw a hundred golden birds. He raised his hands and hollered out, "I know who you are now. You're the Freedom Bird, for you cannot be killed."

And all the birds looked down and sang to him at the same time:

"Nah, nah, nah, nah, nah, nah, nah."

[Audience repeats: Nah, nah, nah, nah, nah, nah, nah]

TELLING TIPS: This story is easy to tell and always works. Although the tale is aimed at children, adults respond to the powerful ending. I usually start out by reminding the audience of our own cultural taunting song. Then I demonstrate how the Thai people sing their tune and get the audience to sing along. You could then mention where you got the story and then launch into it.

Throughout the story, when the bird sings his song, I usually sing the tune first and then motion to the audience to sing it again with me. Some of the singing has a gesture with it, such as shivering or covering your mouth. The audience will quickly catch on and follow your lead.

Classical composer Carl Orff has arranged a version of this story for the Orff instruments. He added the clap at the end of the tune which I have included in my version, as it rounds out the melodic timing and brings the audience together.

Acknowledgments and Permissions

"The Black Prince" reprinted by permission of Laura Simms. From the compact disc/audiocassette *Making Peace; Heart Uprising*, Earwig Music Co., 1818 W. Pratt Boulevard, Chicago, IL 60626. ℗ 1993 Laura Simms.

"The Dead Mule" reprinted by permission of Jim May.

"The Electricity Elixir" reprinted by permission of Chuck Larkin.

"Fox's Sack" reprinted by permission of Bill Harley. From the audiocasette *Come On Out and Play,* Round River Records, 301 Jacob Street, Seekonk, MA 02771.

"The Freedom Bird" reprinted by permission of David Holt. © 1979 David Holt and High Windy Songs (BMI).

"The Golden Arm" reprinted by permission of Jackie Torrence. From the audiocassette *Tales for Scary Times,* Earwig Music Co., 1818 W. Pratt Boulevard, Chicago, IL 60626.

"Honey Bunny" reprinted by permission of Ed Stivender. From the audiocassette *Some of My Best Friends Are Kids!,* Clancy Agency, 5138 Whitehall Drive, Clifton Heights, PA 19018.

"The Horned Animals' Party" reprinted by permission of Diane Ferlatte. From the audiocassette *Favorite Stories by Diane Ferlatte,* 6531 Chabot Road, Oakland, CA 94618.

"How the Turtle Cracked His Shell" reprinted by permission of Robin Moore. From the audiocassette *Fins Furs and Feathers,* Groundhog Press, Box 181, Springhouse, PA 19477.

"Is It Deep Enough?" reprinted by permission of Bill Mooney and David Holt. From the audiocassette *Why the Dog Chases the Cat and Other Animal Stories,* High Windy Audio, P.O. Box 553, Fairview, NC 28730. © 1993 by David Holt and Bill Mooney.

"Jack and the Haunted House" reprinted by permission of Elizabeth Ellis. From the audiocassette *I Will Not Talk in Class,* New Moon Productions, Box 720411, Dallas, TX 75372.

"Jack and the Magic Beans" reprinted by permission of Bobby Norfolk. Available on audiocassette from Earwig Music Co., 1818 W. Pratt Boulevard, Chicago, IL 60626.

"The King's Child" reprinted by permission of Judith Black.

"La Muerta: Godmother Death" reprinted by permission of Doug Lipman. From the audiocassette *Folktales of Strong Women,* Yellow Moon Press, P.O. Box 1316, Cambridge, MA 02238.

"Lazy Jack" reprinted by permission of Gay Ducey.

"The Lion's Whisker" reprinted by permission of Len Cabral. From the audiocassette *Nho Lobo and Other Stories,* Story Sound Productions, 30 Marcy Street, Cranston, RI 02905. Also appears in *The Read-Aloud Anthology* (Macmillan/McGraw Hill).

"Little Burnt Face" reprinted by permission of Milbre Burch. From the audiocassette *The World Is the Storyteller's Village,* Kind Crone Productions, 582 Eldora Road, Pasadena, CA 91104. © 1994 by Milbre Burch.

"Little Hare and the Pine Tree" reprinted by permission of Joseph Bruchac.

"The Magic Gifts" reprinted by permission of J.J. Reneaux. From the book *Cajun Folktales,* August House Publishers, P.O. Box 3223, Little Rock, AR 72203. © 1992 by J.J. Reneaux.

"The Magic Mortar" reprinted by permission of Jay O'Callahan.

"The Magic Pomegranate" by Peninnah Schram. From the book *Jewish Stories One Generation Tells Another* (© 1987). Reprinted by permission of the publisher, Jason Aronson Inc., Northvale, New Jersey. Also appears in *The Read-Aloud Anthology* (Macmillan/McGraw Hill).

"The Magic Pot" reprinted by permission of Pleasant DeSpain. From the book *Thirty-Three Multicultural Tales to Tell,* August House Publishers, P.O. Box 3223, Little Rock, AR 72203. © 1993 by Pleasant DeSpain.

"The Mischievous Girl and the Hideous Creature" reprinted by permission of Beth Horner.

"The Old Giant" reprinted by permission of Jon Spelman. Also available on audiocassette from Public Productions, 1612 Ballard St., Silver Spring, MD 20910.

"Panther and Rabbit" reprinted by permission of Michael Parent. Collected by Erin Garvey and adapted by Michael Parent.

"Rabbit and Possum Hunt for a Wife" reprinted by permission of Gayle Ross.

"Santa Visits the Moes" reprinted by permission of The Folktellers.

"The Storekeeper" reprinted by permission of Doc McConnell.

"The Story of the Half Blanket" reprinted by permission of Maggi Kerr Peirce.

"Strength" is from the book *Peace Tales: World Folktales to Talk About*, © 1992 Margaret Read MacDonald. Reprinted by permission of Linnet Books, North Haven, Connecticut.

"Sweet Harmony Chapel" reprinted by permission of Gwenda LedBetter. Adapted from the short story, "Harmony Chapel," by C. Hodges Mathes, originally published in 1923 in the periodical *Everybody's First in Fiction* and reprinted in a collection of Mr. Mathes's work entitled *Tall Tales from Old Smokey* (Kentucke Imprints and Appalachian Consortium Press, 1975). Also available on Ms. LedBetter's upcoming tape of mountain stories, available from Gwen LedBetter, 55 Beaverbrook, Asheville, NC 28804.

"The Talking Skull" reprinted by permission of Heather Forest. From the book *Wonder Tales from Around the World* (1995), August House Publishers, P.O. Box 3223, Little Rock, AR 72203.

"The Three Dolls" reprinted by permission of David Novak.

"Those Three Wishes" reprinted by permission of Carol Birch and Judith Gorog. Adapted from the book *A Taste for Quiet* by Judith Gorog (New York: Philomel Books, 1982). Also available on the audiocassette *Careful What You Wish For* by Carol Birch, Frostfire, P.O. Box 32, Southbury, CT 06488.

"The Time Jack Got the Silver Sword" reprinted by permission of Donald Davis. From the book *Jack Always Seeks His Fortune: Authentic Appalachian Jack Tales,* August House Publishers, P.O. Box 3223, Little Rock, AR 72203. © 1992 by Donald Davis, Storyteller, Inc.

"Trouble! (or, How the Alligator Got His Crackling Hide)" reprinted by permission of Bill Mooney and David Holt. From the audiocassette *Why the Dog Chases the Cat and Other Animal Stories,* High Windy Audio, P.O. Box 553, Fairview, NC 28730. © 1993 by David Holt and Bill Mooney.

"The Twelve Labors of Hercules" reprinted by permission of Barbara McBride-Smith.

"Urashima Taro" reprinted by permission of Rafe Martin. Based on Mr. Martin's recorded version on the audiocassette *Ghostly Tales of Japan,* Yellow Moon Press, P.O. Box 1316, Cambridge, MA 02238. © 1989 by Rafe Martin and Yellow Moon Press.

"What He Could Have Been" reprinted by permission of Steve Sanfield. From the audiocassette *Could This Be Paradise?: Tales of Sages and Fools from the Jewish Tradition*, Backlog Book Services, P.O. Box 694, North San Juan, CA 95950. © 1984 Steve Sanfield.

"The Wise Judge" reprinted by permission of Susan Klein.

"The Wreck of the Sea Rover" reprinted by permission of Bill Mooney.